If You're Willing

Ivy Symone

Acknowledgments

To my beautiful readers...Thank you for always rocking with me. It means so much. The love and support is something I'm forever grateful for and always appreciating. Thank you to all of the authors out there that show me love as well. Thanks for the support and encouragement.

Nasi and Victorious! You ladies rock! You two are the most awesome-est people I've ever encountered. Not only are you readers of my work, but ya'll have become very good friends. Ya'll are like my therapists in the inbox. I love you two and everything you've contributed to bringing this story to life. You believed in it from day one and was right there whenever I needed to run anything by you. Love you ladies!

Mona, Novia, and Alisa...ya'll already know what ya'll mean to me. Love you my wonderful sisters!

Delores Miles, lady I just love you. Been with me throughout my publishing journey. Knew me when I was just Ada Marie on Facebook. Thanks for being there for me as I brought this here book to life. Thank you!

K. Michelle (lmao), I just don't know what I would do without your crazy ass. It's so crazy when I sit back and think how our friendship started and it just blossomed to what it is now. How long has it been now? A year? Hope to have you there for many more years to come. Love you! Hugs and kisses, hugs and kisses...

My team of friends and supporters, a mix of readers and authors, whom I can depend on to make me laugh, encourage me, support me...Carmen aka Tempis J, Yolanda, Tureko,

Toni, Yo Loni, Elle...thank you so much ladies! Your words keep me going. And it feels good to know I have people in my corner. Love ya'll.

The bum bitches in MAC lol...Amanda, Geneva and Tiffany, I love you hoes!!!

To my family...Thank you for believing in me and getting on my nerves at the same time lol. Love ya!

Chapter 1

With all that Cassie had going on, the last thing she needed was to tend to two grown women and their issues.

When she whipped her car into her sister's driveway, she could see Nicole being restrained by her husband, Parker. At the receiving end of Nicole's deranged state was Colette. She seemed unbothered and even had the nerves to wear a slight smirk on her face.

Cassie got out of the car and headed their way.

When Nicole saw her, she yelled, "Get her Cass! I ain't got time for this bitch's shit. Get her away from me before I hurt her!"

"And I love you too," Colette taunted. She turned to Cassie, "C'mon so we can go."

"Well...hold up," Cassie objected. "What did you do Letty?"

"Tell her Parker," Nicole snarled at her husband. "What did that slut bucket over there do?"

Cassie looked back at Colette who wore an expression that showed her lack of concern. Cassie took the time to study Colette's appearance. Her black spaghetti strap mini dress seemed to be falling off of her, revealing more of her D-cup sized breasts than intended. She had one heel on and the other in her hand. Cassie wasn't sure if that's how Nicole threw her out of the house, or if Colette removed the shoe to attack Nicole.

The way her body swayed, and the glassy look in her eyes, Cassie assumed Colette had been drinking.

"It wasn't even like that Nicole," Parker tried to reason.

Colette scoffed. "I don't want that nerdy mothafucka. I was just helping you out Cole...your husband ain't shit...four-eyed fucka."

That riled Nicole up even more. She was able to go around Parker and jab Colette a few times. Colette screamed and tried to run to Cassie's car, but Nicole was able to grab a handful of Colette's hair jerking her backwards. Cassie then felt a need to intervene and help Parker pry the women apart.

"Go get in the car!" Cassie ordered. She turned to Nicole and Parker with a glower. "What the hell is going on?"

"That bitch was in my house trying to fuck my husband!" Nicole shouted.

Cassie looked at Parker with disappointment. "Did you Parker?"

"No!" he insisted. "I gotta be interrogated by wife and now her sister too?"

"You damn right," Cassie spat. "That's some foul shit. And with Letty of all people?"

"She was drunk." Parker tried to argue in Colette's defense, but neither his wife nor Cassie was trying to hear it.

Nicole started to release angry tears. "I don't even know why I let her in my house. I've tried and tried Cass. But she's fucked up too many times for me."

"I know," Cassie said in a sullen voice. "You and Parker go back in the house and work this shit out. Ya'll neighbors have been entertained enough."

Cassie turned away and headed to her car. The cherry air freshener inside her car wasn't enough to overpower the stench of alcohol on Colette. She sat slumped over, her head resting against the window with her eyes shut as if she hadn't caused problems for yet another household.

"Where am I taking you?" Cassie asked as she backed out of the driveway.

Colette sat up with her eyes heavy. "Shit, I guess take me back to your place."

Cassie shook her head. "No. You can't come back there with me."

"Well, Cassie, I ain't got nowhere to go. Where the fuck am I gonna go?"

"Maybe if you wouldn't burn so many bridges with people, you'd have somewhere to go."

Colette fell back against her seat. "People act like they just so damn righteous as if they ain't never did shit wrong."

Ignoring her statement, Cassie asked, "What the people say about putting you somewhere else?"

"He said that the people said...that they said...some shit," Colette mumbled.

Cassie groaned. Taking Colette to her place was not in her plans for the night. She didn't know of anyone else that would readily take Colette's drunk ass in. So back to her place she went.

After a ten-minute struggle, Cassie managed to push, pull and drag Colette up to her second floor apartment. Once inside, she let Colette fall on the floor. Her dress flew up revealing her uncovered ass and bushy triangle between her legs. It was disgusting and made Cassie shudder.

"Letty, you need to get your ass up," Cassie grumbled. She stepped over her and went to the kitchen.

Cassie didn't have time for this shit. Colette was her least favorite person. She was a wreck, irresponsible, and a whore. And sometimes Cassie felt like she was doomed to turn into Colette. The only difference between the two of them was Cassie didn't have any kids. Colette had three: Cassie, Nicole, and their brother Romyn.

Yes, this lady was her mother. A mother that she was embarrassed to claim. A mother that she had to watch be a whore while she had to play caretaker to her younger siblings. A mother who used to get so drunk from partying all night, then would come home and vomit everywhere for Cassie to clean up. A mother who had slept with everybody's husband. Cassie was so ashamed of Colette.

Colette was a party girl. She was forty-five inside the body of a twenty-five-year-old. Genetics had blessed the woman. Cassie hoped to be so fortunate at that age, but she was almost thirty and people often mistaken her to be Colette's older sister. Talk about aggravating. And all Colette would do was laugh and rub it in Cassie's face.

Perhaps if she had been more of a mother, Cassie could appreciate that Colette looked amazing. But she had no positive words for her. And then she tried to sleep with her daughter's husband? What was wrong with Colette?

Cassie called her brother Romyn.

He answered on the second ring. "If you're calling me about Letty, my hands are tied."

"C'mon Ro," Cassie pleaded.

"Nicole told me what happened," he said. "She had called me to come get her but I couldn't leave work. I ain't in the mood to be dealing with your mother."

"She's your mama too."

"And I don't feel a need to be responsible for her ass either," he sneered. "I didn't come back home to take care of Letty."

Cassie couldn't really blame him. He and Nicole, had less of a connection with Colette as she did. Maybe it was because she was the oldest, but she felt trapped into caring for Colette even when she didn't want to.

"Besides," Romyn continued. "I have a roommate, you don't. You have a whole extra bedroom that she can stay in."

"I just don't wanna be bothered like that," Cassie said. Then a thought occurred to her. Maybe this could work out for her good.

No one really knew this, but Cassie didn't have a job. She had been unemployed for two weeks. Her former employer was a reputable cable company where she held a position as customer service representative. Things were okay; not exactly the best. It was a job and it was paying the bills; but she couldn't stand her superiors and the bullshit she had to deal with. She was always being overworked and overlooked. And her supervisor had one last time to talk to her like she was a child. Two weeks ago was the last time. Cassie's behavior didn't exactly warrant her rights to unemployment benefits, therefore, she had no income at all.

Trying to keep up with her friends spending habits hadn't given her savings much of a chance. It should have been easy being that she had no children to care for; but she had to get a nice two-bedroom apartment in a lavish area with a lavish rent amount. On top of that she had to drive a late model Dodge Charger, which she loved. It was a pretty plum purple, and she couldn't see herself parting ways with it. And since her credit sucked at one point, so did her monthly car payment.

That situation was another stressor in her life. If she didn't get a job soon, she knew she would have to give it all up. Colette got a guaranteed check every month for her spousal survivor's benefits. She lucked up once and got an old man to marry her three years before he died. Cassie remembered the monthly amount being somewhere around seventeen hundred a month. Maybe Colette could be her roomie for a little while and help her maintain her bills; at least for another month while she looked for employment.

———

Rock couldn't believe the shit he constantly found himself stuck in. The more he tried to walk the straight and narrow, it was always some force trying to knock him down. But this one...this one was his fault.

"Are you sure?" he asked.

Melody answered by holding up the white wand with two pink lines in a small window display.

Another baby? That was not in Rock's plans at all. Hell, for him, that was another eighteen years of debt added to the debt already piled high against him.

Melody leaned against the arm of her sofa and folded her arms across her chest. "What are you gonna do?"

"What the fuck you mean?" he asked. He was aggravated by the situation, but he wasn't exactly mad. Melody was already the mother to his eight-year-old son. They've had a pretty decent relationship over the years. He still had access to the pussy even when they were dating someone new. He could even admit that sometimes he got a little jealous when she seemed to be smitten with another nigga. He finally had to admit to himself that there was still love there.

"Well, don't you got that lil girlfriend of yours?" Melody mentioned.

Cassie wasn't exactly what Rock would label as his girlfriend. Dealing with her was a challenge. Rock never thought it would have taken this much effort just to please her. But he knew she was hateful, moody, and a grouch before he pursued her. He knew how she was since meeting her back in their junior high school days.

Presently, he and Cassie weren't on the best of terms. Things had started off great with them. He harassed her and wouldn't let up until she gave in. Even after she gave in, he still had to prove to her he wasn't on some shit. He was able to break through her wall and she gave him a chance. But he didn't know what Cassie's issues were; she started stacking the wall back up and shutting him out. That's why he had been spending more time with his first baby mama, Melody.

"We ain't really official like that," he said. He sighed heavily. "You gon' keep it?"

"I ain't getting no abortion, Rock," she said with firmness. "Now you said six years ago you weren't ready to settle down. You asked me to give you some time to get this shit out of your system. Well, you had another child after that. And now you all lovey-dovey with this bitch Cassie."

"So whatchu saying Mel?" he asked.

"I'm saying, you need to start making grown man choices," she said. There was a pause. As an afterthought, she added, "But if you don't want to, I can go ahead and file for child support for both the new baby and Lil Rock."

The mention of child support made him cringe. He managed to convince Melody for eight years not to take child support out on him. His other baby's mama wasn't having it. She was a hot head like Cassie. If Jerrica knew the type of money he was making at BevyCo, she would hurry up and have his ass in court getting the order amended.

Maybe it was time to make some grown man choices. He would have to make sure Melody was straight. He had to appease her. When she wasn't happy, she could be worse than Jerrica.

"You ain't gotta do that," he said soothingly. He walked over to her to give her an endearing kiss on the forehead. "I'ma be here for you and for them."

"What does that mean?" Melody asked. With hope, she looked up into his eyes.

"We'll talk," he said. He kissed her on the lips. "When I get back, we'll talk."

Melody smiled. "Okay."

They kissed one last time before Rock left.

He had to make a trip to see Cassie now. He didn't know what was up with her lately. She was bipolar as hell. One day she was up and excited to see him, and the next day she was down and didn't want him near her.

When he got to her place the sight of her mama sprawled out on the sofa was a surprise. With the way Cassie felt about Colette, he didn't think she would let the woman set foot in her place.

"What's wrong with her?" he asked in a whisper.

"She's drunk," Cassie replied. She could see Rock getting an eyeful of Colette's exposed twat. She groaned and tapped her mother. "Letty, you need to get up and go in the room up there."

Colette sat up letting her straps fall down her shoulders. She tried to focus on Cassie and Rock through squinted eyes. "Who is that?"

"Don't worry about it. You need to take a shower or something," Cassie said. She was annoyed.

Colette looked Rock up and down. "Is this your boyfriend now?"

"Letty, I swear if you pull that bullshit you did with Nicole, you won't have nobody left that care a little about you," Cassie threatened.

"I don't want his lil ass," Colette grumbled. She grabbed her purse, abandoned her shoes, and staggered down the hall to the first bedroom. "Which fuckin' room is it?"

"On the left. You bet not take your ass in my room," Cassie threatened.

Rock sat down on the sofa. "What's up with her being here?"

"My sister put her out of her house," Cassie answered as she sat beside him.

"She ain't got nowhere to live?"

"Nope. Remember I told you that my mama place caught on fire. It was due to her negligence so the landlord dude ain't tryna put her up in another one of his properties. She messed that up cause he was the only person willing to fuck with her like that. She can't get an apartment in her own name cause her shit fucked up and she got a criminal record."

"So you letting her stay here?" Rock chuckled. "So you do have a heart."

Cassie rolled her eyes. "Please. I'm only doing it cause I need her help."

"Help? What kind of help?"

She released a frustrated blow of air. "I ain't got no job and she's gonna help me out while I look."

It was just like Cassie not to go to him for help. She always wanted to take care of herself to prove a point.

He asked, "What happened to your job? You quit?"

"Naw, I got fired. But it's all good. I'll find me something else," she said without care.

"Like what? The cable company was paying you pretty decent. Where you gon' get another job like that?"

"I'll find one Rock," she said with certainty.

"Cassie, it ain't like you got a degree and qualified to do a lot of shit," he mentioned.

Cassie snapped. "And what the hell that's supposed to mean? I can find a job out there with no degree, nigga! Where the fuck is your degree? Nigga!"

"Damn...chill," Rock said. "I'm just saying. Jazz probably could get you on at BevyCo but I don't know what the hell you could do there. What Jazz do she went to school for."

"So you wanna remind me I didn't go to college like Jazz and Tanya?" Her leg began to bounce.

"Not like that Cass," he said. "You always think somebody attacking you."

She remained quiet wearing a displeased look.

"I ain't come over here to make you mad," he said trying to lighten the mood. He reached for her, wanting to pull her close.

She snatched away from his grasp. "I'm good."

He blew air out in frustration. This was the shit he was talking about. Melody didn't even give him these kind of problems.

"Cass," he spoke carefully.

Cassie got up abruptly and headed towards the hall leading to the bedrooms. She called over her shoulder, "Lock the bottom lock on your way out."

Rock sat there in disbelief. When he heard her bedroom door slam, all thoughts of trying to make her feel better left. He couldn't take much more of her hot/cold ass.

He heard the bedroom door open. He didn't even bother to look at her. He assumed she came back to apologize.

"She mad at you?" Colette whispered.

Rock was rather surprised to see Cassie's mama standing there. He stood up to leave. "Yeah, she's mad as always."

Colette's already fallen straps seem to fall more allowing Rock to see the start of her left areola. If it had been somebody else's mama, he would have been grossed out, but this was Colette. No man in his right mind, could say that Colette wasn't bad. She put her daughters to shame. Even when they were younger, all the boys used to drool over Colette. Back then, Cassie hated it just as much as she did as an adult.

Colette smiled at him. "You cute. You got a pretty lil baby face. How old are you?"

Ignoring her, Rock headed to the entrance area. "Tell Cassie I'm gone."

"Wait," Colette whispered. She stopped him before he headed down the hall. The way Cassie's apartment was made was backwards. The bedrooms were in the front where the entrance was. A short hallway opened up to the living room, dining area, and the kitchen's open space. If Rock made it the door, Cassie would be able to hear them.

"You fucking with my daughter?"

"Kinda," he answered.

"It don't seem like she taking care of you. Take my number. When you need a real woman's company, give me a call okay," she said in a flirtatious manner. She made sure to brush her large breasts against him.

He wouldn't take Colette serious, but the idea of entertaining her seemed rather tempting. He shook his head. "I'm straight." And he left, leaving Colette feeling defeated.

Chapter 2

A few days later, Cassie found herself at one of her best friend's house. She was still upset at Rock for pointing out one of her biggest disappointments in herself. No, she didn't go off to college when Jazmin, Tanya, and the rest of her childhood friends decided to go. She attempted to go to community college, but she wasn't really feeling it. She didn't enjoy those kind of things. Besides, she could barely focus with the shit her mama was doing. That's where a lot of her resentment for Colette came from. Cassie couldn't help but always wonder, if Colette had been a good parent like Paul and Phyllis were for Jazmin, how different her life would have turn out.

That kind of nurturing and love was missing from her household growing up, which could have been almost considered a brothel back then. And she wasn't able to get it from other relatives because people just didn't want to be bothered with Colette and her drama. The only person that would show them some love was their uncle Cut, but he only came through every once in a while to break them off some money, or some goodies he bought hot off the street.

Cassie's eyes traveled to Rock as he talked with Jah, their mutual friend. She didn't even know why she insisted on hopping in the car with him when he came over. He was trying to kiss up and make her feel better, but it wasn't working. When she discovered that he was coming over here, she wanted to tag along.

Jazmin took the cellphone from Genesis before she could bang it on the glass coffee table. "Give me this phone."

Genesis wasn't happy at all. Her face contorted into a frown as she reached for it. "No, no, no," she blabbed.

"Right. No, no, no," Jazmin scolded. "You can't be playing with people's phones—Whose phone is this anyway?" She looked at the display and was shocked. Her mouth dropped open.

Angered, she bellowed, "Jah! What the fuck is this?"

Genesis giggled, "Fuh-ck!"

"What the fuck is what?" Jah asked from the sofa. "Why you yellin' and shit? Got Genni cussin'."

Jazmin's outburst got Cassie's attention. She immediately recognized the phone in her hand as Rock's. "That's Rock's phone, not Jah's. You took it from Genni right?"

"Here, give it to me," Rock said casually. He reached out for it hoping Jazmin's reaction wouldn't pique Cassie's interest. He was sure what Jazmin saw on it wouldn't be something Cassie would appreciate.

Cassie snatched the phone from Jazmin's grip and stared at it. She looked up at Rock with disbelief and disappointment. "Really Rock? And why the fuck ain't your phone locked?"

"Fuh-ck!" Genesis giggled again.

"Ay, I be tellin' ya'll don't let Genni get ahold of ya'll phone. I don't know what the hell her lil ass be doing, but she can unlock a phone bruh. She be on some abracadabra shit," Jah said.

Cassie was beyond pissed. She cut her narrowed eyes toward Rock. All he could do was return with a goofy crooked grin. This shit wasn't funny to her. If he kept this kind of thing up, they would never get anywhere.

"Give me my phone," Rock said reaching out for it again.

"So is this what you doing now, Rodney?" she asked.

"Man, go head on with that," Rock dismissed nonchalantly. He wasn't in the mood to entertain Cassie's tantrum.

"For real?" she asked, feeling a bit slighted. "So it's okay for other bitches to send you pussy pics?"

"I didn't say it was okay. But shit, I can't help that they be sending me that shit. I don't be asking for it," he mumbled. He tried to turn his attention back to the television. Getting the phone back wasn't going to happen on his time. What was the use in trying to get it from her?

"And then this pussy look raggedy." She wore a disgusted contemptuous snarl. "Bitch shit look like roast beef. Arby's pussy looking bitch."

"Shit...Ain't nothing wrong with Arby's. Get some of that Arby sauce and put that shit on there. Good than a mothafucka. Eat it right on up!" Jah said with hilarity. Him and Rock shared laughter in the humorous moment. He continued, "Fuck you talkin' bout. Juicy serve me Arby's every night. Ain't that right baby?"

Jazmin's mouth dropped open and her face flushed with embarrassment. "Jah! My vagina don't look like roast beef."

"You don't be down there, I do," he joked.

Ignoring Jah and Jazmin, Cassie glared at Rock. "Oh you think it's funny?"

Rock waved her off, dismissing her once again.

Jazmin was saying, "No Jah. That right there wasn't very appealing. Rock, tell whoever that is not to ever send out any more pics of her private parts. Or if she must, tell her she need to ask one of her friends to borrow a picture of theirs."

Rock chuckled, "I see Jah rubbing off on your ass."

Jah started laughing. "Let me see."

Cassie stepped closer with the phone facing forward.

"What the fuck!" Jah exclaimed. He turned to Rock. "Nigga!"

Genni said, "Fuh-ck nic-ca."

Jazmin gave Genesis a look that only made her giggle. She said it again, "Fuh-ck."

"See, ya'll got my baby cussing," Jazmin said. "C'mon let's go check on your brother."

As Jazmin left with Genesis scurrying behind her, Jah's face contorted into disgust. He said, "That shit look like it need to be upside down in a mothafuckin' cave some goddamn where. Ol' wolf bat looking ass pussy. Shit look like it'll bite and give a mothafucka rabies. Nigga, please tell me you ain't hittin' that."

Jah's comment only added more to Cassie's displeased attitude. She tossed the phone at Rock hoping to knock him in the head in the process. "And this why I can't take you fucking serious."

Cassie stormed out of the den heading to the front of the house. Rock called out, "Where you going?"

"Call wolf bat pussy and ask her where she going!" she called over her shoulder.

Rock groaned. He knew he had to go after her, but he just wasn't in the mood. Besides, they can say what they want, he was trying to see what "wolf bat pussy" was talking about.

———

Once Cassie got outside, she regretted not driving her own car so that she could leave when she was ready. Maybe she could ask Jazmin to take her home, because how she felt in the moment, she didn't want to be alone with Rock. She didn't trust herself. She was sure she would have him beaten and bruised by the time he pulled up to her apartment building.

Fuming, Cassie stood at the bottom porch step as a bronze SUV swung into the driveway. She kept her eyes on the driver side door wondering who was about to get out. Just then, Rock came out onto the porch.

"Man, why you always trippin' like that Cass?" Rock asked.

Still waiting on the person to exit the SUV, Cassie absently replied, "All you ever do is embarrass me."

"How the fuck I do that? You the one showing people my shit," he argued.

"Jazmin saw it on her own, dumb ass," she said with an attitude.

"And then yo ass showed Jah."

She finally turned to face him. "Who is that anyway? Is that one of your new lil girlfriends?"

"I ain't got no girlfriends," he retorted.

She squinted her eyes at him wishing she could give off lasers that would blow him up. Angered, she said, "So I ain't your girlfriend now."

Rock shrugged aggravating her vexation.

Annoyed with his behavior, Cassie had momentarily abandon her fixation on the SUV. Hearing the door shut, she looked back in the direction of the SUV.

Rock looked up too. "What's up nigga?"

Eli shook his head as if to say "nothing". Cassie was oblivious to the dismal state he was in and said, "Hey."

Instead of returning the pleasantries, Eli turned up his nose. "Damn, do you ever go home? Have you moved in?"

"You always gotta be a smart ass," Cassie said with a roll of her eyes. She looked toward his SUV. "And why you gotta copy Jah? What happened to the Escalade?"

Eli replied, "How am I copying Jah? Mine is *bought* and Jah's is *being bought*. Jah's a fifteen and mine is a sixteen. When was the last time you got your vision checked cause anybody can see that mine is bronze and his is black...well not anybody. Lovely might not be able to. Not at night anyway."

"Whatever," Cassie said playfully. She watched him as he passed by to enter the house. It was then that she noticed, Eli wasn't his usual vibrant self.

When he disappeared, Cassie realized Rock was staring at her hard. "What?" she asked.

"You paying attention to what that nigga driving?"

Cassie let out a sarcastic laugh. "Are you serious right now? You got a bitch's whole pussy in your phone and you worried about me making an innocent observation?"

"Whatever Cass," Rock dismissed. "I'm ready to go."

"I ain't going with you," she said with defiance. "I'll get Jazz to take me home. Fuck you."

"You a mean lil ass. I swear." He brushed by her, purposely making their bodies touch.

For a split second, Cassie reconsidered. She played out the night in her head. He would take her home. They would sit in the car arguing for about thirty minutes. He would shut down. She would get out slamming the door. He would follow her to her apartment door just to scold her about slamming his damn door. She would let herself in and he would follow. They would argue some more. They would calm down. He would apologize and make an empty promise to return. She would go to bed alone. Again.

"Go see about rotten pussy," she yelled at him.

Before hopping into his car, Rock laughed mockingly. "I might just do that."

"That's okay," she spoke out loud as the car's engine revved to life. "I got something for your ass."

Rock sat in the car staring at her. She always wanted to make things so difficult. Normally, he would let her stubborn ass be Jazmin and Jah's problem, but he didn't like how Cassie was looking at Eli. Of course he shouldn't be worried about a soft ass nigga like Eli, but he didn't put anything past anybody.

He opened the door to lean out. He yelled to her, "C'mon man! Stop fucking playing and bring yo ass on!"

She seemed hesitant at first. Still glowering she raised her finger as if to ask for a second. She disappeared back into the house. Seconds later she was coming back with her purse.

"That's what I thought nigga." Rock cut his eyes at her as he put the car in reverse.

"Oh shut up," she said rolling her eyes. "The only reason I'm going with you is because Jah was probably going to bitch about Jazmin bringing me home at night and his ass wasn't going to do it."

"You had to go in there and say bye to your boyfriend, didn't you," he mocked.

Cassie waved him off. She wasn't in the mood for his insecurities. She had enough of her own to deal with. "Don't try to redirect made-up guilt on me because you got caught with a pussy in your phone."

"I don't even know who the fuck that is. It was probably sent to my number by mistake."

"Sure Rock," she said with skepticism. "But what I'm supposed to care for. I ain't your girlfriend, right? So what would it matter if I did say bye to another nigga? Right?"

Rock scoffed with a slight chuckle. He said under his breath in a playful, but serious manner, "Yo ass got fuckin' jokes."

"Yep, jokes for days," she said with nonchalance as she directed her focus out the window.

Twenty minutes later, things went as she predicted, except for him making empty promises to return. He decided to stay a little while to make up for the mysterious wolf bat pussy that showed up in his phone. And since Cassie had her apartment to herself, they both knew what time it was. They wasted no time heading to her bedroom to relieve some tension. They went at it.

She needed Rock to fuck her good; cause her pain. She needed that unbearable pleasure brought on by the pain that was able to bring about a powerful orgasm; and, if he jabbed the right spot, she could squirt. That kind of sex was exciting and invigorating. Not many men had mastered that skill with her. Only one, an older man, had ever brought about that kind of pleasure to her. She longed for it, but no matter how much she tried to teach men that came after him, they just never got it. They were not a master; they were not her *Maestro*.

Her moans were loud and whimperish. She threw it back against him, hoping to encourage him to go harder and faster.

It wasn't working.

Her aggravation manifested quickly. She was done. But he wasn't. He hadn't even busted a nut.

Agitated and no longer into it, she blew a frustrated breath, "Can you hurry up?"

Rock continued to pound her, but it didn't feel the same for her anymore. She felt detached; no longer aroused. She soon began to dry up. Rock could tell, so he proceeded to spit on her.

"No!" she objected. "Don't fuckin' spit on me."

Clearly irritated he sneered, "What the fuck is your problem?"

"Get off me; I'm done," she replied hatefully.

"This the shit I'm talking about Cass!"

She just stared up at him blinking her eyes. His face turned into a scowl. She knew he hated her in the moment. He looked so annoyed and vexed with her. She could even feel his condom-wrapped dick deflating inside of her. She helped him out by scooting away from under him. She scooped up her panties. Without looking back, she quickly made her way to her bathroom.

She couldn't explain why she behaved like that. She couldn't explain her mood swings and irritability. She wanted to believe it was because he was unable to completely take her there sexually. However, it could be other things, such as stress.

After cleaning herself, she proceeded to slip her panties back on.

Walking out of the bathroom, she saw that Rock was fully dressed and glaring at her. He didn't bother to speak of his departure. He just kept moving towards the bedroom door.

She followed behind him. "Where you going?"

Before he answered, she heard thumping and loud moaning. She rolled her eyes and let her shoulders drop. Her new roommate, her mother, was home. Cassie had no idea when Colette had arrived, but she sure didn't waste any time entertaining whomever she brought back to the apartment.

Rock shook his head as if to the situation was unbelievable.

Cassie repeated the question. "Where you rushing off to?"

Rock said, "Out of here. Ain't nobody got time for your shit Cassie. Your ass got some serious issues."

She couldn't argue with him there. She had to ask though. "You going to Melody's or Jerrica's?"

"Why would it matter?"

Cassie walked upon him aggressively, "Because nigga. I know you be going over their house anyway."

"Yeah, I go over there cause that's where the fuck my kids at," he countered.

"But you know what the fuck I'm talking about," she said angrily. "Always talking about you be over your

33

brother's house. You still laying up with Jerrica. Probably Melody too. Or maybe you going over to the bitch house who sent you her raggedy ass pussy."

Rock was done before the argument could fully grow. "Fuck this shit. Ain't nobody gotta explain shit to you...Ol' moody ass. And I damn sho ain't finna sit here listening to yo mama fucking and yo ass playing around."

Before she could come back with something, he had snatched the door open and stormed out. He made sure to slam the door behind himself.

"Fuck him," Cassie said under her breath as she locked the door. She headed back to her bedroom. As she was entering, the secondary bedroom's door swung open. And there was her mama, making a futile attempt to cover herself with her black satin robe. If Rock had been in the hallway with Cassie, he would have gotten an eyeful of melon size breasts and a fuzzy vagina.

"What's going on out here?" Colette asked as if she was concern.

Cassie let out a groan filled with disgust and aggravation, and kept walking to her room. This couldn't be her life; yet here she was living it.

Chapter 3

The following Saturday was Genesis' birthday party and Jazmin had it in the backyard of her and Jah's new home. Although Cassie didn't have any kids to attend the party, she was still in attendance. She even brought her younger brother along.

Romyn was familiar with most of Cassie's friends, but wasn't necessarily comfortable with all of them. Cassie had warned him beforehand that a few of her male friends had homophobic tendencies. Romyn was quite comfortable with his sexuality, but he hated being around people that treated him as if he had the plague.

"Are you okay?" Jazmin asked. She tried to offer him a comforting smile to put him at ease. A few of them sat at one of the tables in the backyard, while others gathered here and there running after the kids. At the moment, Romyn was the only male hanging with the ladies.

Romyn nodded. He stole a glance at Jazmin's husband and his male friends. When he shifted his eyes back, Cassie was grinning at him knowingly.

"What?" he asked. His face blushed with guilt.

"I know who you're looking at," Cassie teased.

"Shut up," Romyn hissed. He rolled his eyes, but not before he stole another glance. This time, the object of his mental inquisition caught him looking.

Cassie lowered her voice. "You want me to hook you up?"

"Will you stop," Romyn whispered.

Jazmin looked at them with suspicion. "What are ya'll talking about?"

Romyn shook his head dismissively, "Nothing. Cassie's being stupid as usual."

"Cassie need to be filling these damn goody bags," Tanya interjected.

"I am," Cassie mumbled. "I don't know why we didn't just fill all of them up at first."

Jazmin said, "Well, I didn't know this many kids were gonna come. Hush Cassie, and just help me out."

Cassie playfully rolled her eyes at her friend. She turned her attention back to Romyn. "So I guess you peeped something, huh?"

"No," Romyn said matter-of-factly. He was about to say more, but paused as he noticed someone making their way over to their table. He was immediately flustered and looked away to avoid eye contact.

"Don't come over here playing," Tanya said to Eli. "Unless you plan to fill these little bags, you can go on back down there."

Ignoring Tanya, Eli looked at Romyn and asked, "Do I know you?"

Cassie watched her brother's light skin turn a shade red as he shook his head emphatically. She sensed her brother's attraction to Eli. She couldn't really blame him. She didn't really know Eli on a personal level, but she had been around him on several occasions. She along with everybody else, had at one time or another questioned his sexuality. He was hard to read. He was every bit metrosexual and meticulous about his grooming. Although he was surrounded by very masculine and thuggish men such as Jah and Rock, he remained comfortable and confident in who he was. Eli was going to be pretty always; that was a given. Cassie had to admit that his flawless appearance coupled with his pretty facial features were a bit intimidating. It was hard to look at him without staring, but it was even harder to not look at him. Like now. He was standing next to her, but talking across her to her brother. She almost didn't want to breathe.

However, Cassie was convinced that Eli went both ways. He just kept that other side of him private.

"Do you know someone named Kreme?" Eli asked.

When he mentioned that name, Romyn's eyes widen and his interest roused. Why would Eli know Kreme unless he ran in that "crowd"? And if he did run in that "crowd", then maybe Romyn's attraction to Eli was acceptable.

"I don't really know him," Romyn answered. "I have friends that know him."

"I've seen you at his club before with Corvell," Eli told him.

"You know Corvell too?" Romyn asked. Corvell was one of Romyn's closest friends who was also openly gay. Both he and Romyn had a bad habit of going after down low men that often broke their hearts. But Eli was fine and he wouldn't mind doing some things with him behind closed doors.

Romyn let his eyes discreetly take in as much of Eli as he could. He loved a man with pretty eyes, and though Eli's weren't a color other than brown, they were the color of sweet lemon tea. His lashes cascaded such a shadow that made it seem as if he had on mascara and eyeliner. Even his natural arched eyebrows seemed professionally etched. Romyn was envious of the wild curls atop Eli's head that qualified as "good hair". His hair was tapered precisely to match the sharp lining of his facial hair that formed into a closely shaven beard. His creamy peanut complexion was free of any blemishes unless the empty piercings counted. Having those were questionable, because not too many straight men had an eyebrow and lip piercing along with a nose piercing.

Romyn guessed Eli to be about six feet with a nice medium build. He could tell he had a muscular body under his fitting shirt. The tattoos on his arms were sexy as fuck to Romyn. And the distressed jeans he had on displayed Eli's nice ass. Yes, if Eli was indeed openly gay or not, Romyn wouldn't mind being his special friend.

"Yeah, I know Corvell," Eli said. "Ain't that your boyfriend?"

And just like that, Romyn had to come to his senses. He did have a boyfriend, but it wasn't his friend Corvell. Lonzo was his heart, and quickly his lust for another man was about to replace that.

"No, he isn't my boyfriend. We're just really close," Romyn replied.

"Tell him I said hey if I don't see him first down there at Bodiez," Eli said casually.

Now Eli really had Romyn curious, because Bodiez was owned by the same man that own Club Jouissance. Romyn wondered if Eli knew about that club too. Both of Kreme's clubs were eccentric, erotic, and risqué. However, there was a difference. Jouissance was for the sexually liberated. It was for the promiscuous, unafraid of sexual exploration. The word *Jouissance* in French is enjoyment, but connotes pleasure and orgasm. It was exclusive to paying members only. Bodiez was a regular night club open to everyone, mostly a mixed crowd.

Cassie was thrown by Eli's ability to speak to her brother so comfortably. Either her assumption about Eli was right, or he simply didn't care about Romyn being gay.

"What is Club Jouissance and who is Kreme?" Tanya asked.

"None of yo business," Eli said in a playful manner. Then he poked Cassie on the side of her head. Her reaction was to swat at him, but he moved out of the way.

"Stop it ugly," Cassie said glaring at him.

"I know you are but what am I?" Eli taunted. He managed to get in another poke and said, "Just cause you got edges don't mean you supposed to keep 'em nappy. If you can't get your hair done at least brush that shit."

And this was the Eli no one could tolerate. Although people laughed they tried not to. It only fed into his silly behavior.

"Fuck you," Cassie mumbled.

Tanya chuckled, "Cassie, your hair is looking kinda rough though."

Cassie smooth her hand over her hair self-consciously. "It ain't that rough. I ain't been able to hit Lita up though. Funds a little low."

"Ain't that nigga over there your man?" Eli asked pointing at Rock. "Get some money from him."

Cassie waved her hand dismissively and turned up her nose.

Tanya teased, "Is there trouble in paradise?"

"What paradise? There ain't never been a paradise," Cassie said.

Jazmin pulled out a chair and sat down. She propped her arm up on her elbow and rested her face in her palm and looked on anxiously. "Do tell. What has happened?"

Cassie chuckled. "Nothing. Things just ain't clicking like it did initially."

"You know what I think," Tanya said smacking her lips.

"Who cares what you think," Eli said rolling his eyes.

Tanya looked at Jazmin. "Getcho cousin."

"Eli," Jazmin chided. She looked back at Tanya. "Okay go ahead with your theory."

Tanya proceeded. "I think Cassie looked at you and Jah and thought she could have the same thing with Rock. Rock and Jah are two totally different people, honey. And you, Cassie, ain't no Jazmin."

Offended, Cassie asked, "And what does that mean?"

"It means exactly what she said," Eli interjected. "You ain't no Jazmin."

Cassie narrowed her eyes at Eli. He responded with an innocent shrug, "What?"

"I don't think she was saying anything bad. It's just that you're not her," Romyn clarified. "I think you need to focus on getting a job and don't worry about Rock. He's a distraction."

"Getting a job?" Jazmin echoed. "She has a job. Right Cassie?"

Cassie cut her eyes toward her brother. "Thank you for telling my business."

Romyn gasped and looked at Cassie apologetically. "I'm sorry. You hadn't told them."

Tanya looked across the table at Cassie like she was crazy. "You ain't got no job Cassie?"

There was no use in keeping it a secret from her friends. They would have known eventually. And her hair was a telltale sign. She got her hair done faithfully when she had income.

"No, I don't," she answered. "But I'm looking though."

A smile spread across Jazmin's face. "Eli needs a new assistant. Maybe he can—"

"He can do what?" Eli interrupted. "I'm good on that; thank you."

Jazmin gave Eli a look. "C'mon Eli. Stop being like that. You know you could use the help."

"She don't look like she can assist with anything," Eli said turning his nose up at Cassie.

Cassie's brow furrowed. "Eli, I can learn to be your assistant. Man, I need a job...for real."

"I coulda sworn I seen a sign outside the McDonald's drive-thru right there on Hillsboro Pike that said now hiring. I think you'll look cute in a McDonald's uniform," Eli said without much thought or care as he walked away.

Tanya laughed at Cassie's discontented frown. "I can't stand his ass either."

Jazmin waved Eli's antics off. "Don't worry about Eli. Just come by Monday."

"Well, shit, I want a job down there too," Tanya said.

"You have a job," Jazmin pointed out.

"*But I don't like it,*" Tanya sang with humor. "*I need anotha one.*"

If anybody was more certified to be an assistant, Tanya was over Cassie. She really hoped Tanya was joking and wouldn't compete with her for an opportunity to work at BevyCo.

———

Kris's expression held the glare of a disgruntled wife as her husband neared her. He already knew she was displeased. The blank look on his face was a testament of that. It was what Eli did when he wanted to disguise how he felt so a person couldn't read him. But Kris had him figured out.

"What are you doing?" Eli asked. He took notice of her with lil man's diaper bag on her shoulder and lil man on her hip. She simply cut her eyes at him and turned to walk away.

Eli followed her and rather than make a scene with his wife, he remained quiet. Instead of going through the house, Kris opted to walk around the side of the house towards the front.

"Are you leaving?" Eli finally asked when he was sure they were out of everyone's hearing range.

"Ain't that what it look like?" Kris said curtly.

"Why?"

She halted her movement to stare at him coldly. "Why do you insist on embarrassing me?"

"Embarrass how?" Eli was genuinely confused.

"You know what I mean," she said.

"I really don't or I wouldn't have asked you."

"You and that boy."

"What boy?"

"You don't think I saw the way ya'll were staring at each other?" she said angrily.

"That lil young nigga back there? Cassie's brother?" he asked for clarification.

"You know exactly who I'm talking about."

Here she goes with this shit, Eli thought. "That's Cassie's brother and I told him he looked familiar and asked if he knew someone I knew. That's all."

"But why is he familiar to you? He's gay Eli!"

"So!"

"You don't think that's inappropriate? People already accuse you of being gay and I gotta deal with the constant questions. And then as soon as a gay man come around, you know them and be all in their face."

"I can't help who I know. But that doesn't mean anything. You need to stop being so damn judgmental. Of all people I thought you understood me and—"

"Understood? Yeah, I thought I did until I see it's something else."

"Something else? You really think I'm gay?" he asked.

"Brother Yosef said that no man—"

Eli interrupted her with a sarcastic laugh. "Oh there it is. Brother Yosef. I knew I would hear his name at least once today. What the fuck else is your *brother* filling your head up with?"

Kris groaned in frustration and began to walk away again.

"Kris," Eli called out. When he saw that she wasn't stopping, he quickened his steps to catch up with her. "Where are you going?"

"Home," she replied over her shoulder.

"What about Avani?"

"She's fine back there with Aunt Livy," Kris said. "She can stay with you."

"Fuck you Kris," Eli spat. He went from trying to be civil to being angered. "I already know where the fuck you going. You think I'm dumb or some shit."

"And why would you care?" she asked in mockery. "Go on back there and throw your dick in that boy's face. He looked like he was dying to get a sample."

"If your ass wasn't holding this lil boy, I would smack you," he returned.

"I wish you would," Kris taunted.

"Don't try me Kris. All the shit you've been doing lately deserve an ass whooping," he said.

"As if your behavior doesn't?" she countered. She continued to walk the distance of the driveway to the street.

At this point, Eli didn't want to waste any more energy on this exchange. Here lately, the number of arguments had increased. He had become good at keeping their problems on the hush, but he knew eventually people would ask. Right now he just wasn't ready to deal with it. The complications of their marriage stared him in his face, but often times he ignored it.

He didn't know where his Kris went. The Kris that he thought he wanted to be with forever. The one he thought would love him for who he was always, just as he had loved her. But she changed. She went from the petite tomboy that would do anything in bed to please him to this very earthy feminine woman that dedicated her whole being to her spiritual beliefs. She had a whole family of sisters, brothers, and elders that she once referred to as her second family. But to Eli, those people had become her first family, and he and the kids were just people that she would make time for when she felt like it. Every time he looked forward to spending quality time with her, she was always on the go to do some studying, mentoring, meditating, worshipping, praying...with Brother Yosef. Eli would need several more sets of hands to count how many times he heard that man's name in a day. And his and Kris' sex life had become nonexistent.

So yes, in the past few months, Eli had turned to "activities" outside the home. And it wasn't just his failing marriage he was trying to get away from. There was an internal suffering he was trying to cope with, and lately he didn't feel much like himself. And he missed his older brother, Abe. Although he got on both his brothers' nerves, they loved him for who he was. Ike was home, but it just didn't feel the same without Abe. Eli wished Abe had listened to his wife, Lovely and not left the country. But if Abe was there, he would be able to help Eli through this trying time.

Eli wasn't a dummy and he knew Brother Yosef was doing more for Kris than just studying their bible. And that was another thing, this Brother Yosef was a founder and leader of this spiritual movement Kris was dedicated to. He was this self-proclaimed prophet, and to his flock, what he said was golden. Eli swore that man was making up shit and Kris believed it with her gullible ass.

He began to rotate the wedding band on his finger absent-mindedly as he made his way back to the others. He had to turn his silly face on to hide the hurt. Known in the past for having little patience when it came to women, Eli was really considering calling it quits on his marriage. He didn't know if he could take another year of the stress.

No matter how hard Rock tried to ignore it, he couldn't help but notice how close Eli had been around Cassie. She always assured him that she didn't even know Eli like that, but whenever he came around they acted as though they had been best friends. Rock didn't like that shit.

"What's up with that nigga?" Rock asked. He nodded in Eli's direction.

"Who?" Jah asked. He looked over at the table where a lot of the women had gathered and was doing a lot of yapping. "What nigga? I see two. That gay mothafucka and Eli."

"I'm talking about Eli. What's up with that nigga? He always hang with girls like that?"

"Nigga, you act like you just coming around. Yeah, nigga," Jah said annoyed. "But when he need to, he roll with me. Why?"

"I think that nigga fucking with me," Rock said matter-of-factly, never taking his eyes off of Eli.

"Fucking witchu how? Nigga, if you don't take yo paranoid ass on from here." Jah was beyond annoyed. He looked at the beer in Rock's hand and shook his head. "How many of them thangs you done had, drunk mothafucka."

"Ain't nobody drunk," Rock chuckled.

"You got to be to think a nigga like Eli fucking witchu. And fucking witchu about what?"

"Cassie."

Jah looked at Rock like he was crazy. "Don't nobody want her mean ass but you. What makes you think Eli of all people would want her? That nigga got a whole mothafuckin' wife and four mothafuckin' kids. And you think he want Cassie beady head ass?"

"I don't put shit past no nigga." His phone began to vibrate in his pocket.

Watching Rock retrieve his phone, Jah asked, "Is that because can't nobody put shit past you?"

Rock tore his eyes away from the screen of his phone and asked offended, "What's that 'posed to mean?"

"You worried 'bout Cassie but whatcho ass be doing?" It was more of a point than a question.

"I don't be doin' nothing. I'm tryna see where things could go with Cass, but her ass crazy as hell," Rock said.

He stared at the picture message he just received a little longer than he needed to before placing his phone back in his pocket.

"I know better than to believe that shit," Jah said.

"Well," Rock started. He gave it some thought about the way he would put his next statement. "Melody pregnant and I know Cassie gon' flip out when she find out."

"Wait. Your baby mama Melody?"

"Yeah nigga. She pregnant. But she talking about getting an abortion cause I won't be with her," he stated. "I ain't settling just yet. I got other shit to do."

"What other shit? Like fucking Cassie?"

"And a couple of other broads too."

Jah shook his head pitying Rock. "Nigga, you sho' do got a hard ass head. You gon' learn one day mothafucka."

Rock chuckled. "Well, until then I'ma have some fun."

Chapter 4

Cassie was having second thoughts. She wasn't sure if she could fulfill the duties of an assistant. She was lazy and didn't like being bossed around. Eli was a difficult person to deal with personally, so she knew he would be worse as her superior.

She had been in his office for five minutes and he had yet to ask her a question. And every time he made eye contact with her, his face was just blank. She was eager though, waiting on him.

He finally said, "You know I ain't really trying to hire you, right?"

Cassie rolled her eyes upward. "Damn Eli. Why not?"

He pointed at her. "See that right there. You already fired."

"You ain't even hired me," she laughed.

"According to Jazmin I have," he mumbled.

"Ain't this an interview? Shouldn't you be asking me questions?"

"I don't have shit to ask you cause like I said, I'm not trying to hire you," he retorted. Then he thought about it. Sitting back in his chair, he asked, "I do wanna know why you lost your previous job."

Cassie lowered her head. Lowly, she said, "I fought my manager and threatened to go to her supervisor's house and beat her ass too."

"You what?" Eli was in disbelief and amused at the same time.

Cassie gave him a wide-eye look. "They were fucking with me. Then they wanted to give Sally Sue next to me all this praise and recognition when I was doing all the work."

"Was her name really Sally Sue?"

"No. It was Mindy Lou," Cassie said with a scowl.

"So why didn't you just say Mindy Lou. They're both country."

"Cause she look more like a Sally Sue and I'd rather say Sally Sue."

Eli laughed. "You got issues."

She poked her lips out in a playful pout. "I know. And that's why I'd rather work here with people that can tolerate me."

"No, you wanna work here cause you think being Jazmin's friend will secure your job. You fuck up, you get fired," he corrected.

Cassie blinked at him.

Eli blinked back at her.

"So do I have the job?" she asked with caution.

"I still don't know yet. How about you go get me some coffee and we'll see how good you do that."

She stood up and ran her clammy hands down the skirt of her dress. "How do you like it?"

"How do I like what?" he asked looking genuinely confused.

"Your coffee," she said with a chuckle.

"Oh. Black—No. Two spoons of sugar and enough cream to match the color of my skin."

Cassie looked at him like he was crazy. She was actually waiting on him to snicker or something to indicate he was playing, but he didn't. He looked at her with a serious face.

"Okay," she said and headed out of the office. Now she had to figure out where the break-room was. She knew where Jazmin's workspace was so that's where she went first.

Jazmin looked up and smiled. "Hey. You finished already?"

"Your cousin is retarded. I don't know if I can really work for him. You don't need an assistant? Can I work with you?" she asked.

Jazmin chuckled. "No. What did Eli say?"

"He's just crazy. Now he want me to go get him some coffee and make it match the color of his skin. What the fuck?"

Jazmin started laughing. "Don't pay him any mind. He don't even drink coffee. He thinks it's disgusting. But what he does drink is Mt. Dew. Go get him one of those and he'll be alright."

"But he specifically asked for coffee though."

"And I'm telling you he's messing with you. The break room is down the hall and to the left. Just make your selection. They're free. Make sure you get the bottle and not the can."

"Is he always particular?"

Jazmin nodded.

Cassie shook her head as she walked away. She went in the direction Jazmin told her. She saw Jazmin's father cross her path and smiled. "Hey Mr. Paul."

Paul did a double take. "Hey Cassie. You up here visiting with Jazz?"

"No, I'm supposedly interviewing for a job," she replied.

"Oh yeah. Doing what?"

"Eli's assistant."

Paul began walking away and laughing at the same time. He called over his shoulder, "Good luck with that."

That was a damn shame, Cassie thought as she made her way into the break-room. She got the drink for Eli and grabbed her one too. As she exited the break-room, she almost bumped into someone who was coming in.

"I'm sorry," she said apologetically. She looked up into a set of pretty brown eyes that belonged to one of the sexiest men she had seen in a long time. She almost forgot that BevyCo was swarming with Italians and other mixed breeds until this very moment.

"No, I'm sorry. I should have watched where I was going," he said. He gave her a once over, then his face frowned with question. "You work here? I haven't seen you before."

"I...uh...I'm working with Eli...I think," she said with uncertainty.

"Oh. So that means you'll be working with me also," he said. He extended his hand. "My name is Gio. Yours?"

Cassie placed the bottle she was holding under her left arm to shake his hand. "My name is Cassie. Nice to meet you."

Gio gave her another inspection and smiled. "Looking forward to working with you."

"Same here," she said. She turned around wearing a big grin. Gio was fine. And he looked like he was interested in her. Rock better get with the program or he would be history.

Thinking of how Gio looked at her, she was glad she chose her black wrap dress that fell right above her knees. She always felt sexy in it whenever she wore it. She didn't consider herself a bad bitch but she could hang with the best of them. She didn't have silky black hair flowing down her back, nor did she desire it. She liked wearing her own hair which she usually kept in an asymmetric layered wrap with side swoop bangs. Today, since she hadn't gotten her hair fixed, it was pulled back into a neat bun, but the side swoop bangs remained. She made sure to slick her hair with some edge control because the last thing she needed was for Eli to clown her about her nappy edges.

She didn't wear makeup but she tried to keep her brows arched and her full lips glossed. A person couldn't have big lips and not keep them moist. Her complexion was a smooth mocha brown that she inherited from Colette. What she didn't inherit from Colette was body shape. Colette had a very shapely body; big breasts and a big ass to match. Cassie wasn't as shapely. If she had to describe her body, it was more athletic than anything. Jazmin had teased her and said her hips were spreading, but Cassie didn't see it. She stood at five feet and two inches, and was around a hundred and thirty pounds. She had a scoop of breasts and a nice bump of an ass. Her clothes fit like they should and shopping for clothes was never a problem.

Still grinning from her encounter, Cassie entered Eli's office. He looked up from his phone and frowned.

"What the hell you cheesing about?" he asked.

"Oh nothing," she sighed. She placed the soda in front of him before taking a seat.

Eli looked at the bottle then at her. "I asked for coffee. Since when did coffee turn yellow and come in a green bottle?"

Cassie dismissed him with a wave. She wasn't going to let him ruin her high. "Jazmin told me you don't even drink coffee."

"Jazmin gon' get your ass fired too," Eli told her.

"Stop being such an ass," she said. She leaned forward wearing a giddy grin. "So you work closely with Gio?"

Eli raised an eyebrow. "Whatchu know about Gio?"

Ignoring his question, she asked, "What exactly do you and Gio do?"

"Residential and commercial property management, but why you asking about Gio?"

"I just bumped into him in the break-room," she said. She was still grinning. "So when do you want me to start?"

"Never. Get out my office," Eli ordered.

Cassie laughed. "What time do I need to be here? Is there anything I need to have for you when I walk in that door? What about Gio? He gon' need anything?"

Eli said, "Why you so thirsty? Rock ain't keeping that throat wet so you looking for something new to drink? You know Gio got a wife right? He wouldn't want your nappy headed ass no way. I see you tried to slick them edges down though."

Cassie grabbed her purse and got up. "Fuck you Eli."

"Whatever," he mumbled.

When she made it to the door, he said, "Eight o' clock."

She turned around smiling. "I'll be here."

———

Cassie couldn't wait to tell Colette she could be looking for her somewhere else to go. Hopefully it wouldn't take her long to get her finances back in order. Then it dawned on her; she didn't even know what her salary would be. She never asked. But knowing Eli he would have said something stupid anyway.

As soon as Cassie entered her apartment, her mother's perfume choked her into an asthma attack, and she didn't even have asthma.

"God! Lady, what are you doing?" Cassie started waving the air. She hit the switch bringing her ceiling fan to life as soon as she entered the living room. She walked over to her sliding glass doors that led to her balcony and slid those open to air the space out.

Colette appeared in the living room placing her earring in her ear. She was wearing a fitting black and white dress that stopped above her knees. Five inch stilettos were on her feet. Her face was heavily made. And her hair was laying perfect in the short cut she was wearing these days.

"Where you off to?" Cassie asked.

"They having a party down there at Bad Habitz," she said.

"On a Monday night?"

Colette grinned. "We party every night baby."

"And you know you need to stop. Letty, you're a grandmother. You need to be home watching reruns of Golden Girls or something," Cassie scolded.

Colette rolled her eyes. "You're so boring. And just cause I'm a grandmama don't mean I'm old. Shit, I'm forty-five. That's not old. You're the one with the old soul. Must've got that shit from your daddy cause you sho ain't got it from me."

"Whatever," Cassie waved off.

"Let me use your car," Colette said.

"Don't you have a car?"

"Yeah but yours is prettier," Colette pouted.

Cassie didn't answer her right away. She walked into her kitchen to retrieve something to drink.

Colette stood at the breakfast bar and looked Cassie up and down. "That dress looks good on you. You should wear stuff like that more often."

Cassie turned to her with a grin. "Actually, I will be. I got a job."

"You did?"

"Yep. And that means I won't need your help anymore."

"Well, that's good. But as long as I'm here I'll still pay something on rent," Colette said. There was a knock on the door and she went to answer it.

"No," Cassie said. "I mean I won't need—"

"Cassie, Rock is here," Colette announced.

Cassie waited in the kitchen until Rock came into view. That was strange. She had talked to him earlier but he never said anything about stopping by.

"What's up?" she asked casually.

"Where were you earlier?" Rock asked. He walked over into the kitchen. He too looked her up and down.

"I told you I had a job interview," she said.

"Naw, I'm talking about after that. Like when I got off from work. I came by here and your car wasn't here."

"Well, maybe if you had told me you planned to come by I would have came straight home," she said.

"So where were you?"

Cassie looked at Rock with question. "Since when have you been worried about where I'm at? Is this something new we gon' start doing?"

"Don't worry 'bout it," he dismissed. "How did your interview go?"

"It went good," she said. Her smile returned.

"Did you get the job or something?" he asked.

"Yeah. I start tomorrow," she beamed.

"Where at?"

"At BevyCo."

"BevyCo? Doing what?" he asked, slightly shocked.

"Why are you saying it like it's impossible?" She was taken aback by his reaction.

"Jazmin must got you on up there. You working with her or something?"

"No. Jazmin is in the finance department dealing with numbers. I can't do nothing like that," she answered. She side-eyed him. "And you got some damn nerves. Didn't Jah get you a damn job up there?"

She hesitated telling him what she would be doing because she was already aware of how he felt about Eli.

"Whatever," he dismissed. "Well, what is it you doing? Front desk? Mailroom? Cleaning lady?"

Cassie's mood soured that quick. She cut her eyes at him and pushed past him. As she made her way to her bedroom, she mumbled under her breath, "Ain't nobody no damn cleaning lady."

Rock laughed. "What I say?"

Colette was waiting in the doorway of her bedroom looking at Rock. Once she heard Cassie's bedroom door slam, she extended Rock's cellphone to him.

He quickly took it and put it in his pocket. He whispered, "I'll hitchu up tomorrow."

Colette smiled and watched him head to Cassie's room.

Once he entered Cassie's room, he closed the door behind him. Cassie was in her bathroom undressing. He leaned up against the frame of the bathroom door.

"You always huffing and puffing about some shit," he stated.

"You think you're funny Rock," she said as she stepped out her dress.

"I was just trying to figure out what it is you're doing at BevyCo." He took his time letting his eyes travel all over her body. She was wearing a matching pink lace bra and panties set. The pink looked good against her light brown skin. She had definition in her abs and toned biceps as if she worked out daily, but Rock knew that not to be true. She explained that it was genetics. The women on her daddy's side were built like that for no reason.

"Why are you looking at me like that?" she asked.

"I can't look at you now?"

She tried to push him away so she could shut the door.

"Why can't I look at you?"

"Cause I wanna take my bra off and slip on my night clothes," she said.

Rock started laughing. "You can do it in front of me."

"No cause I don't feel like being picked on," she said with a pout.

"I won't say anything," he said with sincerity. "Go ahead bae. Get comfortable."

"Rock!" she groaned. She pretended to cry. "You're gonna make fun of me."

"No, I won't. I promise," he said. "Here let me help you."

She turned to face the mirror above her vanity and watched as Rock stepped behind her to unlatch her bra. She hesitated pulling it forward. She kept her eyes on him waiting for him to say something stupid.

Instead of saying anything, Rock held her from behind wrapping his arms around her. They held each other's gaze in the reflection of the mirror. His hands came up to fondle her 32A breasts. He kissed her on her neck. It put her at ease a little bit. She was still waiting on his childish ass to say something about her "itty bitties".

His hands squeezed her breasts gently, pinching her nipples in between his fingers.

"I'm not gonna say anything Cassie, damn!"

She tried to relax.

He said, "Why don't you get them fixed if it bother you that bad?"

"It never really bothered me like that until you started cracking jokes and shit," she said angrily.

"I think you should get implants," he suggested.

Cassie studied her breasts. They really weren't that bad. They were almost perfect if they were about four times bigger. She wasn't exactly flat-chested but she was close. She had never considered plastic surgery before. And for him to suggest implants was a bit bruising to her confidence and self-esteem.

She broke away from him, grabbing her nightshirt. She slipped it on as she headed out to the bedroom.

"If I had known you was gonna be so difficult I woulda stayed my ass away from you," Rock said as he followed her.

"You knew my personality before we crossed that line. We've been friends since we were little," she said nonchalantly.

"But you're a horrible girlfriend," he stated. He sat down on her bed.

"Oh so I'm your girlfriend now?" she smirked.

"I'm just saying...If you were my girlfriend, you'd be horrible," he corrected.

Cassie frowned. She was disappointed because it was clear that Rock didn't want to put a label on what they were doing. At the beginning he acted as though he had to have her. It's like once he got her, the thrill died. What they were doing seemed forced at times. She wasn't exactly the happiest, but a part of her wanted him to want her again.

She thought about Gio at BevyCo. Maybe if someone else was after her, Rock would realize he was going to lose her.

"I'm working with Eli and Gio," she blurted out.

"You what?" A scowl quickly formed on his face.

"I'm Eli's new assistant and him and Gio work together," she said.

"When this happen?"

"Today when I went for my interview."

"So you finna work with that nigga?"

65

Cassie snapped. "What do you have against Eli? What he do to you? Are you mad he don't want you or something?"

"Keep playing," Rock threatened.

"Nigga, you ain't crazy," Cassie shot back. "I ain't never seen Eli do anything to you or say anything about you. Hell, I doubt he care you exists cause that's just how he is."

"So you know how he is, huh?"

Cassie rolled her eyes hard and let out a frustrated groan. "There you go."

"Man, fuck this shit," Rock snarled as he jumped up from her bed.

"Bye nigga," Cassie called after him. She didn't even bother walking his ass to the door. Their relationship wasn't going anywhere and maybe it was time to call it quits.

She heard the front door slam. She ran to her living room to step out onto her balcony. Before she could even see him come into view she shouted, "Don't be slamming my goddamn door!"

"Fuck you," Rock said.

Cassie looked at the empty spot where her car should have been. *Dammit!* Her mama took her damn car anyway.

———

On his drive over to Jah's house, Rock thought of what occurred earlier that day. What he told Cassie had been a lie. He never came to her apartment looking for her; he came by to see what Colette was talking about. She had been trying to get at him for the past two weeks, and up until recently he avoided coming into contact with her physically. She text him and sent him pics of her body as a tease. Honestly, he thought she was playing.

At first he didn't want to go to Cassie's and disrespect her in her own place, but shit, fucking with her mama was already disrespectful. What more could it hurt?

Colette assured him that Cassie wasn't coming home any time soon. Rock couldn't resist and took his ignorant ass over there. He couldn't explain it but it was something about this older woman that piqued his interest. First of all, she was bad than a mothafucka. Her body was right. Her face was on point. She had a wild free-loving spirit. Cassie was the total opposite of her mama. And maybe that was it too. Cassie was driving him away. She was hateful as hell, always angry about something, and boring as fuck.

When he got to Cassie's, Colette was ready to jump his bones. He stopped her. He wasn't quite comfortable. She asked if she could put him at ease. He wanted to know what she had in mind. She showed him...with her mouth. And the shit was good!

That was as far as it went. He started getting nervous that they would get caught so he left only to realize he left his phone behind.

At first he felt guilty about what he done, but after her informing him that she would be working with Eli; the guilt went out the window. But he needed someone to talk to. That's where Jah come in at.

After arriving at Jah's house, they went into Jah's man-cave.

"Nigga, you won't believe what I done got myself into now," Rock said shaking his head.

"I bet I can believe it cause you stupid as fuck," Jah said.

Rock looked over his shoulder to make sure no one else was around to hear. He asked, "Where Jazz?"

"She upstairs getting Ja-ja situated. Whatchu done did?"

"Cassie mama." Was all Rock stated.

"What about her?"

Rock just gave him a shameful look.

Jah looked at him in shock. "You dirty mothafucka. How you gon' do some shit like that? Nigga, you going to hell."

Rock laughed. "I ain't fucked her or nothing, but she did give me some head."

Jah shook his head. He couldn't believe his friend would do something so stupid. He grew angry. Snapping he said, "And what the fuck you telling me for. You dragging me in this shit, cause when Cassie find out—and she gon find out, that's just how women do mothafucka—she gon be fucked up and crying to Jazz. Then Jazz's ass is gonna be mad at me for not saying nothing 'cause she gon' assume I knew what the fuck was goin on. From now on, keep this kind of crazy shit to yo'self nigga."

Rock didn't really have a response.

Jah whispered, "But was the head good though?"

Rock started laughing. "Nigga there you go."

"I bet that bitch can do all kinds of nasty shit. Old ass slut," Jah said.

"She ain't that old. She only bout...twelve or thirteen years older than me."

"Nigga, you gon get caught. I'ma pretend like I don't know shit. And I'ma sit back and watch Cassie set yo mothafuckin' ass on fire. You know Cassie ain't right in the head. Nigga, she gon fuck yo ass up."

Rock dismissed the thought of Cassie as if it left a bad taste in his mouth. "Fuck Cassie. She on some bullshit anyway. Hell, the bitch won't even suck my dick. She barely let me fuck her."

"Damn," Jah said sympathetically. "Ya'll shit fucked up like that?"

"Cassie bipolar as fuck. I swear she need medication."

"Yo dick must be garbage if she don't want you fucking her," Jah laughed.

"Fuck you nigga. Cassie's pussy is garbage," Rock mumbled.

Jah was repulsed. He shuddered at the thought. "Ugh! I don't wanna talk about Cassie's pussy...And see nigga! See how the thought of Cassie is nasty to me? The thought of her mama should have been nasty to yo ass."

"It'd be easier for me to think that if Colette wasn't so damn fine," Rock said.

"Okay, you got a point."

They sat in silence. Since Jah's man-cave was off from the kitchen, they could hear that someone was moving around in there. Rock looked at Jah wide-eyed thinking Jazmin may have overheard them.

Jah got up and headed out the room. Rock was right behind him.

To Rock's surprise it wasn't Jazmin at all. It was Eli. Rock glowered in his direction. Eli didn't pay neither one of them any mind.

"When he get here?" Rock asked.

"He was already here," Jah said.

"Is it a problem?" Eli asked. His tone was almost taunting.

"Don'tchu got a house around the corner?" Rock asked smartly.

"Hey," Jah intervened. "Nigga, you act like you call the shots in my mothafuckin' house. How you gon question him and he at my house?"

"I'm just sayin'. The nigga was probably easedropping and shit." Rock snarled.

"He ain't heard shit. Eli did you hear us talking?" Jah asked.

"I ain't heard shit. I just came in here. What? Is it something I should have heard? And the word is *eavesdrop*. Eaves. *Eavesdropping*," Eli said with an impassive face.

Rock cut his eyes at him. He looked at Jah, "I'm finna head on out. I'll see you in the morning."

Jah walked Rock to the door so he could lock back up. When he reentered the kitchen, Eli was still standing in the same place. Jah waited for it because he knew it was coming.

Unable to resist, Eli asked, "Is that nigga really fucking around with that girl mama?"

Jah started laughing. "I knew yo mothafuckin' ass heard us. Ear hustling ass nigga."

Chapter 5

The following day, Cassie was ready to start her first day. She made sure to look as cute as possible without being obvious. She wore an A-line, belted, eggplant-colored dress that fell right above the knee. It gave her a cute flirty baby doll look. Even though Eli informed her that Gio was married, some friendly flirting wouldn't hurt.

Eli told her to be there at eight, but his ass was nowhere to be found. Was she supposed to just sit at her cubicle twiddling her thumbs? She had no idea what her duties were.

Then she heard a familiar laugh. She knew good and damn well it wasn't who she thought it was. She got up and went in the direction of the laugh. She ended up at Gio's office. He was sitting behind his desk and in front of his desk was a giggling Tanya.

Frowning, Cassie asked, "What are you doing here?"

"I'm working," Tanya replied.

"Don't you have a job?"

72

Tanya's playfulness disappeared. She cleared her throat and glanced at Gio. She said, "Yes, I do; it's here."

"But you were just working at Cigna this past Friday," Cassie pointed out.

"I know."

"So you just quit to come work here?"

"Yeah. Well, Jazmin told me to come up here yesterday. I came because Gio needed a new assistant. Felicia, was promoted."

"So no two weeks' notice or anything? You just quit and brought your happy ass here?"

Tanya could sense Cassie had an issue with her being at BevyCo. She looked at Gio and asked, "Can you excuse me for one second?"

Cassie looked past Tanya as she headed in her direction. She smiled and waved at Gio. "How are you this morning?"

"I'm good," he chuckled. He found the two women's interaction rather comical.

Tanya grabbed Cassie and pulled her down the hall. She whispered. "What is your problem? You can't be talking like that in front of that man."

"Tanya, how you gon' come up here cause I came here?" Cassie asked. She was bothered by Tanya's need to be at BevyCo.

"So I can't work here?" Tanya returned.

73

Cassie put on her petulant face. "But why you get to work with him?"

Tanya's mouth dropped open. Then she straightened her posture, put her hands on her hips, and gave Cassie a scornful look. "So this is about that nigga in there?"

Cassie snickered. "I'll trade."

"We can't do that. Girl you crazy. You getting all mad at me cause you wanna be hot in the ass." Tanya rolled her eyes at Cassie in a playful manner. "Let me take my fat ass back in here before he fire me...Messing witcho ass."

As Tanya walked away, Cassie saw Eli coming down the hall lost in his phone. She noticed he had really been in his phone a lot lately. It was like his mind was somewhere else.

The curvature of Eli's legs in his tapered pants caught Cassie's attention. She hadn't realized that he was bowlegged. She hadn't paid close attention to his body before. But since his pants were orange, who wouldn't notice? And no man in her normal circle of friends would dare to wear orange pants. It was time for her to clown him since he always wanted to point out everything about everybody else.

"Eli, who told you it was okay to wear them pants. This is April, not October," she joked.

He looked up, noticing her for the first time. "Oh it's not October? I assumed since a goblin came and sat in my office asking for a damn job, that it was close to Halloween."

"Fuck you," Cassie laughed as they passed one another. Damn, what was that cologne he was wearing? She had to give it to Eli though, he was always crisp and clean, despite his choice of colors. He had a flashy style but it suited him, and only he could pull it off as effortlessly as he did. She couldn't blame her brother for being so smitten with him.

Five minutes after she sat at her cubicle, Eli came out of his office and tapped her on the shoulder. "We gotta go to the conference room."

"Conference room?"

"Cassie, I ain't got time for you to be acting dumb. Grab something to write with and come on," he said and walked off.

She scrambled to find a notepad and a pen and hurried to catch up with him. He wasn't very good at explaining anything to her. When she sat down beside him, she whispered, "You act like I know this stuff. You ain't even trained me."

He whispered back, "Just shut-up and pay attention."

"Ugh," she frowned. "Why you gotta be mean?"

She brightened up when Gio and Tanya entered the conference room too. They sat across from her and Eli. During the entire boring hour and a half meeting, Cassie daydreamed about Gio. She wondered what their kids would look like. He looked full Italian, and he had that dark olive complexion possibly passing for a light skinned black person. The way his arms appeared in his crisp blue button down, she could tell he was muscular. She wondered if he liked chocolate girls such as herself.

When it was over, Cassie followed Eli back to his office where he proceeded to explain to her that between today and Friday, they would be preparing to move to the fourth floor of the building. He then broke down what was expected of her.

"Wait," she interrupted. "Why it sound like I gotta do everything?"

Eli blew out a frustrated breath. "Listen, I hired you for something you ain't even qualified to do. I'm doing you and Jazmin a favor. So hush."

"But Eli, you—"

"Another thing," he interrupted. "Don't think because we're cool out there that you're gonna get to slack and lollygag and shit in here. I will expect for you to do your job and do it well. Right now you need to acclimate to the way things are done around here."

"Yes sir," she whispered meekly. She didn't realize how serious Eli could be.

"Also, learn how to turn your ghetto-ness off and on. Try talking as close to proper as you can. You've been around me and you know damn well I can talk just as fucked up as Jah, but there's a switch when dealing with these people and taking their money. Now, do you have any questions?"

Yeah, can I switch with Tanya? That's what she wanted to ask but she dared not test his patience. But she was curious about one thing. "Is this what you've always done here?"

"No. I used to be my brother's assistant. Since, he hasn't come back yet, I didn't want to work with anybody else like that. I guess I could have become Lu's right hand but he worked too close with Stefano. I will point him out to you so you'll know not to fuck with him. I hate him."

"Okay," Cassie said feeling awkward.

He continued, "Hell, I guess I had to put my education to use, so property management it is. And you're more like a secretary but if you wanna sound more important than you really are, you can say you're like a closing coordinator."

"Hey, we never discussed salary. What kinda money will I be making?"

"Right now you're making zero dollars," he laughed.

"What?" Her mouth dropped open.

"Calm down. I never sent that info over to our personnel department. Whatchu wanna make?"

Cassie looked at him baffled. "I get to tell you what I wanna make?"

"Well, you ain't getting nothing ridiculous like six figures or something like that. Be reasonable. If you don't suggest something I'ma tell them to pay you eight dollars hourly."

"Hell naw!" Cassie exclaimed. "I need more than that Eli."

"Okay, okay. We'll figure something out."

"So you get to do whatever you want around here?"

"Something like that. And right now, we're about to leave. So get your stuff and meet me by the receptionist desk."

Cassie began to think that maybe this wouldn't be so bad after all. Especially if she got to see more of Gio.

———

After riding around with Eli assessing a few properties and attending a meeting, Cassie was beginning to enjoy her job even more. She didn't know how many times she laughed at Eli's crazy ass and the way he talked to people. He wasn't that bad to be around after all. But she could tell something was eating at him. He kept tapping around on his phone and blowing frustrated breaths of air. By the end of the day, he was so stressed he asked her if she wanted to meet up with Jazmin for happy hour.

They ended up at Sambucas. And it was a pleasant surprise to see that Gio had joined them. Although

Cassie was crushing on him, she felt nervous around him. She wanted him to take interest in her like the way he had looked her up and down when they bumped into one another. But Eli had all of his attention at the moment.

"Are you coming Cassie?" Jazmin was asking.

Cassie snapped out of her daze and looked at her friends. "Huh?"

Jazmin laughed. "Girl, what are you over there daydreaming about?"

"Oh nothing." Cassie shook her head and took a sip of her drink. "What were you talking about?"

"The company cookout at Lu's. It's big and the company's employees bring their families. It's the first quarter Employee Appreciation Day. There's activities for the kids too. Are you coming?" Jazmin asked again.

"I'll be there," Tanya said. "Me and Tyriq."

Cassie lowered her voice and pointed towards Gio. "Will he be there?"

"Girl," Tanya gave her one of her infamous "you got to be playing" looks. "That man don't want you."

"How you know?" Cassie challenged.

"Cause I know," Tanya spat.

Jazmin said, "I'm sure he'll be there. He and his wife and kids come to all of the other events."

Tanya looked at Cassie again. "See there? Wife and kids. He don't want you."

"Oh shut-up," Cassie snarled.

Jazmin grinned. "So how are the two of you liking things so far?"

"Oh bitch! You shoulda been got me on," Tanya exclaimed.

"It's alright," Cassie said dryly.

"What's the problem?" Jazmin asked.

She pointed to Eli. "He's bipolar."

Tanya laughed. "And you ain't?"

Cassie narrowed her eyes at Tanya. "I am not bipolar. Maybe moody."

"Speaking of moody," Jazmin piped up. "What's going on between you and Rock?"

Cassie sucked her teeth and rolled her eyes. "That nigga. He's working my nerves. He act like he mad cause I'm working at BevyCo with Eli. I don't know what it is but Rock got it in for Eli."

"Why? I thought they were cool. I thought they all were cool," Tanya said.

"Me too," Cassie said. "But every time I mention Eli he act like I'm fucking him."

Jazmin fell into thought. "Well, you know Eli got a problem with his mouth. He probably done said some fucked up shit that rubbed Rock wrong."

"Jah got a problem with his mouth too, but Rock don't act crazy when it comes to him," Cassie pointed out.

"But the shit Eli be doing be getting under people's skin," Tanya chuckled. "He purposely fuck with folks."

"Well, that's true," Cassie laughed. "You shoulda seen how crazy he was talking to these people today."

There was a pause in Eli and Gio's conversation for him to turn his attention to them and ask, "What are ya'll saying about me over there?"

"What a great person you are," Tanya said sarcastically followed by a grin.

Eli's eyes went to Cassie. "You talking about me?"

Cassie shook her head. Just then some other people from work joined them. Their space suddenly became noisy and crowded. Cassie sat back and observed for the most part. She especially enjoyed listening to Gio talk and laugh. When this very well dressed, nice looking brown skinned cutie walked over, Cassie forgot all about Gio. But quickly her interest died when Eli seemed thrilled to see him. So thrilled, he actually got up and walked away with this guy.

She leaned over the table and asked in a lowered voice, "Who was that?"

"That's that Kreme guy," Jazmin answered.

"The one Eli asked my brother about?" Cassie asked.

"Is Kreme gay?" Tanya asked.

Jazmin smiled knowingly and looked away.

Tanya whispered, "Is Eli gay?"

"So Kris really is his beard?" Cassie asked.

"I ain't saying all that," Jazmin said. "With the exception of marrying Kris, Eli has always been private about that part of his life. We rarely saw him with anybody. He didn't invite people to family functions or nothing like that. So we were shocked when the twins' mama showed up and said they were his. No one knew he was hitting that back in the day."

"Well, maybe he's bi," Tanya said.

Jazmin said, "I think that's everyone's conclusion. But you know Kreme owns his own nightclub. They say he got this other private club that only members are allowed in."

"Why is it so damn private?" Tanya wanted to know.

"From what I've heard, it's very, very freaky," Jazmin said.

Tanya looked at Cassie excited, and said, "Let's go. You wanna go?"

"To the private one?" Cassie asked. "Girl, you ain't got no freaky bones in your body. Whatchu wanna go to a club like that for?"

"I've heard about them freaky clubs. Is it like swinging? I've always wanted to go to see what they be doing," Tanya said.

"And yo' ass gonna get fucked," Cassie laughed.

Jazmin started laughing too. "Somebody gonna come up to her out of the blue and bend her over."

"Yeah, with a dildo," Cassie giggled.

"Fuck ya'll," Tanya grumbled.

Overhearing their conversation, Gio turned to them and said, "You really should go. At least once."

Now Cassie was interested. Tanya asked, "You've been?"

"A time or two," he said.

"Should you be telling me this?" Tanya asked looking stunned by his admission.

"We're off the clock," he smiled.

Tanya scrunched up her nose. "Hmmm...I don't know. You're my boss."

Gio chuckled, "It's okay."

"So when the next time you going?" Cassie asked out of curiosity.

"When do you need me to go?" Gio returned flashing her a lustful smile.

"Aw sukie sukie now," Tanya said under her breath.

Cassie blushed. "I'm not sure." She looked at Tanya. "When do you wanna go?"

"I wanna go," Jazmin whined.

Tanya gave Jazmin one of those looks of hers. "So Jah can beatcho ass?"

"I know," Jazmin said defeated. She got excited and joked, "Well maybe I can persuade him to go too."

Tanya repeated, "So Jah can beatcho ass?

Chapter 6

Three weeks later, Cassie attended the company's employee appreciation event. The cookout was as amazing as Jazmin said it was. It was also Cassie's first time ever being in someone's home that was so majestic. They didn't spend much time inside, but Jazmin did take them on a tour.

Cassie allowed her brother to accompany her. However, she regretted letting Colette tag along. She could tell her mama was on a mission to snag one of the older rich men on the premises.

"Hey, I know that bitch right there," Colette said. She was eyeing someone keenly.

"Who?" Cassie asked looking around.

"I'll be back," Colette said absently as she began to walk away.

Romyn shook his head. "You know Mama ain't got any sense. You shoulda told her no. What possessed you to bring her? Look at what she got on."

Cassie looked at the rainbow colored frozen treat he was holding. "Where you get that at?"

"Over there," he pointed across the courtyard to a white ice cream stand.

Cassie headed in that direction. There were so many people and kids darting everywhere; she would have sworn she was at a county fair. And the kids had everything a fair could offer too.

She had lost sight of Tanya and Jazmin. However, she stumbled upon Gio's wife. She wasn't all that. Cassie was expecting some breathtaking beauty. To Cassie, his wife looked average. She thought back to his little innuendo that day at happy hour. Ever since that day, he had been giving her these lustful looks when no one was looking. She would blush and play it off. He would say things like, "I'm still waiting." She would laugh him off. She didn't understand why she was evading him when that's all she had been thinking about.

After getting her frozen ice she looked around for her brother. He had moved out of the spot they were sitting at. She spotted her mother talking to an older lady.

"Well, it looks like life is treating you well," the lady was saying as Cassie walked up. She had a snooty way about her. Cassie could tell by the way her eyes looked Colette up and down with her nose slightly turned up.

Of course Colette couldn't just look like someone's mother. She had to be thotted up in her white bodycon dress and five inch heels.

Colette smiled graciously. She said, "And I see life is taking care of you real good. Who did you snag up?"

The lady laughed. "What does that mean Letty?"

"I know you. Remember, we used to run in the same circle. I mean I know you married Esau, but he wasn't taking care of you like this," Colette said gesturing over the lady's body.

Cassie's eyes shifted to Eli walking up behind the lady. "Mama, Lu wants you."

"This is your mama?" Cassie asked surprised.

"Yeah. Ol' Sarah," Eli said.

"Should I know her Eli?" Sarah asked.

"She works with me at the office. And she's Jazz's friend," he answered. He looked at Colette. "Is this your mama?"

"Yeah, Colette. And apparently these two know each other," Cassie said pointing between Sarah and her mother.

Eli uttered, "Tuh. I ain't surprised."

Sarah playfully hit him in the arm. "And what's that supposed to mean?"

"Birds of a feather," was his reply.

Colette's mouth dropped open while Cassie started giggling.

Sarah threw a smile one last time. "It was nice seeing you Letty. Make sure you find me before you leave."

"I sure will," Colette said. She pointed across the way and asked Eli, "Who is that man right there?"

"Which one?"

"The one in the navy blue pants."

"That's Antino."

"I thought so!" Colette said excitedly. "I'll be back."

Eli watched Colette saunter over to the huddle of men. He looked back at Cassie sympathetically, "So yo' mama a hoe too?"

Cassie laughed. "Too?"

"Yeah. You ain't gotta be ashamed. Trust me I understand your pain," he said.

Defeated, she said, "Yeah, I've been dealing with it all my life."

"So Gio wanted me to ask you if you're interested in going out tonight."

Cassie questioned Eli with her eyes to make sure he was referring to what she thought he was referring to. "To the place?"

Eli nodded.

"Tonight?"

"I'll be there so you don't have to worry about anything. And you don't even have to do anything. It's a place to socialize if you want to. For the most part, all I do is sit back and watch people fuck. But I'd be lying if I said I didn't get a kick out of it," he chuckled.

"So you don't participate?"

He hesitated as he looked for the right words. "I'm a voyeur."

"But don't you have to be a member."

"Yeah, but we've already made arrangements for ya'll."

"Ya'll?"

"Yeah, you and Tanya."

"Tanya's fat ass is coming too?" Cassie asked.

"Yes, Tanya's fat ass is coming too. You wouldn't believe how many plus size women be getting their fuck on. And they be sexy too; with their squishy selves."

"Can I invite my brother too?"

"If he wants to come. He might get into some trouble though."

"I'll make sure I let him know that," she grinned.

"We're gonna meet up there at eleven."

"Eleven?"

"Yes, that's when the doors open."

"Where is it?"

"It's...you know what? You probably will never find it your first time. I'll just come and get you and Tanya. Ya'll can ride there with me. So be ready by ten-thirty. And don't wear this shit you got on. Go home and change. You look like somebody's country ass cousin who work at Piggly Wiggly, and be letting all her family come through her line, and don't be ringing up nothing except the milk."

Cassie looked down at her simple capri jeans and blue t-shirt ensemble and started laughing. "Oh shut up Eli. You kill me."

"You should dress more daring," he suggested.

"Daring?" she questioned. Then she suddenly became uncomfortable as his eyes roamed all over her body. It wasn't that his eyes held anything suggestive; she just didn't need him staring too long before he found something else to critique.

"Yeah. I think brighter colors would bring out the color of your skin, brown girl. You have a nice even complexion."

"Thank you," she blushed. That was the first time he ever had anything nice to say to her and actually seemed genuine.

When she looked away, seeing Rock soured her mood. It wasn't the fact of him being present, but he wasn't alone. He knew she would be there, so why would he bring his baby mama Melody along.

"I'll be right back," Cassie said absently. She made her way over to Rock, his baby mama, and their son. "Hey Rock."

Melody turned up her nose as she looked Cassie up and down.

"What's up Cassie," Rock said casually.

Cassie looked between him and Melody. "What's this?"

"What it look like?" Melody blurted.

Rock looked back at her, cautioning her with his hand. "Chill with that, okay."

Cassie cut her eyes at Melody who returned the same despise. Her eyes cut to Rock. "Really Rock?"

"What you mean really Rock? Wait a minute," he said. He looked back at Melody. "Give me a sec."

"I told you don't have me out here looking like a fool," Melody said with an attitude.

"You don't need him for that," Cassie said smartly.

"Fuck you lil—"

Rock interrupted Melody before she could say more. He nudged her for emphasis. "Didn't I say chill?"

Melody rolled her eyes in exasperation.

Rock stepped away ushering Cassie along.

"You must don't want her to hear the lie you about to tell me," Cassie said sarcastically.

"It ain't like that. She only here cause she wouldn't let me just take Lil Rock by himself. She was tripping so I told her to come on," he explained.

"Mmmhmm," Cassie hummed dubiously.

"Fuck it man," Rock said growing irate. "You ain't gotta believe it. I really ain't gotta explain shit to you."

"Yeah, fuck it then," Cassie said angrily.

"Take yo' lil ass on back over there to your boyfriend," Rock dismissed.

"Don't worry," Cassie sassed. "I am, chip tooth bastard."

Rock laughed in an angered manner. "Oh you wanna go there? Don't make me talk about them boils on yo chest."

Cassie was beyond vexed. "Boils? Fuck you nigga."

She could hear Rock's laughter as she stormed away. He made her sick! But she wasn't going to dwell on him or his baby mama. They could have each other. Fuck Rock. Now she really needed to go out and unwind. And she knew just where she was spending her night.

———

There was something exciting about this. Cassie was also nervous as hell. Romyn was a little anxious. And Tanya was having second thoughts.

As Eli suggested, she went home and changed into something a little more provocative. It was a dress that she never got to wear during her friendship with Michelle. They used to hit the clubs all the time together and wear the skimpiest clothing. She hadn't really done anything like that since everybody fell out with Michelle.

The dress was a black Roman toga style maxi dress with high slits going up both sides. Her hair had been freshly done, so she wore it down with the side swoop bang practically covering her left eye. She felt sexy, even if nobody else thought so. When Eli saw her, he gave her a nod of approval. She was glad to at least pass his inspection.

Eli was right. If she tried to find the place on her own she wouldn't have never found it. It was in an old industrial area back in the cut. The brick building showed no signs of life and appeared as if it lacked routine maintenance. They had to go through a series of point checks until they got to the actual club. Once that door open, the music rushed to their ears. The place was dimly lit with colored disco lights circling the room. There were people who looked like normal socializing-people at any other club gathered at tables, laughing and drinking. It wasn't what Cassie had imagined.

"Is this it?" Tanya asked.

"Oh this is just a small reception area. Beyond those curtains," Eli pointed to the far end of the room, "that's where we're going."

Cassie swallowed the lump in her throat. Now she was having second thoughts. She followed close behind her brother.

Once they crossed over into the other room, Eli said to Romyn, "You can stay up here if you want, but there's another area you might be interested in."

"Show me," Romyn said.

Before walking off, Eli said to Tanya and Cassie, "You're on your own. Relax, have a drink, and walk around."

Cassie nor Tanya was listening to what he was saying. They stood there shocked and mesmerized at the same time. Their minds couldn't process any of the activities they were seeing.

"What the fuck is this Cassie?" Tanya mumbled.

"I don't know," Cassie answered absently. Her eyes were focused on a woman sucking a man off. He looked like he had to be at least ten inches and the woman was making his whole dick disappear in her throat.

A waitress with all kinds of "needs" on a tray approached them. Tanya took one of the test tubes, filled with blue drink, and passed it to Cassie. She got one for herself. The waitress smiled and moved on.

Tanya downed hers in one gulp.

"Let's look around some more," Tanya suggested.

Cassie followed Tanya in pure amazement. They walked through a corridor lit by recessed neon lighting.

On either side were private booths with curtains drawn. Despite the music, which was very erotic and psychedelic, they could still hear the sounds of sex taking place.

At the end of that corridor, was a fork. At this point, Cassie was thinking there was something in those test tubes other than liquor. Cassie could feel it. Tanya was definitely feeling it. She had stopped another waitress and this time opted for the red liquid. She passed one to Cassie and they both swallowed in one gulp.

"Alright bitch, you go that way and I'll go this way. If ain't shit popping over here I'll come find you," Tanya said.

"Okay," Cassie grinned. She watched Tanya walk away. Her grin grew wider when she saw a hairy white man approach Tanya and she looked disgusted. She started laughing as she made her way to the other side.

Cassie felt good. She felt extremely sexual and horny. The music and lighting were taking her on a trip. Everything seemed surreal like she was there, but she really wasn't. She smiled at a couple fucking up against the wall like it was the most pleasant thing she had seen all day. It was safe to say that Cassie was high. All her worries were gone. She was totally relaxed. She was in a state of euphoric bliss and felt like she was floating.

She reached a section where it was straight heterosexual fucking. It almost resembled a huge orgy. There was a center lighted stage with what looked to be a continuous bed circling around it. There were people on cushioned benches off to the side as well.

She circled around watching a woman getting fucked in every hole she had. Again, Cassie was amazed...and turned on. Her pussy began throbbing and moisten the g-string she was wearing.

She suddenly felt paranoid as if someone was watching her. She looked up and saw the last person she wanted to see there. But whatever she had drunk in those test tubes wouldn't allow her to care. He smiled her way. She smiled back. She looked back at the performances taking place before her. She continued to walk around the circle.

The sensation of being watched came again. This time when she looked up, she spotted Gio, but he wasn't watching her. She looked back in the direction where she saw her old friend. He was still watching her. She found it funny and started giggling.

She looked to the side of her, and there was Kreme. Now why was he looking at her? Or maybe she was just hallucinating and none of them were watching her. And the old friend wasn't even there. So she made her way over to the old friend to see if he was real.

He watched her as she approached him. Without exchanging words, she poked him in the chest.

"What are you doing?" Sean asked.

"I was just seeing if you were really here," she answered goofily.

"No, I mean what is someone like you doing here?" he asked.

"Well, why are you here?" she countered.

"You know I get down," he said cockily.

"Oh I know you do."

Sean eyed her from head to toe and smiled with approval. "Do Rock know you're here?"

"Who is Rock?" she asked.

Sean laughed shaking his head.

Cassie turned her attention back to the people. Her pussy was aching something awful. Sean's lips were looking rather sexy too. She was about to proposition him when this voluptuous blonde white girl wearing only a red garter belt came up to Sean. She grabbed him by the arm. "I was looking for you. We're ready."

"Okay," Sean said. He looked to Cassie. "Would you like to join?"

She looked across the room and Gio was now looking at her. He smiled. She smiled back. She looked at Sean and shook her head. "Not this time."

"I'll come back for you," he said with a glint of lust in his eyes.

It was the drink. It had to be the drink, because Cassie actually blushed as he walked away.

She returned her focus to the people again. A man was plowing into a woman while choking her. She looked like she was in so much pain but Cassie knew she was enjoying it. She wanted to trade places with the woman. She was so horny she felt like screaming. When she felt like she couldn't stand it anymore, she was touched.

Not someone bumping into her. Not someone tapping her shoulder. But a hand slipped through the left slit of her dress from behind and began to explore in between her legs. She made it easy by wearing a g-string that only needed to be pushed aside. The barely-there material provided little barrier to contain the wetness that already was seeping just from observing, but now her juices flowed onto the fingers of this hand.

She was almost afraid to look behind her. She needed to know who was touching her in such a way, because she gave no one permission to do so; yet, she had no desire to make them stop. She slightly turned to look, but he wouldn't let her.

"Keep watching them," he whispered in her ear.

That's what she did. She kept watching the people while her clit was being rubbed ever so gently. Then one finger began to massage her insides while his thumb stroked her hardened bud.

He kissed her in her most erogenous spot: behind her ears. This caused her to really get into it and grind her ass into him, wanting and needing him to take her. A moan escaped her lips. Her breathing deepened. She felt hot.

"You like what I'm doing to you?"

Cassie nodded like she was in a trance. He picked up the pace, and got more aggressive while his other hand came up to massage her breasts. In combination with kisses to her neck and ears, she felt herself about to erupt. Her arms went back wanting to touch him and steady herself as she ground against the hardness in his pants. She needed to feel him. As soon as her hand found his thickness, she exploded.

Remembering where she was, she didn't hold back her loud moaning and her cry once she went over the edge. Her body twitched as he continued to dig in her pussy and press against her pulsating clit.

"May I have permission to fuck you?"

She needed penetration. She needed to feel a dick spreading her open. She needed the weight of a man on top of her.

She turned around to face him and became instantly bashful. Why would this gorgeous man want her of all people in the room? It was what she wanted, but now that she had it, it was awkward.

"May I?" he asked again.

She nodded.

He took her hand and led her to one of the benches in the corner. He had her to lay down where he proceeded to remove her g-string. He then pushed her legs up to rest on his shoulders and he feasted upon her. She groaned when she felt the flicker of his tongue against her oversensitive clit. She couldn't believe this was happening. She knew it wasn't right. And she knew Sean would run his mouth.

"Oh God!" she moaned. She turned her head to look back at the people in the center of the room. Maybe if she focused on them she could pretend that this wasn't happening.

The sensation of him suckling her clit caused her eyes to close as she relished the feel. She groaned and placed her hands on top of his head. She pulled his head in towards her and brought her hips forward forcing him deeper into her center. His tongue penetrated her opening and it drove her insane.

There was a brief pause. She kept her eyes closed because she didn't want to see. She could hear the faint sound of foil being ripped. Never once did she think of protection but she was grateful that he did.

She allowed her legs to be pushed back, and she held them in place. The next sensation she felt was her pussy being invaded.

Her eyes opened, and her hand went to his abdomen to prevent him from going too deep. He allowed her to keep her hand there. He didn't get aggressive with her while their bodies got acquainted. He kept it slow and easy until most of him disappeared inside her.

Her legs quivered as he filled her up. She looked up into his eyes. He looked back at her and there was something there that she couldn't quite read. However, once he pulled back and plowed back into her causing her to scream out, she realized what that look was; it was an apologetic expression for what he was about to do. He just didn't know that she was very forgiving.

Pushing on his hips and stomach wasn't working. He pounded the shit out of her. Her soaking wet pussy made all his strokes easy. They were hard and deep, something that she needed from Rock but he couldn't deliver.

"Oh God...yes...yes...Oooooh..." she groaned. She opened her legs wide, her left foot pointing east and her right pointing west.

"Damn baby," he groaned. He leaned onto her so he could kiss her aggressively biting her bottom lip. He asked, "Can I go harder?"

Harder? He could go harder? She breathed, "Yes...Please, go harder."

She screamed out in pain but it felt so good, as he plunged into her repeatedly. She was unable to take much more of this beating before she felt it coming. Something that she hadn't had the pleasure of feeling in a long time. She felt her gut tense up. All her senses heightened. She felt like she was lost in time. There was an elation building up within her. She was there. He got her to that place she had longed to revisit. Her muscle clenched around him making him stop. He must have known what was about to happen because he pulled out in time to watch her erupt like a geyser.

Cassie screamed so loud she had the others in the room turning in their direction.

He used his hand to slap her pussy lightly and began rubbing her ejaculate onto her clit. Before re-entering her, he feasted on her again, lapping up the fluids that spilled from her. He then coaxed her to flip over on all fours. He couldn't even get a nice rhythm going before she was erupting again, soaking the bench. It was like once the dam had been broken the first time, she couldn't stop the flow of her waterfall.

She ejaculated once more before it was over. She collapsed onto the bench, forcing their bodies apart. She was spent. She just wanted to lay there and go to sleep. She closed her eyes for a brief second.

"Honey, he really worked you over."

Cassie's eyes flew opened. Before her was a white woman with huge breasts. She was smiling down at Cassie.

She sat up and looked around. Where the fuck did he go? How long did she have her eyes closed?

"You ain't got any more left for me and my husband, do you?" the woman asked.

Cassie didn't even answer her, nor did she look for her g-string. She got up and headed out of the area. She went looking for Tanya. In doing so, she bumped right into Sean. He didn't have on a shirt and the handiwork of his ex-wife's knife skills really stood out.

"Where you hurrying off to?" he asked.

Her high was coming down and she started to feel ashamed. She kept her eyes lowered and mumbled, "I'm looking for Tanya."

Sean's eyes widened. "Tanya? Tanya is here too? Shit, Cassie. Why didn't you tell me that?"

"She ain't gon say nothing," she assured him.

He walked upon her with little space between them. He said, "I didn't know you could squirt."

Cassie groaned regretting even coming to the club. She walked away from him. She hated that he now had something on her he could hold over her head.

Chapter 7

The next morning, Cassie felt everything she did the night before. The part where her leg and hip joint connected ached something terrible. Her pussy was sore. Her head hurt, and she felt completely drained. She didn't even get out of bed unless it was to go to the bathroom.

She lay in bed looking up at her ceiling fan replaying the night before in her head over and over. She wanted it to disappear and be a distant memory. What she did was going to haunt her. She blamed her nasty friends and her nasty brother. None of this was her fault, or at least that's what she tried to convince herself so she would feel better.

But it didn't work.

She found herself groaning in frustration and wanting to kick her own ass. How could she do something so stupid?

After she found Tanya at the club, they went to the front reception area. The two of them both sat there wondering what the hell they had just done.

In a sullen voice, Tanya said, "You smell like sex."

Cassie replied, "Yeah, so do you."

Tanya shook her head pitying the both of them.

About thirty minutes later, Gio walked up to them. "Why are you two sitting up here? You've had enough?"

"Way beyond enough," Tanya said.

Gio laughed. He looked at Cassie and smiled at her with lust in his eyes. "Will there be a next time with you?"

Cassie shook her head. Her eyes went to the curtains that led to Sodom and Gomorrah. Eli and Kreme were coming through. They spotted them and came walking over.

"I've been looking for ya'll," Eli said. He looked between Cassie and Tanya. They didn't look so good. He laughed. "Was it too much?"

"Can we go?" Tanya asked impatiently.

"Where's Romyn?" Cassie asked in a low solemn voice. She was unable to look any of them in the eyes.

"He's...he's getting himself together," Kreme answered.

Cassie didn't even want to know what Kreme meant by that.

A few minutes later, Romyn shamefully joined them. Again no one said much. The only people that were chattering away were Gio, Eli, and Kreme. Eli told the guys that he had been the "newbies" ride there, so he needed to take them home. Everyone said their goodbyes and they left.

When they got in Eli's truck, no one said anything. The smell of inside the club, sex, and alcohol mixed with remnants of their perfumes and colognes was suffocating Cassie. She sat in the front seat with her head damn near out the window.

"Everybody don't talk all at once," Eli joked. "How do ya'll feel?"

Tanya said, "Look man, na'an one of ya'll mothafuckas bet' not tell nobody nothing that went on tonight."

"I don't wanna talk about it," Romyn mumbled. "That place will be the demise of us all."

Silence again.

Eli took Tanya home first. He then dropped Romyn off. Cassie's apartments were close to his neighborhood so they rode in silence for another twenty minutes.

When he pulled up to her building, she tried to get out of the vehicle as fast as possible.

"Cassie," Eli called out.

She stopped to hear what he had to say.

"Are you okay?"

She nodded. She got out and shut the door. She walked up the flight of stairs to her apartment. She noticed that Eli didn't leave until she made it in. When she walked fully into the apartment she could hear her mama fucking. She drowned them out by taking a long hot shower.

Now here it was Sunday and she was trying to think of how everyone would behave at work the next day. Maybe she could call in sick for the whole week.

Her bedroom door pushed opened and to her surprise it was Rock. After how he talked to her at the cookout, she wasn't in the mood for his company.

He walked over wearing a menacing scowl. He sat down on the edge of her bed and looked at her like he knew something.

"What?" she asked.

"Where did you go last night?" he asked.

"Why?"

"I'm just asking," he said.

"I went out. How was last night with your baby mama?"

"Don't make this about me. And I told you what it was with that. You making a big deal out of nothing."

"Maybe I am," she argued. "But it wasn't the fact that you brought her to the cookout, but it was how you talked to me."

"C'mon Cassie," he said dismissing her statement. "Even if I said the sweetest shit to you, it was still gonna be a problem."

"Well, what do you want Rodney?" she asked, perturbed.

"I'm tryna see where your head at. So whatchu do last night?" he asked. His eyes searched the room until it landed on her dress on the floor.

Did Sean go blabbing his mouth already? Even though Rock didn't fuck with Sean any more, gossip still traveled.

"What's that shit on your dress?" he asked.

"What shit?" She leaned over the side of her bed. Once her eyes landed on her dress, she wished she had thrown it in her closet instead of leaving it out on display. Since it was black, it wasn't hard to spot the dried up bodily fluids.

Her heart rate quickened. She wasn't nervous of him finding out because she feared losing him, but she just didn't want him having anything against her. She didn't want him to know she had been a hoe the night before.

"What is that Cass?" he asked again going for the dress.

"I spilled my drink," she lied as she tried snatching it from him.

"What drink is white?"

She could see him growing angry. His glowered deepened as he held the dress up for further inspection.

"It was a pina colada," she said with a straight face.

"I smell sex all on this dress. Who the fuck you been with? Where you go that you had to have on a hoe dress like this?" Rock asked. His face was in a scowl and the tone of his voice was harsh.

"I know you ain't trying to get stupid with me!" she bellowed.

"You fucking somebody else Cassie?"

"If I was...So! Who you fucking?" she retorted.

"What the fuck you mean so? You give me a fucking hard time and don't want me touching you but you can go out and throw the pussy at the next nigga?"

"I ain't threw shit," she hissed as she hopped out of her bed. Her legs were stiff and sore but she tried to play it off.

"Damn, the nigga fucked you like that, that you can't walk." He said more as an observation than a question.

"I can walk," she mumbled. She headed out her room and down the hallway to the kitchen.

Rock followed her. It was clear that he was bothered. She ignored him as she poured herself some orange juice.

"Let me find out you on some hoe shit."

"Or what? You ain't my boyfriend, remember? I'm single so I can be a hoe if I want to. Why don't you worry about wolf bat pussy."

"If I beat bitches, your ass would be choked out," he spat.

Cassie laughed wryly. "I wish the fuck you would."

"Keep wishing," he threatened.

"Get out," she said seriously.

"Who did you fuck?" He was adamant to know the truth.

"I said get out." She was firm in her stance. She knew her smaller stature didn't pose a threat to him, but the carving knife in her knife block did.

"Just answer this, did you go with that bitch Eli? And tell the truth?"

Cassie shook her head in disbelief. "You're so dumb Rodney. And at this point, I think it's best if we don't fuck with each anymore like that. I need to reevaluate this whole thing. So...please just get out."

"For real?" He seemed crushed.

"Shit died between us a while ago," she said angrily. "You and your baby mamas and then you slinging dick everywhere. It ain't what I want."

"You just a hateful ass bitch," he snarled.

"And this hateful ass bitch wanna move on. Now get out."

Colette appeared at the end of the hall with her arms folded over her chest. She looked at Rock and said, "You heard her. Just leave."

Rock shot daggers towards Colette. She stared back at him stone-faced. Without saying another word, he stormed out of the apartment.

Colette looked at Cassie. "What was that about?"

"He's mad cause I went out last night. I always go out and it ain't never been a problem. He don't need to concern himself with what I'm doing now," she said. She headed back to her room with her glass of juice.

Colette eyed her. "Is there a reason you're walking like that."

Cassie threw over her shoulder, "I got the dog shit fucked out of me last night."

Colette laughed. "Ooh! You naughty girl."

———

When Rock arrived at Jah's house, the sight of two Yukon Denalis, one black and the other bronze, in the driveway irritated him. He already knew that bitch Eli was inside.

"What's up nigga?" Jah greeted.

"I can't call it," Rock mumbled as he made his way in. He could hear the screaming of toddlers coming from the family room. Genesis and Avani were running around the dinette table.

Rock looked up and locked eyes with Eli. He didn't care what anybody said, the way Eli looked at him was like he was always fucking with him.

"Hey Rock," Jazmin said from the sofa. She was tending to Ja-ja.

"C'mon," Jah gestured for him to follow him.

Rock asked, "Why he always here?"

"There you go. Stop worrying 'bout that shit nigga." Jah snapped.

Rock made himself comfortable in Jah's room. He looked around and thought Jah had it made. He had a wife that loved the shit out of him. Not to mention Jazmin was a sexy plus size woman with her own hair that flowed down her back. They already had a daughter together, who was terrible but pretty as hell, and now they just had a son to add to their perfect life. On top of that, they just moved into a brand new subdivision where the lowest priced house started at four hundred thousand. Jah had his own room where he could be as untidy as he wanted to be without hearing Jazmin's mouth. And though Jah didn't have the best housekeeping skills, he tried to keep his room straight. It was equipped with quality electronics and furnishings. He had a bar, billiards table, and a poker table. There wasn't really one specific theme; just all of Jah's favorite things. However, he did have a specific color palette which was blue, white and red because his favorite football team was the New York Giants.

Rock wanted what Jah had, but he wasn't sure if he was ready to do what it took to maintain it. His eyes still wandered. He still loved being with different women. He didn't want to be tied down, but he wanted the life that came with it.

"Nigga, you worried about Eli being over here all the time, but why you always bringing yo ass over here," Jah pointed out. "Besides, that's Jazz's and my nigga Abe's family so that makes him my family. Calm down with all that. As a matter of fact..."

Rock watched Jah leave out the room. Two minutes later, he was returning with Eli. Rock blew a frustrated breath. *Why he had to bring this nigga in here*, Rock thought.

"Nigga, don't be looking like that," Jah said to Rock. "Get outcho fuckin' feelings about whatever it is. Eli, whatchu do to this nigga?"

Eli laughed. "I ain't done shit to him."

"What's up with you and Cassie though?" Rock asked.

Eli gave a half shrug. "Nothing. She works with me now. Is that why you got a problem with me?"

"The way you be looking be having me think—" Rock was saying before being interrupted.

"Eli look at everybody funny and shit," Jah said. "That ain't nothing new."

Eli sat down at the bar. He asked, "How do I be looking at you though?"

"Like you fucking with me."

Eli rolled his eyes. "Boy, you ain't that kind of important. You just Jah's friend."

Before Rock could respond, Jah interrupted. "Squash that shit. Now tell me 'bout whatchu was sayin' on the phone."

Rock gestured with his eyes towards Eli. An annoyed grimaced formed on Jah's face. "Nigga, he ain't finna say nothing."

"I don't know if I can trust him," Rock said.

"He straight Rock," Jah said seriously.

"Wait," Rock said before turning to Eli again. He asked, "Did Cassie go out with you last night?"

Eli answered, "She went out with Tanya, her brother, and me. We met up with some *other* people."

"Was she with a nigga?" Rock asked.

Eli shrugged without a show of care. "I don't know. I wasn't with her the whole time. Did you ask her?"

"Yeah but her lil ass got smart and shit," Rock said. Then a thought occurred to Rock. Maybe befriending Eli wasn't a bad thing. This way he could keep tabs on Cassie while keeping her at bay while he did his thing. "Next time she go out with you, make sure you watch her ass. I think she on some shit. Her lil bitch ass had stains and shit on her clothes and walking all funny."

Eli looked at him like he was crazy. "I ain't watching shit and I ain't reporting shit."

Before Rock could voice his comeback, Jah clowned him. "Nigga, I told you yo shit was garbage. Cassie ain't thinkin' bout yo ass. But how you mad and you doin' the dirty shit you doin?"

Eli chuckled. "His shit is what Jah?"

"Garbage," Jah repeated.

"Fuck both of ya'll," Rock grumbled. A sly smile spread across his face. "Her mama don't think it's garbage though."

Jah stopped laughing. "Nigga, you didn't."

"I sho in the fuck did." He said as if he were proud.

Eli gasped dramatically. "You fuck that girl mama?"

Rock started laughing. "Yeah, but this the funny thing. We knew Cassie was going out, so—"

"Wait. It was planned?" Eli interrupted.

"Something like that," Rock said. He continued, "So I stopped through. We was 'posed to just be talking. I was really wantin' some mo' head. But other shit just happened."

"What was funny about that?" Eli wanted to know.

"Oh...The funny part was when Cassie came home. I was in the room with her mama fuckin' the shit out of her. We didn't know she had come home. I shoulda left when we realized she was home. But shit when she came out the bathroom she was still moving around and shit. I couldn't come out the room. Waiting to make sure she had settled in her room, me and Colette ended up falling asleep. So this morning, I just pretended like I had just gotten there."

"So Cassie didn't see your car outside of her apartments?" Eli wondered. He knew he had taken Cassie home and didn't see Rock's car himself. He wasn't looking for it, because he was too concerned about Cassie and making sure she got in safe.

"Naw," Rock said. "I didn't park in front of her building."

"You a dirty ass nigga," Jah said with detest. "And nigga you my friend, but I'm lettin' you know right now, I don't condone this shit. You got all these other hoes out here to pick from, and you wanna fuck with Cassie's mama. Nigga, you foul. You on some Sean shit."

"I might be for now. Shit ain't right between me and Cassie no way. Her mothafuckin' mama more fun than she is. Besides, I'd rather be with my baby mama than her evil ass," Rock said. He added as an afterthought, "Cassie call herself not wanting to fuck with me no more, but I'ma let her lil ass cool off though."

"So you're gonna move on with your baby mama, but you're still gonna fuck Cassie's mama?" Eli asked. He looked confused. "And you think this shit is cool?"

"You heard what he said, right? Nigga selfish. He ain't gonna back down from Cassie's ass like that. Nigga, just talkin'. He gonna hold on to Cassie so she won't go no fuckin' where and when shit don't go through with other bitches, he gon' try to convince Cassie he a good dude," Jah explained.

"Aw nigga, you act like you a mothafuckin' saint or some shit," Rock rebutted.

"I ain't claiming to be no goddamn saint, but I ain't stupid either. You think I'm finna fuck up what I finally got with Jazz?" Jah asked.

"But I ain't got that with Cassie," Rock stated.

"But you fuckin' up yo chances of ever having it," Jah pointed out.

Eli interposed, "If you don't want Cassie for whatever reasons, why don't you try salvaging the friendship and getting it back to a place the two of you were before. But you gotta stop fucking with her mama. Let that be a one time thing and forget it ever happened, never to be talked about again. Then you take your lil happy ass on and find you a new duck."

Rock gave it some thought. He wasn't making any decisions on that issue just yet. If Cassie would act right, he would think about cutting all of the other women off.

However, Colette already said if he stopped their little fling, she would tell Cassie with no hesitation.

Chapter 8

For a man to have everything, Eli felt as if he had nothing. Every day seemed like a struggle to put on this facade of his. To make matters worse, his marital problems with Kris were spiraling out of control. It was why he started spending so much time at Jazz and Jah's house. He was afraid if he didn't get as far as away from Kris as he could, he would put his hands on her.

Jazmin suspected something was going on, but Eli would deny it. He felt like he needed to talk to someone about it though. He just needed to get it off his chest, and every time he tried to talk to Kris about their issues, it would turn into a big argument.

He looked at Cassie at her desk through his office's glass wall. She looked like she was actually working. Usually she spent too much time talking to other employees. Today, however, she was being studious. He was sure she was being quiet and focused to avoid looking any of them in the eye. She was ashamed of her behavior at the club. Maybe even embarrassed. He was surprised she showed up at all.

He dialed her extension from his desk phone.

"Yes?" she quickly answered.

"Come in here for a sec," he told her.

As soon as she hung up, she popped up from her seat and came into his office. He looked her in the face but she refused to make eye contact.

"What do you need?" she asked.

"Have a seat."

She sat down in one of the chairs in front of his desk.

"Why are you looking like that?" Eli asked.

"Like what?" The tone of her voice was sullen.

"Like the way you looking. Smile or something. I haven't heard your loud ass cackling all day. Why you so quiet?"

She shrugged.

He lowered his voice. "Are you still messed up about the club thing?"

Her eyes shifted briefly to his before she nodded.

"Ain't nobody judging you. We're all grown," he said.

"I know...it's just..." she let her voice trail into a deep sigh.

"Would you ever want to go back?"

This time she looked at him searching his face. "I...I...I'm not sure. I don't know...Maybe."

"What about doing the same thing you did Saturday?"

"I don't know. I mean...it might turn into an addiction or something. I felt embarrassed, but I can't deny that I enjoyed it."

"Mmmhmm," Eli hummed with thought.

Cassie's lips formed into a smile. "What does that mean?"

"You a freak," Eli replied casually.

She flushed with embarrassment.

"But hey...do you," he said.

Meekly, Cassie asked, "How do you know about that place anyway?"

"Kreme came to me, interested in a discreet location for his club. I liked the idea of it and wanted to invest. I'm like a silent partner. I leave the operations of the club to him though."

"Oh."

"That's why y'all were able to just come along. It's my shit." Changing the subject, he asked, "How is your relationship with your mama?"

Cassie was confused by his interest in her relationship with her mother. "It's okay...Eli, are you bored or something? You called me in here just to have leisure conversation?"

"What's wrong with that?"

Cassie shook her head with a chuckle. "You're crazy."

"It ain't like I can get fired," he pointed out. "Hell, the owner or shall I say owners, are fucking or have fucked my mama at one point. Shit, I'm blood."

Cassie gasped. "Why are you saying that?"

"Cause it's true!" Eli exclaimed. "That's why I said I understood your pain when it comes to our mamas being hoes. Me and my brothers got different daddies and it's taken her this long to know who fathered who. Sarah was fucking a whole family."

"Stop talking about your mama like that," Cassie fussed.

"She knows she a hoe. She thought I was her late husband's son but she never got him tested. She just assumed I was his because Lu and Antino came back not my daddy. But guess who my daddy is?"

"Who?"

"Lu's daddy!"

"Hell naw!" Cassie started laughing. It wasn't so much of what he said, but how animated he was being. She asked, "How did you find out?"

"Well, both Antino's and Lu's test results came back excluded. However," Eli said inserting a dramatic pause.

"Lu's wasn't exactly zero percent excluded, but the probability wasn't high enough to be considered not excluded by that particular company's procedures. Just knowing that, was enough for us to think it was someone related to Lu. Sarah denied that there could be anyone else in the family."

"So she lied?"

His eyes widen as he said, "With a straight face too."

"But look," he continued. "That nigga is like eighty years old. So he was about fifty when she fucked him. So I'm Lu's brother and my brothers' uncle and brother. Ain't that some hot ass mess?"

"So where is your daddy?"

"He's in Italy. He came for a visit and confessed to Lu that he slept with the *puttana*. That means prostitute whore in Italian."

Cassie couldn't stop laughing. He was telling this information in such a serious way, not once cracking a smile.

"Stop it Eli," she said. "So how did ya'll find out you were his son?"

"We went and got tested. And when it came back that I was his, I was like goddamn! I didn't talk to my mama for a whole month. That doesn't make any sense Cassie. Hell, do you know who your daddy is?"

Cassie chuckled. "Yeah, I know who he is."

"Oh...cause the way your mama was having all of those reunions at the cookout. You sure you know who he is?"

"Yes. Besides, I'm not mixed Eli. I'm straight Black."

"Okay," he said with uncertainty. "You know skin complexion don't mean anything."

"I know. But Charles Stephenson is my daddy. Romyn is biracial though. And our sister Nicole isn't but she's lighter than me."

"So y'all have different daddy's too?"

Cassie nodded.

Eli shook his head pitying the situation. "I really despise a woman who don't know who her children's damn daddies are. Which brings me to why I really asked you in here."

"What?" she asked. She eagerly watched him tap through his phone. Once he got to what he wanted, he turned his phone to face her so she could see the little boy that was on the screen.

"Do he look like me?" Eli asked.

"I don't know. Let me see," she said as she took his phone. She studied the image closer. She had seen Eli's wife Kris, in person. The boy resembled her a lot. They both had those simple faces with not a lot of features that stood out. Whereas with Eli, he had prominent features such as the shape of his nose, his thick eyebrows, his pinkish nicely shaped lips, and high cheekbones like

Sarah. Eli had a golden complexion with brown undertones. And his hair was fine with a wavy pattern. Cassie found it hard for this little boy not to at least look like he had some other race in him.

She handed him his phone back. "I really don't know. Why are you asking? You don't think he is?"

"Well," he started. He leaned forward resting his arm propped up on its elbow on his desk. Placing his face in his palm, he pouted. "I know he isn't."

Cassie looked at him with sympathy. "You do?"

"When she first had him, it was hard to tell. As he started to get older, I wrote it off that he looked more like her. But Avani resembles Kris a little, but you can tell I'm her daddy. I used to look at him like...who yo' daddy? I mean, I had convinced myself that if you back up, turn around three times, blink about four times, hold your head upside down and squint you can kinda see me in him. Abe was the first person to really point it out to me. Lovely said she couldn't see the resemblance either." He laughed at his own joke.

Cassie snickered, shaking her head. "Boy, stop that."

"Okay you see Avani's hair, right? It's like Genni's but you know Jah got that rough shit. With Jazz's input, she saved Genni from looking like you. So my lil boy hair—"

"Hold up! Did you just take a dig at my hair?" Cassie asked feigning insult.

"C'mon Cassie," Eli mocked with a twist of his lips. "You got your hair done now, but if you go too long, that shit get beady."

"Whatever Eli. So what about your lil boy hair?"

"Didn't you just see it in the picture?"

"Yeah, it wasn't that bad. And genetics are fifty-fifty. Every child don't get the same thing."

Eli rolled his eyes and released an exasperated breath. "You would say that. All you nappy heads stick together."

"Ooh! I can't stand you," Cassie laughed. She suggested, "Why don't you get tested if you have doubts."

"That's an insult to Kris, right? I didn't question Avani. We got married and she had lil man. I had no reason to think he wasn't mine when he was born. But...let me show you this picture."

Cassie waited as Eli tapped through his phone once more. He gave her the phone. She was looking at a peanut butter complexion man with dreads standing in the middle of two ladies; one of them being Kris. Eli's son had a strong resemblance to the man.

"You think this is his real daddy?"

His tone began to match the sadden expression of his face. "If he isn't, then I don't know who is. I didn't want to disrespect Kris by going behind her back to find out, but I had to know. And he ain't mine. I got the results a few days ago. Yesterday, I confronted her about it. We argued and I left. I spent all day at Jazz and Jah's house. I couldn't look at her. And the worst part about it is, she named him Elijah. Why would she do that?"

Cassie didn't know what to say. She could see that Eli was effected by his discovery. Now, it all seemed to make sense. It explained his up and down moods, his constant texting on the phone, and his forever presence at Jazz's house.

"So what do you plan to do?" she asked quietly.

Eli shrugged. "I don't know. She won't have a real talk with me. She lashes out and then run...Run right to him."

"So you knew about her affair?"

"I didn't want to believe it. I tried not to believe it and give her the benefit of the doubt. But all she talk about is Brother Yosef. And when she leaves, she never take Avani. I mean, she hasn't really bonded that well with the twins, so I expect her not to take them wherever she go. She's always left them alone for me to handle. But she always takes lil man with her."

Cassie was at a loss for words once again.

Eli sensed the awkwardness Cassie was experiencing. He didn't mean to bombard her with his problems, but it felt good to tell somebody what he was going through.

He said, "I know you can't give me any advice, but thank you for listening."

She offered him a modest smile.

"But back to this other shit," Eli said. He became upbeat suddenly. "Do you wanna go back out there this weekend?"

"There?"

"Yeah. You know...*there.*"

Like a little girl who just made a new friend, Cassie caught her bottom lip in between her teeth and nodded. She wanted to go back without a doubt, but she needed to figure out where things stood between her and Rock.

———

The looks Gio gave Cassie the rest of the week didn't bother her as much as they did Monday. She didn't really know how to interpret the way he looked at her. If she was an overly confident woman, she would think he was lusting after her. She tried to ignore him the rest of the week, but when he told her he would be joining her and Eli Saturday, she eased up. She wasn't feeling as uncomfortable, ashamed, and embarrassed as she was at first.

"So you're going back?" Tanya asked.

Cassie turned her body from side to side to inspect herself in her full length mirror. Into the phone, she said, "Yeah. You ain't coming?"

"I can't go back to that place. It was just...wrong on so many levels. I can't believe you're going again."

"Well, I'm hoping to hook up with my guy again," Cassie said.

"Your guy? Wh-wait a minute. Again? Cassie, you fucked somebody there?" Tanya asked surprised.

"Yeah. You didn't?"

"No!"

"I thought you...Well why did you act like that when we were all in the car?" Cassie asked.

"I let this white bitch eat the kitty," Tanya whispered.

Cassie started snickering.

"Bitch, that ain't funny. I felt so dirty...cause...cause that shit was good. But you didn't tell me you fucked a person."

"I assumed no one wanted to share their experience."

There was silence. Cassie fluffed her bangs a little so they weren't too much in her eye.

"Bitch, I'm waiting on you to tell me whatchu did!" Tanya exclaimed.

"Oh," Cassie giggled. "It was good girl! I mean it was what I needed. And I need some more."

"What if your guy ain't there this time?"

"I don't know. I just wanna fuck him though; nobody else."

"Did you get his name?"

Cassie thought the answer over and responded, "No,"

"Do you even wanna know it?"

"I don't know. Shit, I might need to see him outside of that club. That would mean things would become different."

"But Cassie, you don't know this man's personal life. You don't know if he's married. And if he fucked you there, then I'm sure he's fucking a whole lot of other women. Did you use protection?"

She really didn't feel like getting lectured. And she really didn't want to disclose who it was. She said, "Yes, we used protection."

"Good. Is your brother going? Ain't Eli going?"

"My brother is scared. You know he got that damn Lonzo and he don't want nothing getting back to him. I already told Eli that Romyn wasn't coming. But Gio is supposed to be there."

"You're not afraid of Rock finding out about this?"

"Rock ain't my boyfriend. And Rock is fucking other bitches. Until he's ready to be serious and actually want a life with me, I'm gonna do me."

"Well, just be careful," Tanya said.

"Okay," Cassie said.

"Love ya!"

"Love you also." Cassie ended the call and looked at herself one last time. This time she elected to wear a navy blue form fitting strapless midi-dress with her black five inch stilettos.

Glossing her lips, she noticed Colette's reflection in the mirror. She turned to her. "What is it?"

"You're going out again?"

Cassie was taken aback. "What do you mean again? Is it a problem?"

"No, it's no problem. It's just I haven't seen you fix yourself up like this in a while."

Cassie took in her mother's attire that consisted of the usual ensemble: tight red dress and black platform heels. She asked, "Where are you going?"

"We're having our annual black and red party at the club," Colette answered.

There was a knock at the front door. Colette went to answer it.

Cassie could hear Colette greeting whoever it was. She grabbed her wristlet and headed out into the hall and entryway. She smiled at the sight of Eli standing there. As usual, he was dressed nicely, but rather casual. He toned it down with a pair of white paint-print black pants and a white distressed t-shirt. No matter how toned down he tried to be, Eli still had a way of making everything he wore fashionable. And Cassie was almost salivating at the sight of his bowed legs.

He immediately turned up his nose at her in disapproval.

"What?" she asked as she looked down at herself.

"The dress aight, but them black shoes need to go. You're playing it too safe. Go get something else."

Colette chuckled as Cassie groaned.

Cassie pivoted on her heels and headed back to her room. Of course the man that wore orange pants to work would tell her she was playing it safe.

When she returned, she was wearing her hot pink ankle-strapped heels. She changed out her black wristlet for a floral print one. She even exchanged her accessories to ones that gave off more of a contrast.

Now Eli gave a nod of approval.

Cassie was surprised that Eli had opted to drive his Porsche instead of the SUV. It was very impressive and gave her a feel of luxury, power and importance. As they drove, the both of them were quiet, deep in their own thoughts. Cassie wondered about living a life like the one Eli was privileged to. She always imagined that a lifestyle as his would make all of life's problems go away. But she knew that wasn't true just from hearing Eli's situation. At the end of the day, it doesn't matter how many possessions a person have; if there's no love, they feel empty.

Once in the club, Eli disappeared on her. She turned to say something to him, and he was gone.

Like last time, she walked slowly, exploring and watching. A few guys spoke to her, but she made sure her body language was uninviting. This time, she decided to go the direction that Tanya went. Just like the other side, people were putting on an erotic show.

Then she saw him. His eyes were already locked on her. He waved and smiled. She threw him a quick discreet wave. She then wondered how often Sean came to this place. He liked fucking so it wouldn't surprise her if he came every time they were open. Just as she was about to make her way to him, he walked away heading to a stairwell. She wondered what was up there. She was curious to find out.

"Excuse me Miss."

Cassie turned to face one of the serving ladies with her tray of goodies. She handed Cassie a test tube with green liquid and a note card. Then she walked off.

Cassie walked over to where one of the recessed lights was reflecting off the wall. The note read: *Have a drink then come upstairs. #14*

Feeling like Alice in Wonderland, Cassie downed the shot, but she didn't grow or shrink. Her anxiety shrunk; however, her desire grew. She made her way to the stairwell. Once she got up there, she realized there were private rooms with numbers on the doors. She walked around until she got to fourteen. Her heart began to race in anticipation. She took a second and inhaled deeply before opening the door. Her first observation was that the room was red all over, including the lighting. Then her attention turned to him sitting on what looked to be an oversized sofa, but it was a bed. Not far from him sat a tray of things they might need.

He sat, waiting for her. Cassie's center ached immediately. He was too sexy and the seriousness of his expression was heightening her desire for him.

She walked over to him, placing her wristlet down. He grabbed her hand to pull her down onto his lap. His touch was electrifying. It jolted her mind back to their first encounter causing her heartbeat to pound between her legs.

She straddled him making her dress rise up her thighs. If he leaned back he would have a nice view of her panty-less clean-shaven pussy.

She asked, "Were you watching me the whole time?"

"Yes. You didn't seem to be looking for me so I sent that note." His hands pushed her dress up even more as he cupped her ass. He smiled at the feel of her nakedness. "No panties; I like that."

Feeling coy, she looked away. He kissed her neck then her chin. He was in search for her lips. She turned to face him providing him full access. He pulled back just enough to look into her eyes. He was asking if she really wanted to do this a second time. She answered by kissing him. They entangled in an impassioned kiss as they rubbed here and there. Her hands went under his shirt traveling all over his muscular body. His one hand continued to squeeze her ass and thigh on that side, while the fingers of the other hand were stirring up her sweet drippings.

Cassie became hyperaware of her body's yearnings. Her breast ached and she needed them touched. As if she had spoken out loud, he tugged the bodice of her dress down to expose her breasts. His lips found their way to them to kiss, lick and suck on her nipples. Her body grew mildly hot and her skin tingled. She craved him. She was hungry.

He groaned with disappointment when she hopped off of him. He asked, "You don't want to continue?"

"That's not it," she said. She pulled her dress, that had gathered around her waist, completely off and tossed it. She knelt down before him, flipping her bangs in the process. She needed to clearly see for what she was about to do. This was something that she rarely did, but with him, she felt an urge to do it.

He smiled and began to undo his pants. She helped him because he wasn't moving fast enough. She had an unceasing need to have him in her mouth. And when she was able to wrap her lips around him, it was like taking the first bite of a delectable, rich dessert. He was every bit as palatable as Cassie imagined.

Her method was fierce. She was a savage when it came to fellatio...when she chose to do it. She wasn't neat and orderly with it either. She sucked his dick like she was a feral woman having gone without food, and someone finally threw her a piece of chicken. It was sloppy and wet. She alternated pace and suction pressure, deep throating it to just tending to the head with her lips and tongue, and the usage of her hands.

"Shit," he hissed. He grabbed her hair and pulled her off of him. He lowered his face to hers and placed a soft kiss on her lips.

It was sensual and unexpected. But this gave Cassie the opportunity to look him in the eyes. She wanted to make sure she was pleasing him. At this point, she was his slave and he was her master. Her *Maestro*. She would do anything he asked to ensure his satisfaction.

He stood up towering over her as she remained on her knees.

"Open your mouth," he demanded.

She obeyed. He fed her his dick slowly. She went to wrap her hands around him so she could take control but he smacked her hands away.

"No touching," he told her. "Keep that mouth open."

She let him fuck her in the mouth how he wanted to. He held her by the head and pumped in and out. He got carried away causing her to gag when he jabbed her in the back of the throat.

He pulled away when it got to be too much. He bent down and kissed her again. "Get up here."

Cassie did as she was told. She lay down and watched him remove the rest of his clothing. She was genuinely grateful for the view. His body was perfect. And his dick stuck straight out; no curves or crooks. She was tempted to take him back in her mouth.

Before she could do so, he was on her. They fastened their lips in an intense heated lock. She could feel the hardness of him brush between her thighs. This caused her clit to start thumping. Her pussy started contracting, remembering what he felt like and was in anticipation of having him inside her again. It was like being ticklish, but before being touched, had a person already giggling because they knew it was coming.

She felt for his dick. She tried to bring him to her opening but he pulled away. She thrusted her hips forward hoping to get him inside her.

"You're going to get it; just hold on." There was a tease in his voice that drove Cassie crazy. It was like he was purposely evoking more arousal just from making her wait. He took a second to place a condom on. Again, Cassie wasn't thinking about prophylactics; he just wanted the dick.

Being limber had its advantages. The ability to have wild, rough sex was one of them. She slowly opened her legs and let them fall on either side of her. It left her wide open for deeper penetration.

"Now you showing out," he said with a simper.

She caught her bottom lip in between her teeth and gave him a sneaky smirk. Just as he fed her orally, he fed her pussy the dick. Once she received him fully on one long, deep stroke, the games stopped. There was no sense of personal intimacy. He savagely fucked her. He let her know who was in control. That cockiness she had when she spread her legs, disappeared. Her legs no longer wanted to be at her sides. Just like the last time, her hands tried to prevent the brutal dick stabbing.

"Move…"

She hesitated removing her hands from him.

Politely, he said, "Move your hands please."

She didn't trust him as she whimpered. She held onto his biceps as he plunged into her several times. She tried to resist the urge to push him and take as much as she could, but it was too much.

"Jesus!" she cried out as he eased up.

He started short stroking her while rubbing on her engorged clit. "Are you going to squirt for me?" His voice was thick with seduction.

She could see the drunken lust in his eyes as he looked down at her. It caused a shiver to course through her body. Her pussy started to grip his shaft repeatedly. This only stimulated her clit even more. She could feel it pulsating against his thumb.

"Spread your legs again."

She did. He pulled out of her and began to eat her pie. Her hardened bud was delicately handled by his tongue. Her breathing deepened. Euphoria blossomed from her gut and spread throughout her body. Her hips rocked back and forth. She clutched at the bed with her mouth gaped, letting out a throaty wail as her body trembled with an overwhelming orgasm.

She was still whimpering and convulsing when he entered her again. He kissed her lips in a soothing reassuring way to calm her down. That made her crave him more.

He whispered, "Do I make my Princess feel good?"

Calling her that was so endearing. It made her heart flutter and caused her to gush even more. Wearing an anguished expression, she spoke hoarsely, "Yes."

"Let's see if we can get this pussy to squirt."

She allowed him to push back her legs until her knees were touching her shoulders. He began to fuck her in an unrelenting, unapologetic, deliberate painful manner. But it got his desired results. Her fountain spurted sending her into an orgasmic convulsion. Every time she did it, it drained her.

Her body was still jerking with aftershock as he positioned her on top. She leaned forward as he eased his dick in her. She released a quivering breath as he filled her up with as much dick as he could. He felt even thicker and harder.

She worked her hips, thrusting back and forth massaging his shaft. He began to meet her thrusts causing her to bounce. His arms encircled around her waist, and he began pounding her from underneath.

Her howling turned into the growl of a vicious animal. Her teeth clenched, as she tried to stifle her groans. He groaned with her as the pace quickened.

"Fuck!" she screamed as she poured on him. She released a guttural sound as her body tensed up.

He continued to pump but she couldn't take it. She tried to get up, but he had her locked down. She tried to pry his arms away and raise to her knees. He wouldn't let her go. She hit him in the chest with her fist. "Let me go!"

"I ain't done with you!" he yelled at her.

"So," she said and tried to hop off of him. For a second she thought he was going to let her get away, but he got up with her and grabbed her by the throat from behind. It shot tingles through her body.

He growled in her ear, "Did I tell you, you could get up."

Her heart pounded, her nipples stiffened, and her center ached. The sternness in his voice commanded her body to react. She wasn't ready to stop. Her body needed more. But she wasn't going to let him have it that easy. It would be no excitement in that.

She pushed his arm away and glared at him. He returned the same glare, grabbed her and threw her down on the bed. She tried to get up but he caught her by the throat again. He was able to force her body around and put his weight on her.

"Stay down!" he ordered.

She squirmed under him, but he wouldn't let her up.

"Are you ready to behave?" he asked. He continued to hold her down by the back of her neck.

She could only respond with heavy breathing.

He loosened his grip. "You must want me to hurt you. Is that the kind of girl you are Princess? You like to fight...Damn, you got my dick hard as fuck..." he placed a delicate kiss on her shoulder, "...and I'ma beat this pussy up. You know you fucked up, right?"

She closed her eyes and moaned as his tongue and lips sensually caressed her neck and behind her ears. He nipped at her earlobes and traced her ear with his tongue. She could feel his thick piece of meat grinding on her ass and she was ready for him to take over her body once more.

He worked her over with so much vigor. He brought about two more powerful ejaculations. Once it was over, Cassie lay there breathing hard and heart racing. Her head seemed to be spinning or it was the room spinning around her head. This could be addictive. This was the freaky side of her that she tried to suppress and keep under control. She was afraid if she enjoyed sex too much she would become Colette. A hoe she was not, but here she was fucking this man when she could have been doing all of this with Rock. That was one of their issues;

the sex had fizzled. But Rock never made her feel this satisfied.

Maybe it was the excitement of doing this undercover act, or that he actually fucked her hard enough to get her to squirt, but he was able to bring all of that out of her which was something Rock failed to do.

She turned to look at him. His eyes immediately captured hers. It was something in his that was asking her what did she want. A part of her knew they couldn't do this anymore unless they were ready to deal with the addiction. And with addiction came strong cravings.

Chapter 9

Romyn sat back and followed his mother's movements throughout Cassie's apartment. She carried on as if she didn't have a care in the world. She laughed and talked with his sister, Cassie. Neither questioned his silence, nor did they wonder why his stare was so cold and held disdain.

What both of them were unaware of was that when Romyn came by the night before on one of his uninvited surprise visits, he himself had been surprised. He saw Cassie's car in front of her building so he assumed she was inside. Using his spare key, he let himself in. No one was in the living room but he heard a lot of moaning going on. He peeked around the corner to see if it was Cassie's bedroom it was coming from, but it wasn't. Her door to her bedroom was wide open. It was their mother making all of the noise. Repulsed, he backed out of the house and went back to his car.

He dialed Cassie to see where she could possibly be, but he got no answer. He grew a little perturbed, because he had a feeling he knew where she had gone. She mentioned it but hadn't confirmed if she was actually going. Although he said he didn't want to go back to Jouissance, a part of him wanted to. He wanted to stare at how pretty Eli was and salivate over him and Kreme. But he knew it would only lead to him getting in trouble with his boo Lonzo.

Instead of leaving right away, he sat in his car gossiping with his friend Corvell. Before he knew it, he had been sitting there for an hour. As he was telling Corvell he needed to get off the phone, he watched as someone came out of Cassie's apartment. He was curious to know what man was fucking his mama now. And nothing could have prepared him for who it was. So that's why he was disturbed right about now.

"What's wrong with you?" Cassie asked.

Romyn shook his head. "Nothing."

"Man troubles?" Colette teased.

He shot his mother a contemptuous look.

Colette chuckled, "Well damn. It must be serious. Is it the new person you're seeing?"

"What new person?" Cassie asked. She was curled up in the corner of her sofa with her pajamas still on.

"It's nobody." He tried to suppress the smile that wanted to spread on his lips.

"What's Sarah's son name?" Colette asked. "The one you were talking to at that cookout."

Cassie's eyebrow went up in question. She looked at Romyn. "Eli?"

"No," he said adamantly with a blush.

"Are you fucking Eli?" Cassie wanted to know.

Again, Romyn shook his head.

"I seen you and him together," Colette teased. "Ya'll looked rather...gay together. Is he another down low one? I know how you like them down low niggas."

"I wouldn't know Letty," Romyn said smartly. He cut his eyes at her. "What about you? I know you like messing around with them sneaky niggas. Who's your latest victim?"

"I don't have victims, sweetie," Colette said with arrogance. She walked into the living room with a cigarette dangling between her fingers. "I have willing and eager participants."

Cassie eyed the cigarette. "I hope you don't plan to light that up in here? Letty, what I tell you about smoking in my apartment."

"I'ma go out on the balcony," Colette snarled. She sashayed towards the sliding glass doors and stepped outside.

Romyn turned to Cassie and asked, "How are things between you and Rock?"

Cassie shrugged. "I really have no idea. We haven't really been around each other like that. I told him to leave me alone for a minute. He think I'm fucking around and ain't nobody got time for that."

Romyn gave her a knowing grin. "But aren't you?"

Cassie denied it. "No. I'm just having fun like everybody else at that place."

"That's not what I saw Cassie."

Cassie's mouth dropped as she gasped. "What did you see?"

"You weren't fucking Rock, I know that," Romyn teased.

"Please don't tell nobody," Cassie pleaded.

"Your secret is safe with me sis," he said. "But to be real, anybody is better than Rock. I don't really like him Cassie."

"I know you don't," Cassie said in a passive tone. "I still wouldn't mind being his friend, but this trying to have a relationship with him ain't working. I think when he started working at BevyCo and making real money, he got the big head."

"And you're a bitch, so that wasn't gonna work," Romyn joked.

"Whatever," Cassie giggled.

Romyn's eyes shifted to the balcony. He lowered his voice and asked, "So what's up with her?"

"She won't leave," Cassie said. "All she does is drink, sleep, go to the club, and have sex."

"Still the same Letty," Romyn said shaking his head. "She needs some intervention."

"She needs more than that. Have you talked to Nicole lately?"

"Yeah, last week. She seemed okay."

Cassie nodded in agreement. "Yeah, I spoke to her the other day. She refuses to come over here while Letty is here. Her and Parker are talking now."

"Parker just didn't seem like the type." Romyn was disappointed.

"He isn't. Letty just a hoe," Cassie said. She thought back to her conversation with Eli and laughed aloud.

"What's funny?" Romyn asked.

Cassie shook her head. "Nothing. It's just that—" She was interrupted by the sound of her phone ringing. She looked over at it lying on her end table. When she saw the name that popped up she started laughing even more.

"Hello?" she answered as she hopped up from the sofa. She headed to her bedroom for privacy.

"You heifa!" Eli screamed into the phone. "Don't you ever do that shit no more. Not while you're with me."

"What?" she giggled innocently.

"Hee hee hell! Why in the fuck didn't you tell me you left? I was looking all over for you. Shit, I got worried and thought somebody done carried yo' nappy headed ass off somewhere."

"I left with my friend," she stated. She wasn't sure if he was really angry or just being playful.

"And you couldn't come find me to tell me that? And what friend?"

"Uhm...remember Sean?"

Eli got quiet.

"You know Sean, the one that work at BevyCo and was fucking around with Jazz?"

"Him?" Eli sounded disgusted. "Is he the person I saw you with the first time you went to Jouissance?"

"Yeah. He was there," she answered. "He was there last night too. I left with him. He brought me home."

"So is that why you didn't answer the phone last night? I called you."

She was guilty of ignoring his call. "I saw it...I just...didn't feel like answering."

"Okay," Eli said quietly. "You couldn't text me at least?"

"Eli!" She screamed into the phone. "I won't do it again, so I'm sorry. But there will be no again cause I ain't going back."

"That's fine too," he responded.

It fell quiet. Cassie wondered what he was thinking and why he was still on the phone. Then it crossed her mind to ask him how he was doing. "Are you okay?" she asked sincerely.

"I'm fine," he sighed. She could hear that he was bothered.

She cleared her throat with uneasiness. She asked, "Where is your family?"

"The twins and Avani are here in the house with me. And she's gone with lil man as usual."

"Why do you refer to him as lil man? You never call him by name anymore."

"Because it just don't seem right to refer to him as Elijah. I really hate that she did that," he griped.

"Have she talked to you about those test results?"

"She won't say a word to me."

"Why is she being so difficult? What are your plans? I mean, you have evidence of her infidelities."

He sighed with defeat. "I don't know. I married her after she told me she was pregnant. All she had to do was tell me she wasn't sure who the baby's daddy was. At least I would have gone into this aware of the situation. But she tried to pull some Sarah bullshit."

"Maybe she thought you wouldn't want to marry her if she told you that," Cassie said.

"I wouldn't have cared. You know why?"

"Why?"

"'Cause I felt like I found the only person that understood me and didn't question if I was gay or not."

Cassie fell silent but she was very curious about that subject matter. Carefully she asked, "Eli, why you let people believe you're gay if you're not. But wait...are you?"

"It ain't nobody's business unless I'm fucking them. And if I'm fucking them, it annoys the hell out of me for them to keep questioning it. As far as letting people believe it, I don't know...The mystery of it all just took on a life of its own. It started when I was younger I guess. I wasn't like my brothers. I was labeled effeminate; had no idea what the fuck that meant back then. I don't really think it applies to me in that sense though. I'm just more metro than anything. But when I was a kid I always had a smart mouth. So when other kids would tease me and ask if I was gay, I would throw it back at them asking if their pissy ass grandmama was gay. And if that aggravated them, I would run and get Ike or Abe," he said with a half-hearted chuckle.

"Pissy ass grandmama?" Cassie giggled.

"Yeah, it was this one boy named Bobby that always used to pick on me. I think he wanted my booty for real though. But his grandmama smelled like cat piss all the time. Bitch smelled like she was the litter box and all the cats in the neighborhood just came over and pissed on her ass. Then she had the nerves to want everybody to give her a hug. I was like I ain't hugging you, you funky bitch."

Cassie was dying laughing.

"I'ma let you go cause I'm sure you got more important things to do besides talk to me all day," he said. "I'll see you tomorrow. You are coming to work right?"

"Yeah," she said. "But Eli, if you need anything I'm here. You don't have to get off the phone if you don't want to." She didn't know what it was, but her heart was really going out to him. She felt they had a special bond going on and he let her see a side of him that not many people got to see.

She could hear him hesitating, but he finally said, "Well...can you just come over and keep me company?"

"Do you think that's a good idea?"

"I know you ain't worried about Kris. She thinks I want your brother anyway. Just come on and if you get uncomfortable, me, you, and the kids can walk around to Jazz's house."

"Speaking of my brother...why did Colette say she saw you with Romyn?" Cassie asked.

Eli responded, "Because she probably did. And stop being so damn nosy. If your brother want you to know what that was all about he would tell you."

"You're such a smart ass," she said.

"It ain't what you think though."

"Mmmhmm," she said with playful doubt.

"You know it ain't. Now are you coming over here or not?"

She thought it over before smiling. "Give me a few minutes."

Chapter 10

When Kris returned to the house that Sunday night, she wasn't surprised that Eli had company. He told her he would start living a life without her. She had no problem with that. He had been living a whole different life anyway. What she was curious about was who all showed up in the purple Charger she parked beside in the driveway. She knew it belonged to Cassie, but she was aware that Romyn was Cassie's brother. If he was indeed inside the house, then she knew she had to move on.

She got out of her car and went inside the house. She immediately heard talking and laughter sounding off from the kitchen. She slowly made her way to them. She knew it. It was Cassie, Romyn, Tanya, and Eli. The ladies sat at the kitchen bar counter, While Eli stood on the other side. Leaning over the counter next to him was Romyn.

Cassie and Tanya looking in her direction alerted him to her presence. He turned around and for a minute she thought she saw a glint of elation. But that was not Eli. He didn't care about her like that.

"Where is lil man?" Eli asked, after noticing she was alone.

"He's with Camilla," Kris answered. She didn't bother to speak to his company. She continued her journey towards the bedroom she once shared with him. Of course he had to follow her.

"Kris, can we talk?" he asked.

She was surprised at the soft, sincere tone of his voice.

"There's nothing for us to really talk about," she said. She busied herself in her closet.

He stood at the doorway and watched her as she picked through her belongings.

"Are you planning to be away from the house for an extended time frame?"

"Yeah," she murmured.

"Are you taking Avani?"

"No," she said.

"You know, she asks where you are all the time. I don't understand why you're abandoning her but you drag lil man with you all the time," he said.

"Well," she said passively. "After you did that shit behind my back and discovered he wasn't yours, I assume you wouldn't want him around."

"Okay, you just made that about him and completely skimmed over the fact that you have a daughter that would like to spend time with her mama too."

She didn't have an explanation for him.

"Is it because she's my child and not his?"

She remained quiet.

"I can't believe I married my mama," he scoffed.

"I am not Sarah," she spat.

"I can't tell," he argued.

"Fuck you Eli," she said. She brushed past him with the things she wanted to take.

"You haven't done that in a long time," he said under his breath.

"And I'm not. Ever again," she said curtly.

"Why? I've been trying with you. I've given you space. I don't hound you. I don't even try to argue with you. I don't know what happened, or how Yosef got in your head, but this isn't what I wanted."

"No, you've proven that. I wasn't what you wanted. I don't know why you married me—"

"Wait," he interrupted. "Who told you that? Those aren't my words. That's that Malcolm X, Mahatma Gandhi wannabe nigga putting that shit in your head. You know where the fuck I messed up at?"

"Yosef ain't got nothing—"

Raising his voice, Eli spoke angrily. "That fake fucka got everything to do with this. Isn't he lil man's daddy? But I fucked up when I tried to respect your beliefs and let you be you. I should have intervened when I saw the shit getting out of hand."

"Don't raise your voice. Where are the kids?" she asked.

"Why do you give a fuck?" He was now furious.

"Because you're being loud. Oh wait...that must be for your company. Go back to your boyfriend in there," she said sarcastically.

Eli let out a disbelieving chuckle. "Is that the only thing you've created to hold against me?"

"It's all I need," she retorted.

"I've been a good father—it took me a while, but I got the hang of it. I was a good husband—"

"Exactly. *Was!*"

"I said was because you no longer want to acknowledge that anymore. You're trying to paint me as this bad person so you can feel better about this dumb ass shit you're doing."

She rolled her eyes in aggravation. She headed out of the room. "I'll be moving out permanently next week."

"Huh?" Eli followed her.

She bypassed his friends in the kitchen and went to the living room throwing her things on the sofa. She headed up the stairs to go to the kids' room to retrieve some items for Elijah. In doing so, she realized Avani was in her bed sound asleep. She made sure to be quiet as she moved about the room.

"Hey Kris," a child's voice said softly.

She turned to the doorway and saw Bria standing there. She offered the young girl a smile. "Hey."

"Where's Elijah?" Bria asked. She saw the clothes in Kris' hands and asked. "Are you going somewhere?"

"Yeah for a lil while," Kris answered.

"Just you and Elijah?" Bria asked.

Kris nodded as she headed out of the bedroom. Bria was following her.

"How come you always gone?" Bria asked.

"Ask your father," was all Kris could say.

"He said you ain't shit, but he told me not to repeat that," Bria said.

Kris stopped and looked back at Bria. She was such a pretty girl, but had picked up her father's foolish behavior. And Bria wore the same emotionless expression as Eli.

"Go back to bed Bria," Kris told her. She turned away and continued her journey back downstairs. Of course he would say something like that to a ten year old. He had no couth about himself at all. That's inappropriate parenting which Yosef had spoken to her about.

Naturally he didn't want his son being raised in the same house as Eli. She couldn't really blame him.

Their three-year-old daughter Avani was all Eli's. It was obvious. At first she wasn't even sure about her. She had been with Yosef before, but once Avani turned out to be Eli's she felt it was only right to be with him. She had left Yosef heartbroken but she thought she was making the right decision. But at one point she was confused, especially since she kept communication with Yosef. She discovered she was pregnant, and once again she wasn't sure who the father was, but she didn't bother to tell Eli. By then they were married, and he gave Elijah his last name. Now Yosef wanted his son with him. She planned to get a divorce. She also would get the Masters name removed from Elijah's birth certificate.

Eli waited for her at the bottom of the stairs. She ignored him and gathered her other things.

"You don't have to leave Kris. I got this house for you and the kids. It was what you wanted, remember?" He spoke in a low voice. "I can go back to the glass house that you hated so much."

"I don't want this house. It's all yours," she said.

"I really hate you right now. You know that?"

"I really don't care," she mumbled. She went for the door but paused. She turned to him so that he could watch her remove her wedding ring set. She placed it on the entryway table, then proceeded to exit out the front door.

———

Tanya, Cassie, and Romyn all exchanged looks when they heard the front door close. Eli never came back in the kitchen.

"I'ma go check on him," Cassie whispered. She got up from the stool she had been sitting on and headed towards the front of the house. She spotted Eli sitting on the stairs with Bria.

"Are you okay?" Cassie asked with concern.

He nodded, but he didn't look at her. His eyes were focused elsewhere. Bria wiped his face and that's when Cassie saw the wetness of his lashes.

Bria said, "It'll be alright Daddy. She'll come back when she realizes she stupid."

"She ain't coming back," Eli said. "And I don't want you worried about it. But I'm fine Bria. Thank you for caring about me though. Now go back to bed."

Bria gave Eli a hug before she ran back upstairs.

Cassie asked, "What did she say?"

"She took her ring off and put it on that table," he said nodding in its direction.

"What does that mean?"

"It means she don't wanna be married to my ass no more, Cassie. What the hell you think it would mean?" Eli said smartly.

"Okay...dang. You ain't gotta snap on me," she said. She sat down beside him on the steps.

"I'm sorry," he mumbled.

"It's fine. I know you're fucked up right now. For what it's worth, I think Kris is crazy. She doesn't realize what she has right here. And what about Avani?"

"Kris is Sarah all over again," he said.

She remained silent. Hell, sometimes she questioned if she was Colette all over. It felt like the inner Colette in her wanted to bust out on the scene. It was why she couldn't go back to that club. It would only provoke it.

Her eyes shifted to Eli and watched him fidget with the gold chain around his neck. Him doing that was equivalent to her knee bouncing when she was bothered.

A warm smile spread on her face and she couldn't resist the urge to ruffle his hair.

Eli pushed her hand away playfully. "Don't touch my hair lil girl."

"Are you going to keep this much length to it for a while?" she asked.

He combed his fingers through his hair, flattening it a little. "You don't like it?"

She absolutely adored his hair. She always found herself staring at it. Whenever she stood at his desk at work to show him something, she always admired its shine and wave pattern.

She said, "I love it. It's you." Her heart swelled as she inhaled deeply before speaking her next words. "Eli, you know you deserve to be happy. You don't have to accept Kris' shit just because you think she's the only one that understood you at one point. Don't let her dumb ass upset you or make you feel like you're not worthy, or even feel like you've failed at this marriage. She's just stupid. Fuck her and if you want me to, I'll kick her ass."

Eli started laughing. "You so stupid, you know that?"

Cassie grinned and traced his facial hair with her fingers.

"Why are you touching me like that?" Eli asked amused.

Ignoring him, she asked, "Why don't you grow this out like everybody be wearing nowadays?"

"I thought about it, but that shit look like it catch all kinds of shit. Food, spit, boogers, booty crumbs, pussy residue...Ain't nobody got time to be washing out their beards all damn day long."

"Booty crumbs?"

"Yeah, you know niggas is eating ass now, Cassie," Eli said with a hint of humor.

Cassie's stomach was cramping up from laughing so hard. A person never knew what would come out of Eli's mouth. Although he tried to keep a straight face, he couldn't refrain from laughing either. But that was Cassie's mission; to get his mind off of Kris and hopefully her kind words made him feel better.

Cassie's phone started buzzing in her hand. She looked at it and saw it was a message from Rock. **Whr u at?**

Why was he always trying to keep up with her whereabouts? They weren't together.

She text back: **where you at nigga?**

"Who is that?" Eli asked.

"Rock's stupid ass. I don't know why he's texting me wanting to know where I'm at," she said with a hint of annoyance.

Eli looked at her clearing his throat with uneasiness. With regret, he began, "I need to tell you something."

"What?" she asked. Another text came through. **I wanna tlk**

Eli hesitated. "It's about—"

The doorbell sounded followed by knocking. Eli frowned, "Who is this? It bet not be Yosef's ass coming to my house."

Cassie watched as Eli answered his door.

"Where Cassie at?"

Cassie stood up and looked around Eli. "Rock? Who told you to come over here?"

Eli stepped aside so they could have a clear view of each other.

"Can you come out here real quick?" Rock asked.

She could see the vexation in his face.

Eli said, "You can come in here if you want."

Rock snarled, "I don't wanna come in your house nigga. C'mon Cassie."

Eli was taken aback. "What the fuck is your problem? You act like I done fucked your mama or some shit. Bye nigga!" And he slammed the door in his face.

Cassie started snickering. Rock was cussing on the other side of the door. She went for the knob. "Let me see what his problem is."

"I'ontruss it," Eli said. "He talking all crazy and shit, nose flaring. Why he so angry?"

"I don't know, but I'll be alright," she said. She exited the door, closing it behind her. She glared at Rock. "What is your problem?"

"My problem? Now I see what yours was. You and this nigga fucking? Is that why you can't act right with me?"

Cassie groaned with exasperation. "Rock, if you don't go on with this shit. What possess you to come over here anyway?"

"I was on my way to Jah's house and I saw your shit sitting in his driveway. Why the fuck you over here at night?" Rock questioned.

"Why? I don't know. Cause I'm grown and I have free will," she said smartly. "You ain't got no right to be asking me anything. I told you to leave me the fuck alone. If and when you see my car over here again, keep it moving. I owe you nothing."

"So that's how you playin' me?" Rock asked. "You can't do shit with me but you all in this nigga's face. You here at his house. You can't tell me ya'll ain't fucking."

"Hey, if you had a house I probably would have visited you too," she said wryly.

"I hope the mothafucka give you AIDS," Rock said with hate.

Cassie snapped. "You one dumb mothafucka. You know that? If anybody get the shit it'll be your hoe ass sticking your dick in every goddamn thang that smile at you. I ain't with your stupid ass because you can't fuck worth shit, lil dick bitch! Always fucking whining and shit. I think I know why you don't like Eli now. You wanna fuck him, don'tchu? Or maybe you want him to fuck you, you bitch!"

Rock palmed her face and pushed her as hard as he could sending her flying backwards. The only thing that kept her from hitting the ground was the bushes by the porch steps.

"You mothafucka!" Cassie screamed before she lunged at him. She was so enraged that she didn't realize the door had opened and Tanya, Romyn, and Eli had come flying outside.

When Rock went to repeat his actions, Eli swung on him and connected with his jaw. Not only did the hit stun Rock, but the fact that Eli had been courageous enough to hit him. Infuriated, Rock retaliated.

Tanya started trying to break them up and screaming at the same time. Then out of nowhere, they heard someone shouting at them. It was Jah running towards the house.

"Goddamit, ya'll mothafuckas stop this shit!" Jah shouted. He ran up on Rock and Eli, trying to pry them apart, but something snapped in Eli. He wanted to seriously fuck Rock up. It was evident that people really underestimated Eli's masculine capabilities.

Cassie stood back actually impressed. It took Jah having to restrain Eli and push him back towards the house.

"Bitch! Putcha hands on her again!" Eli shouted angrily around Jah.

"Fuck you, faggot mothafucka!" Rock spat.

"C'mon nigga. Take yo' lil strong ass back in the house," Jah urged. He was out of breath as he pushed Eli. Over his shoulder he said, "Rock, getcho dumb ass off this man's property!"

Rock wiped at the blood oozing from his busted lip. Nostrils flaring and glaring at Cassie, Rock began to walk away.

Tanya looked at Cassie. "Are you okay?"

Cassie nodded. "Let me go in here and check on Eli." She shot Rock one last look. She didn't know what had gotten into him, but he was no longer her concern. He fucked up big time.

Chapter 11

Being at work for two days without Eli's presence felt weird to Cassie. She ended up working close with Tanya and Gio while he was gone. She called and checked on him, but he assured her he was okay; he just wasn't in a talking mood.

"Is he alright?" Tanya asked. She waited for Cassie to end the call with Eli. It was Wednesday and Cassie had called him every day.

"He sound the same as he did Monday," she said. She looked troubled. "I wonder if he's mad at me."

"Why would he be?" Tanya asked. "You're not the one that acted a donkey, Rock did. Rock had no business coming over there asking anybody shit."

"I know, but Eli was defending me. He probably mad cause I got his pretty face bruised up. You know how he is," she chuckled.

Tanya laughed. "Oh yeah bitch. He mad about that shit."

Gio came walking around the corner wearing a big grin. In his hand was a bouquet of yellow red-tipped roses.

"Somebody is very special today," Gio teased.

"Who them for?" Tanya asked.

Gio walked up to Cassie and handed them over. "They're yours. I was up front when they came. There's a card in there."

Cassie was flabbergasted. She had never had a man to give her flowers. She took the roses from him and plucked the card out.

"Bitch, these are pretty. Who sending you flowers?" Tanya said excitedly.

Cassie shrugged. She looked at Gio. He was still grinning and waiting for her to read the card.

Silently she read: *I crave you Princess*

Cassie's breathing quickened and her heart began to pound in her chest, sending its echo to her pussy. God! She said she wasn't going back to that club. She told him Saturday, that she didn't think they should continue this. He act as though he understood. She tried to clear her mind of him, but every night when she closed her eyes, he popped into her mind leaving her having to satisfy herself. Now he was sending her roses making her panties wet.

Tanya snatched the card from her. "Let me see this."

Cassie wondered if Eli planned to return to the club the upcoming Saturday. He probably wasn't in the mood after what went down Sunday night. She could go on her own now, but it would feel weird arriving there by herself.

"Damn!" Tanya exclaimed. "They craving you. What the fuck you got between them legs? Whatchu done did *Princess*, got a nigga craving your ass?"

Cassie blushed. "Nothing."

"Are you going to tell me who he is?" Tanya asked.

Cassie's eyes shifted to Gio. He was smiling knowingly. She got up from her chair at Tanya's desk and walked into Eli's office. She sat behind his desk to use his phone and dialed his number.

He answered, "Hello?"

"Hey Eli, it's me," she whispered.

"Cassie? I thought it was somebody important calling from the company. Didn't we just get off the phone?"

"Yeah, yeah...we did. But I just got a delivery of roses, right? They're from my maestro. And even though I said I wasn't going back to the club, I think I need to go this Saturday. Are you going?"

"Time out. Your what?"

"My maestro," she giggled.

"What the fuck is that? Ain't that like a music conductor or some shit?"

169

"Well, it can also mean whiz, master, expert...In my case, it's master. Maestro of my body," she said.

There was a pause on Eli's end.

"Eli?"

"You dumb as hell, you know that? But anyway...Why are you calling me?"

"I wanna go back to the club. Are you going?"

"Why are you whispering?"

"Cause I'm at work nigga. Should I be screaming this shit letting everybody know I want my boss to take me back to a sex club?"

"And you bet not either," he threatened. He said, "I'm not sure if I'm gonna feel like it, but I'll let you know."

She was disappointed. "When will you let me know?"

"Probably Saturday," he said.

"Okay."

With a curious tone, he said, "I thought you said you weren't going back though. What changed your mind?"

Cassie's smile grew so big, her face ached. "The flowers; he's thinking about me. And now I'm thinking about him."

"What color did you get?"

She was confused. "Huh?"

"The roses."

"Oh," she giggled. She looked at them and said, "They're yellow with red tips."

"What do you think your *maestro* is trying to convey with that color choice?" he asked.

She had no idea. She shrugged as if he could see her. "I don't know. I'll have to look it up."

Eli laughed. "Bye Cassandra."

She snickered as she placed the phone back on its base. She went back out to Tanya's desk and sat down. "Hey, look up rose color meaning."

Tanya pecked away at her keyboard. She clicked on a link that took them to a list of various colors of roses and their meaning, with a diagram of each. They found the one that resembled hers. It said: friendship and falling in love.

Tanya's mouth dropped open. "This nigga falling in love with the pussy. No wonder Rock tripping. Cassie must got that snapper."

"Shut-up," Cassie said playfully hitting her. She wanted to gloat and enjoy the giddiness bubbling inside, but she had to keep her feelings in check. This could go in a direction she might not be ready to go in.

She got up again, with the roses. "I'll be back." She went back in Eli's office. This time she called her friend. She couldn't let Tanya hear her conversation, because she would be shamed for even talking to him. But she had to go back to the club just to see her maestro.

———

The following day in the office, Cassie was glad to see Eli had returned. He was there before she got there which was unusual. Leave it to Eli to return looking runway ready. From one day to the next, they never knew what they would get from Eli. One day, he could wear black slacks with a black button down and look completely normal. The next day he could show up in some bright ensemble that didn't match in pattern or color, but he made it hot. Today, he wore pink slacks with the matching vest over a baby blue dress shirt finished with a solid navy tie. The beige leather belt matched the beige Versace loafers on his feet. She only knew the shoes were Versace because of the gold-tone logo in the front. The gold logo complemented the gold chains and buttons of his vest along with the gold of his jewelry.

Tanya's eyes were glued on him as he made his way into his office. He was intently focused on the papers in his hand. A delighted smile crept across her face. She leaned back in her chair to look at Cassie. "You see that shit?"

"See what?" Cassie whispered.

"You don't pay attention to nothing," Tanya waved off. She moved closer and whispered. "Eli look like he packing. You see his dick print in them pants?"

Cassie gave Tanya a chastising look. "Tanya. You need to stop. You must need some dick looking at people's prints and shit."

"You right about that. I do. It's been a long time coming...but I know..."

And they both finished together, "A change gon' come!"

"Praise him!" Tanya raised her hands to the ceiling. "He'll make a way out of no way! He may not come when you want him, but he'll...."

Together they said, "Be there right on time!"

Tanya grabbed her phone. "Girl, let me show you what this nigga sent to my phone."

Cassie looked on eagerly. Tanya showed her a picture of a man's penis. Cassie started laughing. "What's wrong with it?"

Tanya side-eyed her. "That's what the fuck I asked. Shit look like it need some Proactiv."

"What did he think he was gonna accomplish by sending you that? Whose dick is that anyway?"

"Girl, you remember Bruce? This nigga call hisself trying to entice me with this shit."

"It look like it itch," Cassie laughed. "Look like a chicken nugget with eczema. Girl, don't you let him stick that up in you."

"I ain't. I already told him I'm practicing abstinence, but he sent me this shit," Tanya grumbled.

"Aw...you're still doing that?" Cassie asked sympathetically.

Tanya laughed. "Why you act like you feel sorry for me?"

"Cause I do. I mean, how long has it been since you had any? So Ricky ain't had none of your caramel pie yet?"

"No. And we're cool being friends. He still come over and chill with Tyriq when he's there from time to time, but that's it."

Cassie smiled. "But that's nice of him. He ain't nothing like his big headed brother."

"Girl, they so different."

As they continued to play around, Cassie didn't see Eli standing at his office's door. When she gave him her undivided attention, because of Tanya, her eyes dropped down to his crotch. Now she understood why Tanya made such an observation. It was right there. And her twat twitched.

Bad girl, Cassie thought. She asked, "You need me?"

"Yeah. Come here for a minute," he said quietly.

Cassie got up and went in his office. She didn't bother asking if he needed the door closed. From the expression on his face, she had a feeling it would be personal.

"How are you today?" she asked as she took a seat.

"Better," he sighed.

She noticed his left cheek was faintly bruised. "I'm sorry about all of that Sunday."

"How many times are you gonna apologize for how that retard acted. That wasn't your fault."

"I know but...you ain't no fighter. And I shouldn't have put you—"

"Thanks a lot," he said dryly. "Just tear me down even more."

"No Eli. You know what I mean. You don't go around puffing out your chest to prove a point."

"But I will beat a nigga's ass if they keep fucking with me. Rock just happened to come at the wrong time. I was imagining him being Yosef. I really wanna kick that nigga's ass."

"Speaking of that...Have you spoken to Kris again?"

"She won't talk to me. And she didn't come by the house Monday or yesterday. I think I hate her 'cause of how she's doing Avani. What do I—I mean...how do I explain this to a three-year-old?"

"I doubt she's even thinking about how this is effecting or will affect Avani. Dude really got her fucked up like that?" Cassie asked.

"Crazy, isn't it?"

With a teasing smile, Cassie asked, "So...I didn't know you could fight like that for real."

"You think I'm a punk too?"

Cassie shook her head emphatically. "It's not that. You just come off as..."

"Weak? Scary?"

The smile faded from her face as she gave him a pensive stare. Apologetically she said, "No and I'm not trying to offend you."

"I don't fight. I don't want to have to. I leave that kind of shit up to my brothers, but Abe and Ike made sure I could handle my own if they weren't around. They used to kick my ass all the time until I got tired of them getting the best of me. I could never seriously whoop their ass— cause you see how tall them niggas are? And then Abe all swoll and shit. He was like that when we were kids. Big ass nigga. I call on him for every damn thing...but I can't right now."

Cassie saw a flash of sadness in his eyes. Her heart really went out to him. "He'll be back soon Eli."

"I hope so," he answered solemnly.

"I was just trying to point out that I was impressed, especially since you came to my defense," Cassie explained. "I just didn't realize you would do that for me."

"If a person make me mad enough, I can get just as ig'nant as the next. But I am too pretty for all that. I ain't got time to be doing all that sweating, huffing and puffing, and getting bruised up."

A slight smile returned to her face. "I know that."

A knock on the door interrupted them. The door pushed open and in walked Jazmin.

"Am I interrupting business?" she asked.

Eli shook his head. "What's up?"

Jazmin walked over. "I was just coming up here to see how you're doing?"

"I'm good," he said.

"You ain't really talked to no one these past couple of days," she said.

Cassie added, "Yeah, I was worried too."

"I think you were more distraught than anybody," Jazmin said.

Eli looked at Cassie and smiled. "You were that worried about me Cassandra?"

Cassie rolled her eyes upward in a playful manner. "Please."

Eli looked at Jazmin, "Where is Jah? I wanna fuck with him cause that nigga came from nowhere. How did he even know what was going on?"

Jazmin laughed. "Well, Rock was supposed to come to our house. He was on the phone with Jah when he saw Cassie's car at your house. Jah was telling him he bet not stop by your house with some shit. I think Rock said something stupid and wasn't listening to Jah. And you know if we walk out on our porch we can see between the houses that's across the street and see your yard. He was already coming outside to make sure Rock came straight to our house. But he saw when he pushed Cassie and took off."

"What did he say to Rock?" Cassie wanted to know.

"He cussed him out in our driveway. Rock didn't even come in the house. He's crazy. Like, why is he worried about you Cassie when he's living with his baby mama and they're expecting another baby," Jazmin said casually like it was a known fact amongst them.

Cassie's mouth dropped open.

Eli looked at Cassie, then at Jazmin. "I believe she wasn't aware of that."

Jazmin gasped realizing her mistake. "You didn't know that? I assumed you did and that's why ya'll stopped messing with each other."

Cassie frowned. "No, this is my first time hearing this. And Jazz, don't you think I would have come to you if I knew that?"

"Yeah which is why when I overheard Jah fussing at him about it the other night, I was wondering why didn't you tell me. I thought maybe you didn't want to talk about it."

Cassie's face relaxed. "It doesn't matter. That's his life."

"Well, why don't we get a round of drinks after work today," Jazmin suggested.

"That's cool. I'll see if my brother wanna come," Cassie said getting up.

Jazmin gave her a teasing smile. "Cassie, do I see your booty growing?"

Cassie blushed and smiled coyly. "Is my booty growing girl?"

"Yeah. Ain't her booty growing Eli?"

Eli looked disgusted. "I mean...what am I looking for? Like...there's nothing there."

Cassie started laughing. "Fuck you Eli."

———

Saturday came and Cassie was disappointed to know that Eli hadn't made up his mind about going to the club. Cassie still wanted to go for some reason. She informed him that she was going in case he changed his mind. And since she had a complimentary membership from the owner, she could go by herself.

She paid attention the last time they came to the club to know how to get there on her own. She parked and got out her car. She saw a few people dressed as if they were going to the same place she was going. She hesitated before walking away from her car. She looked around to see if she could spot Sean's car, a red Challenger.

"Princess."

Her head snapped in the direction of the voice calling out to her. When she saw him, a big smile spread across her face. She walked in his direction as he met her halfway.

"What are you—" she started but was cut off by him grabbing her by the hand and pulling her along.

"We're not going in there tonight. You're coming with me," he told her.

She didn't object as he led her to his car. Once she was buckled in his passenger seat she asked, "What about my car?"

"I'll bring you back to it."

"Where are we going?" she asked.

"I got us a room. I didn't feel like dealing with that environment tonight. I hope you don't mind."

She shook her head.

"What were you looking for when you got out of your car?"

She smiled. Instead of answering, she asked, "Why are you always somewhere watching me?"

He smiled. "I don't know."

She looked over at him. "You're a trip."

"Why do you say that?"

"The roses and now this."

180

He took her hand in his. That gesture alone gave Cassie butterflies. She was unsure of where all of this was going. It would feel awkward meeting with him somewhere that wasn't the club. She like the idea of the club, because she could pretend that they were other people. She was his Princess and he was her Maestro. But getting a room, was different.

What she appreciated, was that he didn't get just any room. They were at the Gaylord Opryland in an executive suite with a view of the open atrium and the Cascades waterfall. The view was awesome. She stood out on the balcony taking it in. And though it was night, it was lit creating a very quiet and tranquil atmosphere.

He came and stood beside her. His presence next to her sent a chill through her body causing the hairs on arms to stand.

"Have you ever been here before?" he asked.

"Not in one of these rooms," she said in amazement. Her eyes sparkled. "I mean, I've walked through the gardens before but never been up here."

"You haven't done much have you, Princess?"

She blushed every time he referred to her as that. She shook her head. "No, not really. I always said when I get my shit together, I was gonna start doing things. Living for me. Doing grown woman things."

"How old are you?"

"Twenty-nine. I'll be thirty in a couple of weeks."

"Will you let me do something special for you?"

She turned to him and was at a loss for words. "Like what?"

"I don't know. Let me take you to another city and show you a good time."

Her mouth dropped open to say something, but she was too shocked to respond.

"C'mon," he said grabbing her hand. He led her back inside the dimly lit room to the suite's bedroom.

As he took her in his arms, without her heels, Cassie didn't realize how much taller he was than her until now. But she had to admit it felt good to be so close to him. There was a sense of love, affection, and even security that she never felt from a man; at least not all three of those qualities in one man. She had a guy that she felt love from, but he didn't make her feel protected. She's felt protected with one, but he lacked affection.

This was different. And because of who it was, she didn't want to enjoy it as much. She realized sooner or later, they would have to stop this. She was scared of how it would look to everyone. And most of all, she wouldn't want to bring about hurt for anyone else.

"What's the matter?" he asked her.

"Nothing," she mumbled.

"I could feel you tense up. Are you sure?"

She nodded. Using his finger, he lifted her face so that she could look at him. She searched his eyes as he did hers. Lovingly, he placed an affectionate kiss on her lips. She felt like melting right there. God!

"Let me give you a massage so you can relax."

What! She wanted to ask him why. Again, no man had ever offered her a massage. This was so different for her.

She slowly removed her clothes as he prepped the bed for them. He placed thick towels down where she would lay. Once she got in the bed on her stomach, he undressed. She laughed inwardly causing a smile to spread. He was supposed to be giving her a massage, yet his dick was already up and ready. And that was what she felt against her ass when he straddled her backside.

But his hands were wonderful. And where did the oil come from? He had shit hidden. Again, Cassie laughed to herself.

It was so relaxing she could have gone to sleep until it was time for her to flip over. She kept her eyes on him as he tentatively massaged her. When he rubbed on her breasts she wondered what he thought of her little mounds. The way he sucked on them didn't give her any implications he wasn't pleased.

Quietly, she asked, "Do I need implants?"

His eyes shifted to hers. In a serious tone, he said, "You're perfect the way you are."

Instead of opposing him and showing how insecure she was, she opted to remain quiet as he continued to tend to her body.

His hands traveled down her stomach. She quivered under his touch and her honey pot was in need of a stirring. When he opened her legs so that he could place them on either side of him, her pussy jumped in anticipation, but he skipped over it. Instead he kneaded at her thighs.

Then he finally came back to her center. Instead of massaging her there, he positioned himself so that he could massage her with lips and tongue. Her breath caught in her throat and she arched her back at the feel of him stroking her bliss button. He didn't let up until she was calling out to the gods and trembling from an orgasm.

"You like that shit, don't you?" he asked cockily as he slipped his finger inside her.

"Yes," she moaned. She spread her legs further wishing he could just fuck her with his whole body.

With two fingers now massaging her insides and his thumb caressing her clit, he leaned forward so that he could kiss her. She assumed he enjoyed how succulent her lips were because he loved to suck and gently nip at them just as he did to the lips in between her legs.

"Can I have you to myself?"

Before she could process the question and carefully respond, her head was nodding.

"Princess, I want you to fill my hand with all this pussy juice. Okay baby?"

Just from how sexy he said that had her on the verge of cumming. He began to finger fuck her deeper and rougher, hitting that spot while applying pressure to her clit.

Despite how aggressive he was, he still managed to remain soothing in her ear, whispering encouraging words in between kisses.

"Let that shit out," he coaxed. "It'll make me happy. Make me happy, Princess."

"Oh God!" she cried out. She grabbed the arm of the hand fucking her. She could feel an eruption building up. She didn't even know she could do it this way. She pushed his arm right before she squirted. She screamed out and started quaking.

Her pussy was still convulsing when he entered her. Her spilled fluids lubricated them both, keeping their love making enjoyable and pleasing.

"Fuck," he hissed angrily. He had to pull out of her to interrupt his own explosion. He tapped her pussy with his dick and rubbed his head in her wetness.

"Damn Princess, you can't keep pussy like this a secret...Fuck! You feel so good. You should've been given me this."

"I didn't know you wanted it."

His lips formed into a slow, sexy smile. He ordered, "Turn around."

She got on her knees and tooted her ass in the air. It started out doggy style, but the way he was pummeling her, had her flat on her stomach. He hovered over her and continued to slam into her.

Slowing down to just a grind, he whispered in her ear. "Will you let me have some of this ass?"

She was hesitant. She didn't know if she could take that. She done anal in the past, but it had been a while. Her ass wasn't set up like that.

"Can I?" he asked again.

"If I say stop, will you?" she asked.

"I don't want to hurt you. If you tell me to stop, I won't continue."

"Okay."

He pulled her body back up so that he had easier access to her hole. Before he even attempted to enter her, he started eating her from the back running his tongue up and down her slit and finding his way to her entrance. It made her squirm but it felt good. Then he lubed her up with the oil and put some on him too.

She held her breath as the head of his dick knocked on her backdoor wanting in. He took his time working in a little at a time. Eventually he had the head in. She tried to relax more so that he could at least get another inch in.

"Are you okay?"

She nodded keeping her eyes closed. She had to concentrate so she wouldn't quit. She felt him pushing with a little more force. He was in enough to be able to work up a rhythm. His short strokes continue to open her further until he was long stroking her ass.

"Fuck," she groaned.

"How do it feel?"

She didn't know. It felt good but it was still uncomfortable. The pained expression on her face gave him cause enough to stop.

He chuckled, "You ain't really ready for that, but you tried."

She was so relieved. He left her on the bed. Seconds later she could hear the shower running.

"Princess," he called out. "Come in here with me."

She got up and went to him. He escorted her into the shower. As they soaped up and tended to the other, she realized he didn't use a condom this time. When she was about to question him about it, he distracted her by picking her up. She wrapped her legs around him and held onto him by wrapping her arms around his neck. The next thing she knew, he had her against the shower wall with his naked dick in her once again.

He felt too good to ask him to stop, both now and earlier. It made her wonder why he was so cautious their first two encounters, but chose not to be this time.

After their fervent exchange in the shower, they tenderly dried one another off. She tried to keep her eyes averted from looking into his. The way he was looking at her made her uncomfortable.

"Stop that," he whispered softly. He offered her a comforting smile. "You're looking scared. What's to be scared about Princess?"

She shook her head, and walked out of the bathroom. She began searching for her clothes.

He stopped her as he embraced her from behind. "Baby, what are you doing?"

"Trying to get dressed," she replied as she gripped his arms.

He placed sensual kisses along her neck to put her at ease. "You're not getting dressed yet because I plan to keep you all night."

"All night?" she asked for clarity.

"Mmmhmm," he moaned as he continued to kiss her.

She closed her eyes and allowed herself to get lost in his affection.

He whispered in her ear, "Are you mine?"

She nodded, this time she was sure.

He sucked her neck. He spoke softly. "I hope you're okay about me not using a condom. I just needed to feel my Princess, and let you know that this what we got is special. You've been marked."

She smiled, turning her head so they could share a kiss. She didn't mind being marked, but would he mind dealing with the consequences of his actions? Should she inform him now that she wasn't on any contraception?

Chapter 12

Momentarily, Cassie forgot where she was. She assumed it was morning, but the room was still dark. After what her body went through the night before, she fell into a deep slumber. Despite being exhausted, she awakened with a strong need. She couldn't explain exactly what he had opened up within her, but she couldn't get enough.

She flipped over to see if he was awake. He lay on his back but his head was turned away from her. She watched his chest rise and fall. She took the time to admire his body. Her eyes traveled from his neatly trimmed beard, down his neck, over his chest, and across his stomach. That's all that was exposed; the sheet covered the rest of him. The hair on his lower abdomen traveled down disappearing under the sheet. Even though he was clearly asleep, she could see his manhood was awake. It wasn't exactly sticking straight up but she could see the outline of it.

Cassie was extremely taken with him. But she wasn't supposed to be with someone like him. She wondered how Jazmin would feel about this? Hell, she didn't even want to hear Jah's reaction. He could get ignorant and embarrass her to a point of no return. And though she knew she needed to end this, she didn't want to. She wanted him to herself, freely. But was he available for that? Was he ready to be public although he asked her to be his? Would she care about what the others thought if this could be the love of her life?

She moved closer to him pushing the sheet further down. It was nothing like pleasing a man first thing in the morning. She began sucking him, but more so in a loving passion as opposed to the hungry devouring she had previously done. His dick expanded in her mouth and he stirred out of his sleep. Moaning, he placed his hand on her head, intertwining his fingers in her hair softly.

Why did he have to be so endearing? He was making this hard for her. He was supposed to be mean and uncaring. Wasn't that how most men approached flings? Was this the reason women were drawn to him? Was this how he reeled women in, only to disappoint them because he wouldn't commit?

Tears came to her eyes. She didn't understand her sudden rush of emotions. She tried to blink them back as she removed her mouth from him. Unable to look at him, she proceeded to straddle him, easing him inside her. As she rode him, she could feel him willing her to look at him. She refused to.

A lone tear rolled down her cheek.

He sat up, instantly falling in to protective mode. "Cassie, what's wrong?"

"Don't call me Cassie!" she snapped. She tried to push him away from her, but he had a tight hold on her.

"Okay, but tell me what's the matter with you. I don't want to see you upset."

"It's nothing," she said, looking away. She asked, "Do you wanna finish or what?"

"Do you?"

She nodded.

The rest of their session felt like she needed it to feel. Straight fucking. None of that affection and love in his eyes. It seemed as though he got angry with her and flipped her over onto her back and punished her. She squirted but he didn't seem as fascinated anymore. He just wanted his nut to get it over with.

They remained awkwardly quiet while cleaning up and getting dressed. There was no hand holding on the way to his car. Once she was settled in, she realized how bipolar she was. She didn't want to hurt him, but she didn't want to be strung along and get deeper into it.

"I'm sorry," she said. "I just think this isn't a good idea anymore. But no matter how much I try to convince myself of that, I just don't feel it. I wanna keep seeing you but I don't know what will become of this. I'm afraid."

He remained silent and focused on driving.

She said with a slight laugh. "I wonder what my friend Eli would think of my behavior."

He looked at her. "Your friend?"

"He's my boss too."

"Why are you worried about what he would say?"

"Because we've become close and what he says matter to me now. Besides, he's always saying something that'll make me laugh. And I wanna laugh right now."

"Well, call him up and get with him so he can make you laugh."

She caught the attitude in his tone, although he tried to remain indifferent.

She waved off the notion. "I don't think he's in the mood to make anyone laugh. I probably should be trying to make him laugh."

"Why are you talking like that when you're here with me?" he asked.

She shrugged. She blinked back tears and said with uncertainty, "I don't know. I just wanted to lighten the mood I guess; get off the subject since you weren't responding to me."

He didn't say anything else. She looked at him and could see his eyebrows pinching in a frown. She really made him mad.

"I said I was sorry," she said softly.

"You cool," he mumbled.

"What do you want to do?"

"I don't know...ask Eli."

Cassie stopped trying. He wasn't going to let her get very far anyway. With the exception of the radio, they rode in silence all the way to her car. He didn't even wait for her to get in her car, before he was pulling off. The sports car's tires even made a screeching noise as if he couldn't wait to get away from her.

Sadly, she got in her car and drove home.

Colette greeted her as she walked in her apartment with a smug look on her face.

"You didn't tell me your hot ass was going to stay out all night," she said.

"I'm sorry, but I thought I was grown and didn't have to answer to anybody," Cassie said smartly. She stepped into her room.

"Was you out with your new lil boyfriend?" she asked following her to her room. She stood in the doorway watching Cassie walk towards her walk-through closet.

"None of your business," Cassie said. "When do you plan to get out of my place? I need my space."

"Your space? I don't get in your way. I'm barely here," Colette argued.

"Yeah, I just wanna come home and not see your face or hear you fucking," she said flatly. She walked further into her closet in search of something to wear for the day.

"I guess the nigga didn't do a good job. If he did, you wouldn't be so fuckin' grumpy," Colette joked.

Cassie ignored her. She heard the door to the bedroom Colette was staying in open. Colette leaned back and waved at the person. "I'll be in there."

Cassie looked at her mother in an annoyed way. "You have company?"

"He'll be gone in a minute. Hey, do you think you can run down to the store and get me a pack of cigarillos?" Colette asked.

Cassie rolled her eyes. Her phone rung. She answered it when she saw it was Tanya.

"Hey," she said.

"So?"

"So what?"

"I know you went to go be nasty at Jouissance. What happened?"

Cassie's eyes went to Colette. "I'll tell you about it. What are you getting into today?"

"Supposed to be meeting with Jazz for brunch at Saint Anejo. You coming?"

"What time?"

"One o' clock. Just meet us down there so you can fill us in. Oh, ask Romyn if he wanna come too."

"Okay," Cassie said. "I'll see ya'll then."

Once she ended the call with Tanya, she dialed Romyn.

"Hey lil boy," she said into the phone. "What are you doing today?"

"I was waiting on Lonzo but it seem like he got family duties," he said. She could hear the disappointment in his voice.

"You wanna go to brunch with us?"

"Who is us?"

"The usual. Me, Jazz, Tanya..."

In a hushed tone, he asked, "Will Eli be there?"

"I don't know. Probably not," she said.

"I'ma call him," Romyn said with playfulness.

"What's up with you and him? Ya'll done became buddy-buddy or something."

"He's just a friend," was all Romyn said.

"Well, Saint Anejo at one o' clock. Do you want me to scoop you up?"

"You can. What's that hussy mother of yours doing?" he asked.

Cassie looked at Colette still standing in her bedroom's doorway. "Being a hussy."

Romyn laughed. "You need to get that bitch out of your place."

"I'm working on it. Bye boy," Cassie laughed.

She looked at Colette and asked, "Is there something you need?"

"Are you about to go somewhere?" Colette asked.

"I am, so ask whoever the john is in that room to go fetch you some cigarillos," Cassie said.

"That's fine," Colette said with a huff. She walked away.

Cassie shook her head. She couldn't get rid of the premonition that Colette was up to no good. She no longer wanted her at her place. She didn't want Colette bringing any drama her way. She was known for causing havoc in other people's lives. It was why no one wanted to deal with her.

Cassie dressed in a pair of floral print leggings with a cap-sleeved white hi-low top. She slipped on a pair of gold gladiator style sandals. Since her hair had been destroyed in all of that bedroom wrestling she done, she decided to brush her hair up into a bun.

She didn't bother letting Colette know she was leaving. She was really hoping she got the hint and would find herself somewhere else to go.

After grabbing Romyn, they headed over to Saint Anejo. Jazmin and Tanya were already inside waiting. When Cassie's eyes landed on Eli, she looked over at Romyn.

"Did you ask him to come here?" she asked.

Romyn smiled. "No, he was already coming."

"Hey Cass!" Jazmin greeted. She stood up to give Cassie and Romyn both hugs.

Tanya followed suit. Eli didn't bother. Cassie sat down in front of Jazmin at the end of the table.

She looked over at Eli and cautiously spoke, "How are you Eli?"

He gave a listless response and focused on the menu in his hand. She looked at Jazmin and Tanya for an answer. They both shrugged.

It was surprising to see Gio had joined them as well. With all of them at the table, it became noisy with chatter and laughter. Cassie kept looking at Eli to see if his mood had changed. He was talking but not really one hundred percent present. At this point in their friendship, Cassie was always concerned about Eli and what he was going through.

Cassie was nursing on her third round of sangria, when she happened to look up and saw Sean walk in with Michelle. They were with two more couples.

"Oh shit," Cassie mumbled.

"What?" Jazmin asked. She turned around to see what had Cassie's attention.

Tanya did as well. They both turned back around with scowls on their faces.

"Of all places in the city, he had to come here today," Jazmin griped.

"That's what I'm saying," Tanya said.

Gio said with his never going anywhere smile, "Hey, ain't that Sean."

"You know what," Tanya said. "I keep forgetting he work at BevyCo too."

"Yeah," Jazmin rolled her eyes. "I tried to get my daddy to have him fired, but instead of firing him, they transferred him to the Brentwood office. I guess that was alright as long as I don't have to look at him."

"How many kids that nigga got now?" Tanya asked.

"He should have three now," Jazmin said.

Cassie's eyes followed Sean and his group as the hostess led them to the table across, but three down. As he was being seated, he did a double take and locked eyes with Cassie. He smiled. He whispered something to Michelle which caused her to look their way. Her messy tail just had to get up and come over to speak.

"Hey ladies," Michelle beamed.

Tanya turned on the phoniness and grinned. "Hey Michelle. You're looking good. How old is that baby now?"

"Should be the same age as Jazz's new one," Michelle answered letting her eyes tease Jazmin.

Jazmin scoffed and looked the other way.

Michelle looked at Cassie with her head cocked to the side. "Hi Cassie. You're looking pretty. You either got a new job or a new man, cause I know Rock ain't taking care of you like that."

Cassie gave her a quick sarcastic smirk.

Sean walked over standing behind Michelle. "Hey everybody. What's up Gio? Eli? Ladies, ya'll look lovely. Hey Cass."

Cassie let her eyes shift to him. He looked as if he wanted to open his mouth and say the wrong shit. She just stared at him.

"C'mon baby so we can order," he told Michelle.

Once they walked away, Eli got up excusing himself. Cassie's eyes followed him as he went out on the large patio where the outside dining took place. He began talking on the phone.

"What's wrong with him?" she asked.

"He ain't really been saying much," Tanya said. "I hate when he's like that cause he don't be no fun. I miss stupid Eli."

"I do too," Jazmin said.

Cassie stated, "There's more to Eli than always being silly, y'all know that, right?"

"Yeah, I know," Jazmin said with thought. "But when he's silly Eli, he seems to be happy."

"Or masking how he really feels," Cassie posed.

Jazmin nodded. "I think you're right. I be glad when this Kris mess is over with. I would have never guessed her to be so stupid."

"He told you?" Cassie asked.

"What?" Tanya asked. "What's going on with him and Kris?"

Jazmin explained, "He broke down this morning and confided in me and Jah. He said that they're getting a divorce. And he just looked so sad and he started talking about Abe. Eli is really hurting ya'll. So I insisted he come along with us. I don't want him sitting up in that big house all alone."

"Where his kids?" Tanya asked.

"They're at Lovely's," Jazmin answered. "He's talking about going to Italy for a few weeks to clear his head. I told him that might be a good idea."

"Shit, I need my head clear. I'ma ask him can I go," Tanya joked.

Gio said, "You don't have vacation days for that."

"I'm just playing. Dang!" Tanya said in a playful scowl. She added, "But if I go and if Eli's gone, you and Cassie can work together."

Cassie shook her head at Tanya as she got up. "I'll be back."

She headed to the restrooms on the other side of the restaurant. Before she could reach the door she heard him calling her name. She stopped and glared at him.

"Why you looking like that?" he asked.

"Cause you look like you wanna say something. I ain't playing. Don't say anything in front of them," she warned.

"I said I wasn't," he insisted. He nodded towards the open outside bar. "Ain't that your friend Eli?"

She looked towards Eli. He was really wrapped up in his conversation. He happened to turn in their direction, but he quickly turned back around.

"Yeah. Now can you get far away from me?" Cassie said as she went in the ladies' restroom. She handled her business and exited the stall. She halted when she saw him in the restroom. He pushed her back in the stall and closed the door.

The thing she liked about the stalls was that they were more like little closets with a toilet. There was an actual door that went all the way to the floor for added privacy.

"What are you doing?" she whispered.

"I'm still mad at you, but I want you."

He attacked her with unrestrained kisses. She reciprocated the same passion. He tugged at the waist of her leggings. Her hand went to his to protest.

"We can't. We'll get caught."

"Just let me feel you. I *need* to feel you Princess."

She couldn't tell him no. She turned around and bent over the toilet. Because of their height difference she had to raise up on her toes. He still had to dip a little to access her opening. And she was wet, warm, and inviting.

She had to stifle her moans as he stroked her. He said he needed to feel her, but he was going for an actual release. He quickened the pace to get there fast. Her legs shook and stomach quivered. She wanted to scream but she couldn't. Her breast ached and she needed them fondled, but they didn't have time for all of that.

His pace slowed as his arm went around her pulling her into him. It caused her to be almost upright and she felt him bite her on her shoulder. That sent all kind of chills through her body. She realized that was his way of stifling his own groan as he came inside her.

This was what she was talking about. How would she rid him of her system if he kept doping her up this way?

She quickly wiped herself. She hoped the pantyliner she wore was enough to soak up what was still running from her yoni.

"You go first," he told her.

She turned to go out, but he stopped her by grabbing her by her wrist. She looked back at him only for him to give her a quick kiss.

She went out of the stall and washed her hands. She hurried out of the restroom knowing Tanya and Jazmin would be wondering where she had been for so long.

On her journey back to their table, she spotted someone she knew from her old job who wanted to catch up. She apologized for cutting it short, but she had to get back to her friends. That was her perfect alibi though.

"Damn Cass," Tanya said as she took her seat. "Where you been? Taking a shit?"

"No, I saw someone I used to work with and she wanted to talk me to death," Cassie responded. Although that was the truth, she felt so self-conscious as if they could see she was leaving some details out. She looked across the table and Eli was giving her this pensive stare. She ignored him and looked beyond to Sean's table. He grinned her way. She didn't bother catering to his teasing.

Besides the squishiness in her panties, Cassie enjoyed the rest of the evening with them. Even Eli opened up a little and was responding with more than three words.

After sitting there talking, eating, and drinking for three hours they all parted ways. Once in the car, Romyn teased, "I saw you."

"Saw me what?" Cassie asked with innocence.

"You know what you did. I saw him go in the restroom too. I'm just glad ya'll didn't come back at the same time. I think that would have been a dead giveaway."

"You're so nosy," Cassie laughed.

"So where is that going?"

"Nowhere. Right now we're just fucking, but he has somebody and I ain't playing side chick. So I'm cutting this off."

"But didn't you say that after the second time you went to see him?"

"I did and—"

"And didn't you go back last night?"

"I did and—"

"And what was that in the restroom? Ya'll were talking? That was a long ass talk."

Cassie laughed guiltily.

"Again I ask, where is this going?"

Cassie shrugged. "I really, really like him. Hell, I think I might be falling in love. I think he got strong feelings for me too. I don't know Ro. I'm kinda scared."

"Well, don't rush into it. Tell him what you expect and that if he want things to go further he need to take care of that situation."

Cassie thought she should just leave it alone altogether. It was heartache and pain waiting to happen.

Chapter 13

The following day at work, Cassie couldn't do much concentrating. She had her situation on her mind. She had her brother's opinion and considered his advice. The only other person she thought she should confide in was Eli. His opinion mattered a lot to her.

She tapped on his opened office door. He was on the desk phone. He motioned for her to have a seat while he wrapped up the conversation.

She waited patiently. In doing so, she took the time to examine Eli. There was still a troubled look in his eyes, but she could tell he was trying to play it off. She was his friend now and hated seeing him hurt.

After the call, Eli turned to her. "What can I help you with?"

"I wanted to talk to you about something personal. You got a minute?"

"A few."

She smiled bashfully and averted her eyes. "So there's this person I like, right?"

He nodded for her to continue.

"The one I told you that sent me the roses. I find myself falling for him. I think I might even love him. I don't know how he feel about me exactly. I feel like he likes me...but sometimes I think he wouldn't want someone like me. It keeps me from truly enjoying him."

Eli gave her one of his infamous blank stares.

"I want to stop seeing him but it's something that's there that I can't shake. This is the thing though, he has someone. And even if we could be together I'm not sure how the people in our lives would take it."

Again, another blank stare.

"Eli!" she cried out. "Say something."

"I don't know what you want me to tell you," he said.

"Something, anything."

"If you love him then tell him that. If you don't want to leave him alone, tell him that. Who gives a fuck what people will think or say. And as far as him having someone...is he willing to let that person go so that he can move on with you?"

Cassie didn't have an answer. She waited for Eli to continue.

"Ask him and see what he says. You'll never know unless you communicate these things. Cassie, you're grown so stop acting like a silly high school girl who's ignorant to the world. And life goes by so quick. People are here one day, and the next day they could be gone. Live. Be happy."

She nodded in agreement. "You're right. And if he's not willing to move on, I guess I should."

"Make sure you ask him first. He could be feeling the same way about you."

"I will. But Eli, you mention live and be happy. I don't see that in you lately."

"I know. Those words were for me too. I gotta move on from this Kris mess. I gotta accept that this is what it is. I also need to know that it's not totally my fault, but I did play a part. I have to prepare myself to be a single father...again. You know when I went up front earlier, I was served this," he said. He pointed to the big envelope in front of him.

"What is that?"

"Kris had divorce papers drawn up," he said. "She doesn't want anything. She wants to forfeit her parental rights to Avani..."

Cassie's heart broke for Eli as he fought against the tears.

"I hate her," he said in a low sullen tone.

Cassie got up and walked around the desk to console him with a comforting embrace. "I'm sorry Eli. I didn't realize you were suffering like this."

His arms went around her and it made her nervous. She didn't want this moment to turn into something. She guessed he didn't either because he pushed her away.

"I need to be alone," he said quietly.

Confused, Cassie slowly walked away. "Eli, I'll just be right out—"

"I know," he said. He couldn't even look at her.

Cassie closed the door behind her. She stood by the glass wall and peered in at him through the privacy blinds. He got up and closed the blinds on her. She chuckled because he was such an ass even when he was upset.

"What's going on?" Tanya asked.

"It's Eli. He's upset. Kris served him divorce papers."

Tanya gasped. "For real?"

Cassie nodded. She took a seat at her desk. Her office phone rung. Seeing who it was she hurried to answer. "What's up?"

"Okay," Jazmin said excitedly. "I would have come up there but that's doing too much. So I was thinking since your birthday is two days after Tanya's and Jah's will be coming up, why don't we just have one big party."

Cassie leaned back to get Tanya's attention. "Jazz wants to have a big joint birthday party."

"That's cool," Tanya said.

"Okay, what are you thinking," Cassie asked.

"I'm thinking let's have a nineties party. House party style," Jazmin said.

"The nineties. Okay. That might be cool."

"So not this Saturday or the one after, but the one following that."

Cassie didn't give it much thought. "That'll work."

"Okay, I can get Desi to help me plan it. She's good at that kind of stuff especially with it being such short notice."

Cassie's cell phone vibrated on her desk. She looked at it and saw that she had a new text message. She smiled when she saw it was from *My Maestro*.

"Okay, just let me know what we need to do to make it all happen," Cassie said.

"Okay," Jazmin said before ending the call.

Cassie opened the message and it read: **I need you...NOW!**

She flushed with heat and knew she had to slip away. She looked at the time. It was almost lunch time. She text back: **Give me a minute and I'll be there**

———

Rock looked at the picture he had of Cassie in his phone. It was from a few months ago when things seemed like they were going in the right direction. He wished he could rewind to then and do some things over. He really fucked up and he was trying to undo what he had done.

It was impossible to undo the baby growing in Melody, unless he persuaded her to get an abortion. It was a headache trying to keep her happy. Then there was Colette. That was his biggest mistake. All of the other hoes he could simply cut off, but not her. She wanted to be petty and threaten to tell Cassie. He shouldn't care about Cassie's feelings but the truth of the matter was he did care. If he didn't, he knew that seeing her at Eli's that night wouldn't have bothered him. He just hate that Cassie could be willing to give another nigga a chance, but hold back and shut down on him.

Hell the more he thought about it, at the beginning Cassie's sexual appetite was just as intense if not greater than Colette's. And he remembered the feel of her which was what kept him coming back. Even though Cassie had bipolar tendencies, if he had just been a little more patient, they could have worked through that.

And Colette was nothing more than a petty hoe. He looked away from the phone to look at her smug expression. He sighed with defeat. "What do you want?"

"Give me about two thousand and I won't say nothing," she said.

"Two thousand?" He grimaced.

"Nigga, that ain't shit. I only asked for two because I know your lil bitch ass won't have nothing more to give."

"Keep calling me names," he warned.

"Or what?" she taunted.

He released a defeated sigh. "When you want it?"

"I need it now. I'll give you until next week though," she said.

She pissed him off with this blackmail shit. Normally he would want her to break him off real quick, but he had to end this situation immediately.

"Aight," he said. "Get out my car man."

"I can't get no goodbye dick?" Colette asked.

He hated the amusement in her face. He wanted to slap her, but he got himself into this. "Get out Letty."

"Fine," she said before getting out. As she got out, Rock got an eyeful of ass when her dress flew up. He would miss that.

He talked to Melody during his drive to Jah's house. They hadn't really talked much since the little brawl he had with Eli. He felt Jah was more disappointed in him than being angry.

When he got to Jah's house, he was a little happy to see Cassie's purple Charger sitting in the driveway. Maybe this visit could kill two birds with one stone.

"What's up nigga," Jah greeted.

"Nothing much," he mumbled. "Where Cassie at?"

"They down there in the den. We ain't gotta go that way though," Jah said.

"Naw, I need to speak to her," Rock said heading towards the back of the house.

Jah tried to stop him. "Naw, nigga. Don't even bother her. Leave that shit alone."

"It ain't like that," he mumbled. He could hear the chatter and laughter before he made it to the kitchen. But when he arrived he understood why Jah wanted him to avoid the den.

Rock wasn't happy to see Eli there, but this wasn't about Eli.

"Hey Rock," Jazmin called out.

"Hey," he uttered. Tanya ignored him as well as Cassie. He wasn't feeling how Eli was staring at him though.

"Ay Cassie," Rock called out. "Can I talk to you for a minute?"

Without looking at him, Cassie said, "There's nothing for us to talk about."

He wasn't going to beg her, but he would put his ego aside. "Look man, I just wanna tell you I'm sorry about how shit happened. Sorry Eli for what happened between us too. That's all I wanted to say."

Cassie looked at him with curious eyes.

Eli murmured, "You cool."

213

Cassie got up and made her way to him. He had to admit, she was looking good. Her clothes were of better quality. The purple high-waisted pencil skirt was flattering to her small figure. She must have been wearing a special bra because she looked like she had more breasts than he remembered. Her hair looked fresh although she had it pulled up into a bun. The heels she wore gave her some added height giving her a svelte sexiness.

"What's up?" she said.

Before Rock answered, Jah eased by. "You good?"

"Yeah," Rock nodded. He and Cassie moved a few feet down the hall for a little more privacy.

"You look good," he said.

"Thanks," she replied dryly.

"Eli must be paying you good."

Smugly, she said, "Something like that."

"Like I just said, I'm sorry. Can we start this thing over?"

Cassie shook her head slowly. "I don't think so Rock."

"We can put all this other shit behind us and make it work this time."

"You put your hands on me," she pointed out.

"Technically I only pushed you. I would never just hit on you like that Cassie. As much shit as you talk, there's been plenty of times I could've snapped off and fucked you up, but hitting on women ain't something I do."

She folded her arms across her chest. Her body language clearly expressed she wasn't letting him in.

"You have a baby on the way."

He figured that news would get to her. He was prepared for that one. "Yeah, I do."

"So that mean when we were trying to make it work the first time, you were still sleeping around."

"I was. And it was fucked up. I was wrong."

"I mean since you didn't want to put labels on what we were doing, you could have kept it real and just told me you were seeing other people. We could have agreed to not be exclusive, which would have meant you couldn't get an attitude because you think I'm getting close with another man."

"You right."

She shifted her weight on one foot and her arms began to loosen. "So what do you want Rock?"

"I want us to start over."

"Why?"

"Because I miss you and I want another chance."

"With a baby on the way?"

"That doesn't mean I wanna be with Melody."

"Oh! It was that one. I should've known with her sneaky self."

"I'll just have to deal with her ass and work something out," he said.

"I wouldn't be able to trust you though. I would always think that you were fucking her when you're not with me. I would be insecure and I don't wanna feel like that. I hate that feeling. I'd rather be alone."

"I get that, I guess. I would just have to ask you to trust me."

She sighed. "I'm about to be thirty years old. Never married, don't have any kids, ain't got no degrees, ain't went nowhere...I'm ready to live now. And unless you're willing to help me make some of that happen, I don't need you getting in my way."

Defeated, Rock said, "I can't guarantee any of that, but I respect it."

She smiled. "Can we just work on being friends again?"

"That's cool too. I still wanna take you out or something. I owe you that."

"Well, my number is still the same. When you're ready, call me."

"Can I get a hug?" he asked.

She uncrossed her arms completely to embrace him. He held her tight. And when he saw Eli approaching, he kissed her on the lips.

She pulled away giggling. "You think you're slick."

Rock caught the saltiness in Eli's eyes as he passed by. Cassie noticed him and she broke away from Rock.

"Hey, you're leaving?" she asked.

Eli slowed his stride long enough to tell her, "Yeah. I gotta go get the kids. But I'll see you in the morning."

"Okay," she said. Rock noticed that she seemed disappointed and the smile disappeared from her eyes.

He didn't want to bring it up at the moment, but he knew something was going on between Cassie and Eli; the evidence was in Eli's eyes.

Chapter 14

Since that first time during that one lunch break, Cassie found herself using her lunch hour to get it in with her maestro over a span of three weeks. Some days, it was very quick and fast. Other days, it was sensual and prolonged. She had to start carrying wet wipes, extra pantyliners, and extra panties. She would have to grab a quick bite to eat or bring it back to her desk to eat on.

And if they didn't hook up during the day time, she was meeting with him at night. He was wearing her out, but there wasn't a time she wasn't willing. It was during this time, that they really became close as lovers. They even argued, but he somehow managed to win her over every time. It didn't hurt that he had roses delivered to her every week either.

They even managed to sneak away for a weekend to Miami. It was her first time ever riding a plane. He was right there beside her soothing the whole flight. They had plans to go other places, which excited her. At this point, she would go anywhere as long as he was with her. But, she was still afraid. She wanted him, but he still had someone. And she hated the idea of giving him so much of herself only for him to abandon her one day.

It was the Friday before the party. It was lunch hour and she was in a hotel room on her back getting her pussy ate. He exchanged one pair of lips for the other pair. When he kissed her, she could smell and taste herself on him. It aroused her even more.

She gasped when he entered her aggressively. Sometimes she had to make sure he wasn't mad at her when he did that. She could always tell by the way his eyes either brightened or darkened. Today, they brightened which caused her to smile at him. He smiled back. Damn, she was loving this dude. But she was afraid to speak it out loud.

Cassie wasn't sure why she didn't notice before, maybe because she wasn't looking for it, but where his left ring finger had been vacant all this time, now it housed a diamond wedding band. What the fuck was this?

She had never been turned off when in the act with him, but this right here soured her mood.

"Get off me," she said angrily. She pushed him with as much force as she could to let him know she wasn't playing.

He looked genuinely confused. "What did I do this time?"

Cassie hopped out of bed and scrambled for her clothes.

"Baby, what did I do?" he asked. His voice was pleading.

"Why you got that on?" she asked pointing to his hand.

He looked at it and guilt etched across his face. "Let me explain—"

She saw him getting out of the bed, but she didn't give him the chance to touch her. She ran to the suite's bathroom and locked it. She didn't even have all of her clothes. She had only her pants and one shoe.

"Will you let me explain?" He was on the other side of the door.

She yelled, "I don't care!"

"It ain't even what you're thinking. I promise it isn't."

"It doesn't matter..." she teared up. Her voice cracked, "This is why I don't need to be with you."

"Baby, open the door."

"No! Just go away. Please!"

"I'm not. I need you to come out. I want you to look me in my eyes and know that I'm telling you the truth. Having this on means nothing to me."

"Then why do you have it on?"

Silence.

She said, "I'm gonna be late getting back to work. So can you please don't try to keep me here to feed me a bunch of bullshit."

"You're just gonna be late then."

"I hate you!"

"I love you."

She was speechless. Hearing him say it gave her butterflies. She wanted to open the door but it was a trap. He didn't mean it. She cried, "Don't do that."

"What? Love you? Why are you so afraid of that?"

"I'm not afraid. You're lying and you need to stop because I know you don't."

"You are afraid to let someone love you. Let me please."

"Go away."

"Come out here."

"I will when I know you're gone."

"Cassie, you're the—"

"Don't call me that!"

"It's your name!"

"No, not when I'm with you like this. I don't wanna be Cassie."

A few seconds passed before he replied, "If you don't wanna be Cassie when you're with me, then I guess none of this is real. And that's fucked up...because I love you."

She could tell he moved away from the door. He was quiet. She strained to hear him moving about. Five minutes passed and she felt the suite's room door slam.

She waited about two more minutes before she opened the door. He was gone. She didn't trust him. He might try to come back. She gathered her things and went back in the bathroom to clean up and get dressed.

Needless to say, when she got back to the office she was grumpy. She was hungry and pissed off.

Tanya placed a Snickers candy bar on her desk on passing. "Bitch, eat that. You ain't yourself when you're hungry."

Cassie laughed and threw her middle finger at Tanya.

Eli appeared at her desk smelling good as ever. He said, "You've been gone all this time and didn't eat anything?"

"I was running errands," she answered curtly.

"Hmmm," was all he uttered before walking away.

Tanya said, "You know, it's some doughnuts in the break room."

"From this morning?" Cassie asked.

"Girl, they Krispy Kreme. They still fresh."

A doughnut sounded good at the moment. Cassie got up and went to the break room. No one was in there and the boxes of doughnuts were stacked up nicely on the back table. She opened one and it was a variety box. She grabbed a chocolate glazed one that seeped yellow custard, and grabbed a cruller while she was at it. The glazed blueberry looked tempting too. She also grabbed a regular glazed. She wrapped all four—because she got that blueberry one too—in napkins and headed out the break-room.

She got to her office space and before she could get to her chair, she was stuffing the blueberry doughnut in her mouth. *Still fresh.* She stood right there and ate the glazed one in three bites. She was going to have a doughnut orgasm right there. She ate the cruller next. She was famished. He worked her intensely earlier. She came so many times and he made her squirt twice. That wiped her out and she didn't get anything to eat. She needed carbs or something to fuel her body.

She finally took her seat taking a bite of the chocolate glazed with the custard inside, and it oozed its contents on her blouse. *Damn!* She swiped it up and licked her finger. Then she dipped her finger in the hole to gather more custard and licked her finger again. Then she heard someone clearing their throat.

She slowly turned around and saw she had an audience. They were standing off to the side dying with laughter. She was embarrassed. She knew her mocha skin was turning a deep shade of cherry. She placed the almost hollow doughnut on her desk.

"Goddamn Cassie," Tanya said in disbelief.

"Fuck ya'll," Cassie grumbled playfully. Gio and Eli were turning red, they were laughing so hard at her.

"Bitch is you hungry or is you hungry?" Tanya asked.

"She fucked them doughnuts up!" Eli clowned. "Cassie, I didn't know you could eat like that."

"Again, fuck ya'll," Cassie said cutting her eyes. "That shit was good."

———

The 90s party was everything. Cassie didn't think they could have done a better job with it on such short notice. Everyone dressed the part, the dj had 90s music blaring from the speakers, and everyone was having a good time.

Cassie wore a pair of acid washed denim booty shorts with a black bra top under an open black leather vest. She had to complete the look with a pair of black Lugz. She had her hairdresser to give her a 90s inspired hairstyle that incorporated the present day look. She had soft waves in the front while the rest had been sculpted into a retro victory roll updo.

Jazmin wore a champagne colored satin polyester wrap skirt with the matching halter top that tied in the front. She wore her hair with a side swoop in the front for mock bangs that tucked into the high ponytail atop of her head. On her feet were brown blocked-heeled sandals.

"Where's Tanya?" Jazmin asked.

"She's on her way," Cassie told her. She asked, "Did Desiree and Damien come?"

"They're here somewhere. They're wearing matching spray painted overalls. They look cute," Jazmin giggled. She looked over at Romyn with his busy rayon shirt tucked into loose fitting blue pants. She said, "You look nice Ro."

"Thanks," he smiled.

"Who got Desiree's baby?" Cassie asked.

"Damien's mother. Desiree almost didn't want to come cause she ain't been away from the baby more than two hours. Damien, my daddy and Phyllis had to convince her to go out tonight."

"Who else is here?" Cassie asked.

"Oh girl, come look at these fools. Jah, Rock and Ricky looking like they're extras in Menace to Society," Jazmin laughed.

Cassie, followed by Romyn, weaved in and out around the cluster of people to follow Jazmin. She ended up taking them to an upstairs tiered VIP section. It was where their circle was. Cassie laughed as soon as she saw them because Jazmin was right. They all had on khaki colored dickies. Jah's matching khaki shirt was open exposing the white tee he had on. Rock had on a blue flannel shirt over a white tee. And Ricky paired his with just a black tee.

"I told you," Jazmin said.

Rock acted as if he was excited to see Cassie. He came up to her to give her a hug. "What's up baby?"

She could tell he had been drinking, but he was enjoying himself. Everyone was in merriment, and that was the intention.

Jah was holding an Old E 800 beer bottle in a brown paper bag. Cassie asked Jah, "Is that a prop or is there something in there?"

"It's something in here. I've been pouring it out for my homies all mothafuckin' night," Jah said.

"He's stupid," Jazmin said under her breath to Cassie. "Somebody gon' come through here and break their neck slipping on that shit."

Cassie and Romyn started laughing. As she fell against Rock in mirth, she saw Eli walking over. She immediately stopped laughing. They made eye contact but he looked away first.

Of course he wasn't going to go along with that khaki mess. He was looking mighty scrumptious in his all white overalls over a black shirt. On his feet were black boots. There was not a thing about him that was out of place. His facial hair was so precise it looked painted on. He wore a thick white gold herringbone necklace that gave off a shine that matched the twinkle of the diamonds in his earlobes. He had his nose ring in too. One wrist was adorned with a matching herringbone bracelet and the other a white gold diamond Rolex.

Looking at him made her uncomfortable. She was starting to become aware of her attraction to him once again. And if she didn't know any better he was giving off some jealousy vibes. He looked bothered that Rock was hugged up with her.

Cassie was thankful that Tanya showed up to distract her from thoughts of Eli. But he was the first one to blurt out something about Tanya's choice of attire.

"Look at Blossom," Eli laughed.

Cassie had to laugh. Tanya had on a dress with a denim bodice and floral print skirt, which flowed landing at about her knees. She even had on a denim boat hat adorned with a daisy. On her feet were white classic K-Swiss with thick white socks.

Jazmin said with hilarity. "Is that what you were going for?"

"I loved Blossom," Tanya said in her own defense.

"We can tell," Cassie said.

Tanya looked over at the guys. "Who ya'll supposed to be? A bootleg version of Bone Thugs-N-Harmony."

"Menace to Society extras," Jazmin repeated.

"Aight Juicy, and don't you start Thickumz," Jah warned.

While they clowned around, Cassie removed herself from under Rock's arm.

"Where you off to?" he asked.

"Just looking around and to get me a drink," she said.

"I'll go with you," he offered.

"Okay."

They walked away from the others and headed to the bar on that level. While waiting for her drink, Rock asked, "When can we go out? I feel like you been avoiding me."

"I haven't. I just been busy," she said. *Busy fucking*, she thought.

"Can you make some time for me?"

Cassie took her drink from the bartender. She said, "I can try."

"Ay, I need a favor from you too," he said.

"Like what?" She was leery.

"Can I come by and talk to you about it?"

He was determined to get back in her place. She gave in and said, "Yeah. Just text me before you come Rock."

"I will. I won't get in between you and your dude," he said passively.

"You fishing," Cassie laughed.

He was guilty. Smiling, he said, "I am. I know it gotta be somebody."

"I don't know why you think that."

His eyes traveled over her hair and down to her face. "Whoever it is got you glowing. It's something different about you."

"Same ol' Cassie," she stated matter-of-factly.

He asked, "What's up between you and Eli, for real? This ain't on no jealous type shit but I'm curious. Like, I seen that look ya'll gave each other."

"We're friends. And Eli's been acting funny lately. He's going through some stuff and between me, Tanya, and Jazmin, we've been kinda looking out for him. Hell, my brother too."

"You don't think he has feelings for you? He look at you like he wanna fuck you or some shit. And now I mothafuckin' know I wasn't imagining things. Plus, he was too quick to come to your defense that night."

"Too quick? Maybe he just didn't approve of you treating me that way. It don't have to be about anything else but that. Like I said, we consider each other friends."

"You don't like him just a lil bit?"

"Rock!" she said firmly. "Stop with the questions."

"Okay, okay," he surrendered. He nodded towards where everyone, including their friends, was dancing. "Come out there with me."

"Dance?" she asked sheepishly.

Rock nodded. He didn't wait for her to respond. He grabbed her arm and started pulling on her.

"Hold on," Cassie said as she gulped her drink down.

They headed down to the main dance floor. They squeezed through the thick crowd of people getting lost in the thick of it. Biggie's *Juicy* was playing. As they danced, Cassie was beginning to think Rock only asked her to dance so he could feel her up. She laughed at his blatant attempts to molest her.

They were so into playing around on the dance floor and being goofy with Jazmin, Jah, Ricky, and Tanya, that it took Cassie by surprise when Gio walked up to her and asked Rock to let him cut in. At this point, Rock had been territorial of her.

Rock gave Cassie a puzzled look. She looked back at him with a goofy grin. He was hesitant but he backed away. Shai's *If I Ever Fall In Love* started playing. Cassie shot Jazmin a wide-eyed look which caused Jazmin to giggle before turning her attention back to Jah.

Gio pulled her close and smiled like he always have done. "How are you tonight?"

Bashful, Cassie said, "I'm good. I didn't even know you would be here."

"I had to," he said.

She chuckled, "You're looking very *I Wanna Sex You Up*."

"You like it?"

She continued to laugh as they swayed. "It's a good look on you."

"I like your look too. Showing this much leg is too tempting," he said. "You had to know you were gonna get some attention tonight."

"Yeah, if I had one of those huge booties and an overflow of breasts," she joked.

"You have just enough. I appreciate it at least."

"Thank you," she said. She asked, "Where is the wife?"

"She didn't want to come. She's not into parties and clubs."

Cassie nodded knowingly. "That's why you can go be naughty. Is she aware of that?"

"She's aware that I'm involved in activities outside the marriage."

She discreetly looked down at his left hand. There was no ring. She asked, "And she's okay with it?"

"I think she just don't care. We live different lives. It's safe to say we weren't really made for each other."

"It's a lot of that going on," she said. "Makes me almost not want to get married."

"You wouldn't want to?"

She shrugged. "I don't want it to end in a disaster."

"Well, it's not like that for everybody. I just feel like maybe if I had met someone like you, before I married her, things would be different."

"Like me?"

"Yeah. Stop thinking you're not good enough."

Cassie grew uncomfortable. She didn't know she was so transparent. And why didn't she think she was worthy?

"Excuse me. Can I cut in?"

Both Gio and Cassie looked at Eli standing there. Cassie was shocked as her mouth hung open. Gio grinned and handed her right on over and walked away. She was unsure if this was a good idea. She glanced in Jazmin and Jah's direction, but they weren't paying attention.

Luckily Montell Jordan's *This Is How We Do It* started blaring from the speakers. She couldn't imagine herself dancing slow with Eli. However, she found herself having a good time with him. It was one of the things she appreciated about his company; they could be silly.

Then SWV's *Weak* started playing. Before she could escape, he had pulled her in close.

"Why are you running away? Who said you could leave?" he asked.

"Because..." she said as she searched her brain for an excuse. But when he started singing the words along with the song, it did something to her. Like a magnet, she literally was drawn into his arms.

"Sing it to me Cassie," he whispered to her.

Her heart thudded heavily in her chest. Why was he doing this? *Now*? Of all places and times? *Now*?

As she softly sung along with the song, the words began to get the best of her. Eli could sense it as her grip tightened on him.

Sean happened to come along at the right time to cut in. "May I?" Sean asked.

"What's up Sean," Eli greeted. He looked Cassie in the eyes before handing her over. He said to Sean, "You gotta give her back though."

She didn't want to be left with Sean. She groaned in aggravation and tried to walk away. He grabbed her by the arm to stop her.

"Why are you running away from me?" he asked.

"Why are you even here? Who invited you?" she asked.

"Ricky told me about it. But I came with someone else. It's not completely private Cassie. The club is open to everybody."

"Well, you need to go find whoever you came here with and harass them," she cut her eyes.

"Why you act like you can't talk to me?"

"Because…How would that look? Jazz is here. I don't want her seeing me talking to you, but it's too late and now I gotta look stupid trying to come up with a lie. I told you we can't talk like that out in the open."

"It's not that serious Cassie," he said.

She caught a glimmer of the ring on his hand. "What's that?"

"Nothing," he replied.

Cassie pulled away from him and pushed her way around people until she got to the bottom of the stairs leading her back up to the others. He was following her anyway.

She stopped before ascending the steps. "Will you stop please?"

"You don't have to be that way. I just wanna ask you something."

"What?"

"Are you with him?"

"Who?"

"Eli."

"Why is everybody concerned about me and Eli?" she asked annoyed. She narrowed her eyes at him with suspicion. "You're jealous?"

Sean started laughing. "Would I be wrong if I said I was?"

She shook her head as she tried to suppress the smile threatening to form on her face.

"You look cute," he said as his eyes danced about her body.

She blushed then remembered where they were. "I gotta get away from you."

"Come holla at me before you leave," he called after her.

She waved over her shoulder. When she turned around, a few of her friends were standing by the rails overlooking the lower level. She looked at Rock with his cold expression as if he was ready to punch her.

She cautiously went up the steps keeping her eyes on them.

"How the fuck you gon be all in Sean's face like that?" he asked angrily.

She was thrown off. She looked past Rock at Tanya who seemed to be waiting for an answer. Coming up the stairs behind her, was Jazmin and Jah.

"He just came up and started talking to me," she explained. "I didn't know he was here."

"It looked like more than that," Rock said.

"Why are you watching me like that anyway?" she retorted.

Tanya interjected. "Don't nobody fuck with that mothafucka like that. Cass, that don't look good."

She pointed down to the lower floor. "Well, Ricky's the one that told him about the party being here. And the club is open to the public, but I asked Sean myself what was he doing here. It wasn't shit to that. So stop making it seem like I'm doing some dirty shit behind ya'll's back."

"It seemed like ya'll were having a little lover's fight," Jazmin said with disappointment.

"No!" Cassie responded as if she was appalled. "Jazz, don't do that. I wouldn't do that."

"That's foul Cass," Rock said.

Eli's face scrunched up with confusion. "Foul? But ain't you—"

Jah walked up in time to pull Eli away before he could get out the rest. "Nigga, shutcho ass up!"

"Well, I would hope you wouldn't be falling for his shit," Tanya said. "The way you dogged him out and now ya'll buddy-buddy."

Cassie couldn't believe this. It was infuriating her. This was the exact reason why she didn't need Sean talking to her. "This is supposed to be a celebration of our birthdays and ya'll wanna ruin it?"

"You ruining it by talking to the enemy," Jazmin spat. She added, "I knew something was up when we ran into him at Saint Anejo's."

Cassie's mouth dropped open in disbelief. "I'm leaving," Cassie said angrily. She stormed away from them. She had no idea where anything was or what led to what. She ended up at a corner table in the dining area of the club.

"Hey!"

She looked up and saw Jazmin and Tanya.

"We weren't trying to upset you," Jazmin explained. "It's just him popping up here was unexpected. He knew better than to creep his ass in this party. And Jah bout to smack the shit out of Ricky."

Cassie chuckled giving Jazmin the side eye. "Jazz, you been drinking? You know you be sounding like Jah sometimes."

"Yeah, she been drinking," Tanya said. "But back to you. What was that all about? What did he say to you?"

"He came on purpose knowing none of us would like that shit," Jazmin snarled. "He's caused enough problems amongst us. But just tell me this Cassie...Are you messing with his dirty dick ass?"

Cassie released a deep frustrated and defeated sigh. "Let me explain, but I'm asking that you be understanding and don't judge me."

Tanya groaned with disappointment. "I know you not fucking him Cassie!"

"Remember when we went to that club?" Cassie asked.

"The nasty one?" Jazmin asked.

Cassie nodded. She went on to explain. "Sean was there. And me and Tanya kinda took some shit that got us all horny. He was—"

Tanya gasped. "It's him? He's the one you've been sneaking around seeing. Why didn't you tell me Sean was there that night?"

Jazmin threw her hands in the air with exasperation. "I'm done. I don't wanna hear no more."

Before she could walk away, Cassie stopped her. "No, just hear me out. I need to get this out cause some days I think I'm gonna explode holding it all in."

With reluctance, Jazmin stayed. She folded her arms across her chest and looked at Cassie with a disinterested face. "Talk."

Chapter 15

Cassie asked Jazmin and Tanya to keep what she disclosed to themselves. Surprisingly, they both understood and had nothing bad to say after she told them. She explained that it was a mistake that just kept going. And now it had turned into something else. Of all people, Cassie expected Jazmin to understand.

The remainder of the party, Cassie chose to stay to herself and work through her thoughts. She wasn't enjoying the party as much. She was glad everyone else was though. Rock acted like he was still upset with her. Jah had let it go. As long as Sean stayed away from them, he was straight. Eli took Romyn where Kreme was and he has been MIA ever since. Tanya and Jazmin were getting completely wasted.

She continued sitting at the table. It was dark but where it was situated, she could still people-watch if she could stay focused. Her mind began to wander and the people became a blur.

She needed to get rid of Colette. She didn't know why she felt a need to help her or even be concerned about her. Colette only cared about one thing: Colette. And she wasn't even going to entertain the idea of her and Rock making another attempt at a relationship. And now that Jazmin and Tanya knew what was going on between her and Sean, she didn't feel as stressed. He didn't have anything to hold over her head anymore.

She wished she could have a relationship with her father. Maybe it was time to seek him out and try. It's been years. She was now thirty and she remembered seeing him only one time when she was five. She remembered hearing him say to Colette that he couldn't take her and that his wife couldn't know about her. He looked at Cassie and smiled giving her a teddy bear. He told her to be a good girl and to take care of her mama.

Between a party-going, alcoholic sex fiend for a mother and a wealthy lawyer father who didn't want to claim her, Cassie felt like she didn't have a chance. But because of friends like Jazmin and Tanya, she felt like somebody. She couldn't mess up things with them.

"Can I sit right here?"

She was snapped out of her thoughts and realized Eli was standing before her.

"Yeah," she said lowly.

"Why you sitting over here in the dark?" he asked. He sat beside her in the booth making sure to put space between them.

"Just thinking," she mumbled.

"Why you so bipolar Cassie?"

"You got your nerves. You moody too," she argued.

"I've been dealing with some shit. But you're moody all the time. I think I can agree with Rock when he says you're hot one day and then you're cold the next. Mixing those temperatures like that can cause a storm."

"Okay, I admit I'm bipolar. But I be dealing with stuff too." She looked at him with question. "Why are you over here talking to me anyway? Where's Romyn?"

"He's in good hands. And I came over here because you looked all sad. Did they make you feel bad earlier?"

"I don't wanna talk about that," she mumbled.

"Can I ask you something? I guess you don't have to answer because it's none of my business, but what's going on with you and Rock?"

"Nothing. He keeps asking me what's going on with me and you. He suspects that we're fooling around."

"Rock is just paranoid and insecure," he said. Then he contemplated his next words. "We've been around each other for the past couple of months right?"

"Yeah."

"And in that time we've grown close. I believe we share mutual feelings when it comes to the other. And I don't wanna see you get hurt by him. He ain't no good. If

241

you need to be with somebody, try stepping outside this circle and find someone new. I think you deserve that."

Where was all of this coming from? It left her confused and somewhat hurt. What were these mutual feelings he spoke of? Hell, she was attracted to him, and if they could take it to another level she would seriously give it some thought.

She felt herself getting emotional and looked away from him. "I guess I need to fix me before I attempt anything else. I want a relationship but I don't know how to be. My moodiness push them away. I ain't never been in relationship longer than four months. And most of those were nothing but a lot of sex. It's like I can't offer nothing else but my ass. I'm just like Colette."

"Don't compare yourself to that woman," he said with disgust. "And I think you have a problem with letting someone love you. I used to be like that and that's why I never had a real relationship until Kris. And even that took a while. I used to only want to think of me. I didn't really want to do love, but I think I grew up when I became somebody's daddy. And I wasn't afraid to give love a try anymore."

"Okay and as soon as you gave it a try, look what happened," she pointed out.

"Yeah and maybe I acted too soon when I made her my wife. I felt like it was the right thing to do. I wasn't exactly in love with her, but I loved her. But it doesn't mean that I can't be hopeful of ever being in love one day. Like you told me that one night...it's somebody out there for me besides Kris. Just like it's somebody out there that will understand you and have a little patience—cause God they gon need it!"

"Whatever Eli," she grumbled.

There was a moment of silence. So many thoughts were racing through Cassie's head. And whenever anybody had kind things to say about her, it made her mushy.

Eli cleared his throat with uneasiness. He said, "I'm leaving in the morning."

"Where to?"

"Italy. I'm going with Lu for about two weeks. Cosimos ain't doing that well. Remember, I am that man's son and Lu is my brother."

"Two weeks?" That was all Cassie heard.

"Maybe three. I'll be back...I think. I might get over there and don't wanna come back."

"What will I do at work?" she asked as she fought back tears.

"Work. Gio will be there to help. So will the others. You'll have stuff to do. And if I don't come back, I'll make sure you'll have a position somewhere."

"Are you taking your kids?" she wanted to know.

"Yeah, they're going with me."

In a sullen tone, she said, "I wish I could go."

"You need a passport first," he told her.

"Yeah, I guess I gotta take care of that. You tell Kris you're leaving?"

"I signed and returned those papers. Kris is no longer my concern; not until we go to court. I have no words for her."

She fell quiet. She then mumbled, "You won't be here for my actual birthday."

"I know. It wasn't my original plans, but...I just need to get my head straight. My emotions are all over the place and I don't want to make any impulsive decisions; especially based on the wrong things."

"I guess I understand," she said solemnly.

"Oh I wanted to tell you that you look nice tonight. Whoever done your hair is a miracle worker. She got them edges looking like baby hair."

Cassie laughed and nudged his side. "Oh shut up!"

"I'm so serious," he said. He touched her face at her hairline, and let his finger trace the fine hairs that swirled.

His touch made her body hairs elevate and she tried to resist the shiver that went through her. She turned to him and her heart began pounding. The way he was looking at her was as if he wanted to devour her right there. Her leg began to bounce out of control. He placed a hand on her knee and squeezed to make her stop. His touch was about to make her scream.

She begged with her eyes. "Don't."

"Cassie..." His voice was low and desperate.

She looked away and said, "You're leaving, so don't."

"But—"

She slid out of the booth seating and tried to get as far away from him as she could. She wasn't ready to go there just yet; especially with him leaving her the following day. Why would he pick that night? She needed for him to keep how he felt to himself.

———

The following day when Cassie awaken, she felt dispirited. She felt alone. She felt empty. Most of all, she was in pain. Not physical pain, but the kind a person suffered from heart break.

She thought back to the night before. After walking away from Eli, she decided to leave altogether. She went to say her goodbyes although Jazmin, Desiree, and Tanya tried to convince her to stay. They argued that she hadn't even gotten any cake. Jazmin cut a big chunk of cake and insisted she take it with her.

When she got home, she was surprised Colette wasn't there fucking somebody. She had her apartment to herself and it was so quiet, and so still. Then she thought about him. She had never considered having him at her place because of how nosy Colette was, but that night she didn't care. She just wanted to be with him. She sent him a text: *I need you*

It took him a while, but he text back: *I'm not doing this with you anymore*

Seeing those words sent her spiraling. She text back: *please*!

Him: *no*

Cassie: *I love you*

Him: *stop*

She grew irate. *I hate you*

Him: *exactly*

Cassie: *come to my place*

Him: *go to sleep*

Cassie: *I'm sorry. I'm stupid. I'm scared. I don't know how to let a man love me. I don't know how to love a man. I need you. teach me*

No response. Then there was a knock on the door. Startled, she jumped up from her sofa and looked through the peephole. He had to have been on his way before she even started texting him because he was standing outside her apartment door. She tried to compose herself before opening the door.

Before she could say anything, he came in and shut the door behind him. His vexation shown on his face as he attacked her aggressively with kisses. He tugged at her clothes, groped her breasts, and rubbed on her yoni.

Before she knew it, she was completely naked in her hallway.

He backed her up against the wall. Now it was his turn to come out of his clothes while they hungrily devoured one another. As soon as he tossed the last article of clothing, Cassie lowered to a squatting position, grabbed his erection and guided it to her mouth.

"That's all the fuck you want," he said angrily. "You just want the dick."

His tone only drove her to get lost in pleasing him.

He wanted to be angry, but she made him weak. He groaned, "Cassie...Dammit! I can't stand you." He grabbed a handful of her hair and yanked her off of him. She looked up at him with desperate wet eyes. He took her face into his hands, leaned down, and placed a delicate kiss on her lips as he helped her to stand to her full height.

"I love—" she started but he silenced her with another kiss that evolved into a deeper passionate one. While they tongue wrestled and lip suckled, he was lifting her legs to place around him. She held onto him while pinned under his weight against the wall. He leaned into her guiding his dick to her wetness. Before sliding inside her, he rubbed his dick head in between her slit arousing her clit and stirring her honey.

She moaned in his mouth as he caressed her insides. He was being gentle and loving. Each deep stroke caused small orgasms to ripple through her body. She knew she loved him. She didn't want to let him go, so she held onto him tightly.

The pace picked up. The strokes deepened and got harder. Her body bounced up and down against the wall in an even rhythm as he dug into her.

He panted into her ear, "Hold onto me Princess."

She held tight both around his waist and neck as he carried her into her bedroom with his dick still inside her. He lay her on her bed, still in position, and didn't hesitate to start grinding into her again.

"Yes...baby..." she breathed heavily with pleasure. "Please...don't stop."

He raised on his haunches while holding her legs high and wide apart, rocking in and out of her. He admired the sight of his dick being gripped by her ridiculously wet pussy.

He commanded, "Rub on that pussy for me."

Cassie began to rub on her clit as she was told. She watched him as he delighted in the sight of her touching herself.

Releasing her legs, he moved over her to kiss her. He asked, "Do you want to hurt, Princess?"

She nodded with desperation and eagerness. She closed her eyes as he pushed her legs back and began to plow into her.

She began to cry and couldn't even form a comprehensible word. Her arms tried to push him back but his weight wouldn't budge. He knew her. He knew she would resist. Her face would contort into one expressing pain and discomfort. She would beg with her eyes for him to stop. But it wasn't what she truly wanted. She needed him to continue. She needed him to hurt her. It wasn't one hundred percent satisfying if she didn't hurt.

The sensation became immense as it always did. But this one was really intense and forceful. As her body forced out a stream of ejaculate, it shook. Normally he would watch the fluid spurt, but he kept his eyes locked on hers. She looked so vulnerable, so wounded, scared, and in her eyes she was asking him to rescue her.

Instead of re-entering her, he placed affectionate kisses all over her body. He wished he could rescue her, but he couldn't. Not right now. But for tonight he would make her feel good.

For the rest of the night, he made slow, sensual, aggressive love to her.

She remembered drifting off to sleep with his arms around her. She wasn't sure when he left, but when she woke up he wasn't there. The only thing that reminded her that he had been there, was how sore her body was and how her sheets had captured his smell.

She finally got out of bed, took a shower, dressed, and shuffled to the kitchen with her phone in her hand. The sight of Colette passed out on the sofa angered her.

"Letty! Get up and go to the room," she yelled. "All your parts are spilling out your clothes. Ugh!"

Colette groaned and mumbled something.

"Get up!" Cassie shouted.

"Okay! Damn, you ain't gotta do all that yelling," Colette said. She slowly picked herself up from the sofa. She staggered down the hallway.

"Letty, you need to be finding somewhere else to go."

"Don't think cause you got that job that you don't need me," Colette called.

"I really can think it," she retorted.

Colette stood outside the bedroom door and said, "So now that you don't need my money I'm not good enough to stay here?"

"You've been here for two months. You can't go stay with Gerald or Eddie Lee, whatever their names were."

"I don't stay with no man," Colette sneered.

"That's cause you can't just fuck one," Cassie said under her breath but loud enough that Colette caught some of it.

Colette walked back down the hall. "What did you say?"

"You know what I said," Cassie said. She started moving about in her kitchen, not caring about Colette.

"And what about you?"

"What about me?"

"Why is it that you ain't got a man?"

"This ain't about me. I'm trying to get you out of my place. Besides, I'm considering moving and you're not coming with me."

"And why is that?"

"Cause I don't want you in my house!" Cassie said adamantly. Her phone rung from the counter. She answered it, "Hey."

"Hey Cass," Nicole said. "What are you doing today?"

"Nothing."

"Granny asked about you. She cooked and wanted you to come by. She made your favorites since your birthday is tomorrow."

"And I haven't had Granny's cooking in a while," Cassie said. She could feel herself salivating already. "Let me get ready and I'll be over there."

"Okay. I'll tell her."

Cassie ended the call then stared at Colette. "What are you looking at?"

"You're such a hateful ass girl," Colette said shaking her head.

"You helped to make me that way," she countered.

"You going over Mama's?"

"Stop being nosy," Cassie said rolling her eyes.

"Tell everybody I said hello," Colette said nonchalantly as she walked away.

Then there was a knock on the door. What the fuck! Cassie thought. She went to the door and opened it without checking. "What?"

"Damn, that's how you answer doors now?" Rock asked as he stepped inside.

"What are you doing over here?" she asked eyeing him suspiciously.

"I've been texting you and you ain't responded. So I just came by," he said. Colette coming out of the bedroom caused him to turn that way. "Hey Letty."

Colette smiled and waved.

"You should have called then," Cassie said. "What do you want? Cause I'm bout to leave."

"To talk to you..." his voice trailed as he looked back at Colette. She was still standing in the hallway. He looked back at Cassie. "Let's go in your room real quick."

Cassie led the way. They closed the door. She crossed her arms over her chest. "What is it?"

"Remember I mentioned to you about a favor."

"Yeah. What is it?"

"You got two thousand you can let me hold?"

Cassie's eyes widen. "Are you serious?"

"I'm dead serious. I really need it," he said desperately.

"For what?" she asked.

"I gotta go to court and the judge ain't gon let me walk away without having those two stacks to apply to my arrears."

"Arrears? Like in child support?"

"Yeah."

Cassie let out a wry laugh. "You shit out of luck."

"C'mon man, I know you got it. You bring that home in a week," he said.

"How the hell you know what I bring home?" she asked.

"I know. Shit, Tanya told me."

"Me and Tanya don't get paid the same thing. So you don't know what I bring home." If he really knew the truth, he would know that Cassie got way more than Tanya. She just let Tanya believe they were in the same pay bracket.

"Do you have it or not?" he pressed.

"Maybe," she said. "When can I get it back?"

"Next month. I just don't wanna go to jail."

"And I guess you're expecting for me to care?"

"Something like that. Would you help me if I was your man?"

Cassie gave it some thought. "Probably. But you're not my man."

"C'mon Cassie," he whined.

Giving in, she said, "Okay. Give me a minute and we can go to an atm. I should be able to give you eight hundred today, unless you wanna wait until tomorrow."

"Naw, I'll take eight today," he said. He smiled with relief.

Cassie looked at Rock waiting for him to leave. "Can you get out?"

"Damn, I can't stay in your room now?"

"Not while I'm taking a shower," she said. "Now go on."

He sucked his teeth and reluctantly walked out. She shut and locked the door behind him. As she gathered her things in preparation for her shower, Eli popped in her head. She wondered if he had already taken off for Italy. And why hadn't he called or text to let her know he was gone? Feeling a little hopeful, she thought maybe he changed his mind altogether.

———

Rock eased his way across to Colette's room. The door was opened and she was standing there about to remove her clothes. She looked up and saw him. She grinned. He motioned for her to come to him.

"Come in here," she said.

"I can't," he said glancing back at Cassie's bedroom door. He eyed Colette's body, licking his lips.

Colette could see the lust dancing in his eyes. She teased, "You want one for the road?"

"Come out here," he whispered.

She listened for Cassie's shower. She looked at him seductively. He was such a trifling ass, but she loved it. She dropped to her knees before him. He eagerly obliged, unfastening his pants to release his dick. Colette devoured it.

Everybody knew Cassie loved taking long showers, but they still had to listen for her. Being sneaky excited the moment and Rock got a kick out of it. On top of it, he was about to get the two thousand dollars for Colette from Cassie.

Without wasting more time, he motioned for Colette to stand up and bend over against the hallway wall. Once Colette got this money, he was cutting her off. That's what he kept telling himself. If he didn't, then giving her this money was a waste. So he enjoyed it as much as he could.

Colette panted in a breathy whisper. "Don't you cum in me this time."

"Well, get ready to catch it," he said. He felt his nut coming but then the shower stopped. The thought of getting caught threw him off and released inside of Colette.

"I thought I told—"

"Ssh," he cut her off. He removed himself from her and fixed his pants. He shoved her in her room and closed the door. He walked back to the living room and sat on the sofa to wait for Cassie.

Five minutes later, Cassie was opening her door. She walked to Colette's room and knocked on the door.

"What is it now?" Colette said as she answered the door.

"Did you take my black sandals?" Cassie asked.

"Hold on," Colette huffed. She spun around and went to the closet. When she bent over, Cassie got an eyeful of her naked bottom and her ran-through vagina. The wolf bat Arby's pussy flashed in her mind at the sight of Colette.

Cassie turned away. "Ew! Letty, you need to stop doing that. And spray some freshener in here. It stink. It smell like stale balls and rancid pussy."

When Cassie got to her Granny's she was a little thrown by a special guest. Waiting for her, was Charles Stephenson. No one had to tell her who he was or make any introductions. She knew she was looking at her father.

She didn't know what to think or what to say. His presence didn't move her one way or the other. She spoke and moved on to speak to everyone else. It wasn't that she was ignoring him, she just didn't care to say anything to him.

Charles approached her cautiously, "Can we talk?"

She looked at Nicole and her granny. They gave her subtle encouraging nods. "Okay."

They stepped out on the front porch. Before he began to speak, he studied her. With an appreciative smile, he said, "You look like my mother."

That was probably true, giving that she resembled Charles so much, she probably looked like his mother.

"You two are about the same height," he said.

Cassie remained quiet. The vibe was awkward for him.

He released a nervous breath. "Well, I came by just to see how you were doing."

"Why now?" she finally asked.

"Because the two of us having some type of relationship is way past overdue," he replied.

"But I'll be thirty tomorrow. It's taken you twenty-five years to see me again. What is so special about now?"

"I don't know Cassandra," he said with a shrug. "Maybe because I'm trying to right all my wrongs in my life. And I thought maybe I could begin with you."

She didn't say anything.

"I know that doesn't mean much to you. And I can see that you could care less about me showing up now. I don't know what I expected...Is it possible that we can establish a relationship?"

"It's possible, but I don't know if I really want to," she said.

He got quiet this time.

"I'm really hungry," she said. "And there isn't much I'm prepared to say to you. So if you don't mind—"

"I was there when you graduated high school," he blurted out. "Whites Creek High School, out there on the football field. You had on your blue cap and gown and got embarrassed when your granny, aunts, and cousins screamed your name."

She halted. He had been at her graduation?

Charles continued, "Remember that big arrangement that your granny gave you for graduating? That was from me. The bike you got when you were six, ten, twelve...from me. I even sent Christmas gifts every year."

"Why are you telling me this?" Cassie asked. She couldn't stop the vexation building. "If all that came from you, then why couldn't you have given it to me yourself?"

"Between Brenda and Colette, I felt stuck."

"Who the hell is Brenda?"

"My wife."

Cassie sat down in the rocker and her knee started bouncing. "I can take a guess at what part your wife played in this. What did Colette do except want you to take care of your child?"

"Colette didn't want you. She wanted me to take you but I felt like I was stuck between a rock and hard place. Brenda wouldn't have gone for that. She would have made things difficult for me."

"So you picked your wife over your child?"

"I'm not proud of it. There were other things to consider as well."

"Like what?" she asked with an attitude.

"My career. It was her father that made me partner at their firm. And there were your siblings—"

"Siblings? How many do I got?"

"You have two brothers and a sister."

Cassie asked, "So your family, career, and all that prevented you from being my father?"

"Cassandra, I'm admitting I was wrong. I'm asking for an opportunity to fix it."

She let out a mocking scoff. "Let me guess, Brenda is dead, huh?"

Charles' silence was enough for her to know the answer.

"So now that you've gotten everything you wanted out of life including a dead wife, you figure you could come into my life and make it all better?"

"No. I know it will take some time," he said.

"What if I said leave me the fuck alone and to never come by here looking for me again?" she asked.

"You know your mama used to tell me that every time she found out I came by your granny's," he chuckled. "I tried Cassandra. I even confessed to Brenda that I had another daughter. She didn't care and she didn't want me to care. I went along with it because she had my life in her hands. But I tried to do what I could. I don't know what your mother told you about the gifts. I'm not even sure of what she told you about the money I gave to her for your college tuition. She—"

"Hold up!" Cassie interrupted. "What money for college?"

"Your mother would tell me to stay away one minute but then ask me for money when things came up. She said you didn't have all of your tuition money. It didn't cover room and board. I gave it to her as long as it meant you being able to do whatever it is you wanted."

"I didn't go off to college. I tried a semester of community college and that's it. She never told me about having tuition money," Cassie said flabbergasted. That must've been how Colette was able to stay nicely dressed, getting her hair and nails done, and drive around in nice cars.

They both fell into silence.

Cassie couldn't stand Colette. Charles was just as wrong, but she would give him credit for trying. But Colette was the absolute worst.

She suddenly lost her appetite. She got up and mumbled, "Tell my granny I had to leave."

"Wait, Cassandra," he called out.

She ignored him and hurried to her car. She wanted to cry. She wanted to scream. She wanted to go to her apartment and punch Colette in the face.

Chapter 16

Cassie didn't get to confront Colette that night. She could only assume that Colette got drunk somewhere and passed out there. She was glad that she wasn't there the following morning ruining the start of her birthday. Since it was Memorial Day and her actual birthday, she spent it house hopping. She celebrated both occasions a little here, and little there consuming as much barbecue food as she could.

After the day she had, she was glad Colette still hadn't found her way back to her place. When she got to work Tuesday, she was delightfully surprised that her desk had been decked out with colorful decorations and balloons. There even a banner going across her overhead cabinets that said Happy Birthday Cassie. She really appreciated it since her birthday had fallen on the day before, but the office was closed for the holiday.

The only sad thing about the day was looking at Eli's dark office with him not in it. It was after lunch when she heard from him. It wasn't a call or a text, but he had a floral arrangement with balloons and a teddy bear delivered for her birthday. The gesture was touching. She sent him a text: **Got your gift, thank you...Hope all is okay with you**

He hit her right back: **You're welcome and I hoped you enjoyed your birthday**

That was it. She kept staring at the text waiting for it to turn into different words. His message seemed so impersonal. She wanted something there between them that didn't exist. She needed to get it out of her head before it consumed her.

But she couldn't help it.

Here it was at night and she was preparing for bed. Still nothing else from Eli. She dialed Jazmin.

"What?"

Cassie grimaced. "Why you answering Jazz's phone?"

"Cause I can," Jah said. "What the fuck you want? Juicy in the shower."

"Can you tell her to call me when she gets out," she asked.

"I will. By the way, happy birthday hateful ass girl," he said.

She smiled, "Thanks." Then a thought crossed her mind. She asked meekly, "Have you talked to Eli?"

"I think Jazz did earlier. It was like midnight there or some shit. Why?"

"I haven't spoken to him since he left. Do you know when he plan to come back?" she asked.

"He ain't," he answered.

Her heart dropped. "He isn't?"

"No," Jah said. "He's listing his house for sale this week."

"Why? I mean...did he say why he's not returning?"

"Naw. You know that mothafucka weird too. All ya'll mothafuckas crazy," Jah said with a chuckle. "I'm just fuckin' with you though. I don't know what his ass doing. That's yo nigga ain't it?"

"Why you say that?" Cassie asked taken aback.

"I see shit," was all he said.

"Whatever. Tell Jazz to call me," she said.

"Bet."

She laughed to herself. Jah was crazy. She looked at the phone. If it was ten at night now, then it was five o' clock in the morning there. She wanted to talk to him and attempt to tell him how she felt again. The only thing was she was terrified of him rejecting her.

———

After Cassie was able to confront Colette about keeping Charles away from her, they had a big blowout. There was tension between them. She had given Colette three days to get out. It was the third day and Colette hadn't packed one bag.

"Letty," Cassie said patiently. She remained calm. She wasn't really in the mood for a bunch of yelling and cussing. She was tired, her head hurt, irritated, and the little bumps on her chest were hurting. Her period was right around the corner. "How come you haven't got your stuff together?"

Colette lay across the bed in a dismal state. She looked up at Cassie. "Look baby, I know you don't like me. But I honestly don't have anywhere to go. On top of that, I just found out I'm pregnant."

Cassie almost fainted. "You're what?"

"I'm pregnant. I'm fucking forty-five years old. I don't need no babies."

"Then why didn't you do all that you could do to prevent it?" Cassie asked angrily. "This is so fucked up Letty."

"I know. I ain't gonna keep it. But let me stay here just a little while longer. I'ma have to get this abortion and I don't wanna be moving around from house to house."

"Why don't you get your shit together?" Cassie said angrily. "Stop acting like you're nineteen. Get a job. Fix your credit. Buy a house. You're a grandmother to two kids. You ain't never done a damn thing that a grandmother would do. You're nothing like your mama. And I swear to God, I hope I'm nothing like you."

She mocked Cassie with laughter. "The only difference between me and you is you ain't got no goddamn kids."

"I'm not a whore," Cassie corrected.

"Aren't you the one that was fucking that woman's husband? Or what about that older man that used to give you money for fucking him? And don't think I don't know about you going down to that lil raunchy sex club. How many dicks did you fuck down there?"

Cassie was incensed.

"You can't get mad Cassie," Colette taunted with a grin. "You're just like your mama. Accept it and embrace it."

"I ain't embracing shit!" Cassie hissed. She hurried to her room and slammed the door. Why was she letting Colette's words get to her? Were they true? Was she any better than Colette?

She desperately needed her maestro back in her life. The mention of the sex club made her miss him. But that last encounter had been the end of them. Shit! Why did she ruin that? And why didn't she tell Eli how she felt when she had the chance?

———

It was within the second week since Eli had been gone. She was finally adjusting to the fact that he wouldn't be coming back any time soon. He still hadn't bother to call her. She got the message loud and clear. He didn't think of her in the same way. His feelings stopped at the surface. Hers went beyond the surface. Or maybe she was obsessed with liking him she felt like he should like her back with just as much zeal.

"What are you over there doing?" Tanya asked.

Cassie was counting weeks and days on the calendar. She was confused. Although she had an irregular regular menstrual cycle, she always knew when to expect it. She referred to it as irregular regular because it didn't come in a cycle of every thirty days like normal women. It alternated in a pattern. According to her calculations, she should have had one by the middle of May. It was the middle of June. At first she didn't think anything of it because she thought it was doing one of those adjustments to get on a different cycle. All of the premenstrual signs were there. And her breasts were so tender, but no cycle.

Cassie turned to Tanya spooked.

"What is it?" Tanya asked with concern.

"Tanya, I think I'm pregnant," she yelled in a hushed whisper.

"Are you sure?"

"I ain't had no period in forever," she said.

"What's forever? Maybe it's just running behind."

"Forever is April tenth. It should have been here."

"And your ass just now paying attention and counting up days and shit?" Tanya asked.

"It didn't dawn on me until I really became aware of how hot and painful my titties are."

"Oh bitch, you is pregnant. Who's the daddy?" Tanya asked.

Shit! She hadn't even thought about that either. Was she being punished? This couldn't be happening. She leaned forward on her desk, arms propped up and her forehead resting in the palm of her hands.

"You don't know, do you?" Tanya asked. She seemed to sympathize with her.

Cassie looked at her with worried eyes. Yes, she knew, but she wasn't going to tell Tanya who it was just yet. "Don't you know Letty told me she was pregnant last week? We can't be pregnant at the same time!"

"Well, before you panic," Tanya started. "Let's make sure you are and then we'll go from there."

"What's gonna happen to me?" Cassie cried.

"Cassie, stop being so stupid. Ain't shit gon' happen to you except in nine months you gon be pushing a big headed baby out your pussy. Now get it together. You want me to call Jazz up here?"

"No, don't bother her. I might not even keep it," she said.

"What do you mean? You're gonna get an abortion? Cassie, don't do that. Aren't you the one that's always complaining that you don't have a baby yet?"

"Yeah, but I was hoping a husband came along with it," she said. Tears began to spill over her lids. "My life is just stupid. One minute I think I'm on the right track and I can handle whatever comes my way. And then the next minute, I hate everybody and everything. And nothing goes right. And people show up out of nowhere, and people disappear. And I got a stupid pregnant forty-five-year-old mama that's homeless in my apartment."

Tanya rubbed her back. "You're already hormonal. Why don't you take the rest of the day off and get it together. I'll tell Gio you didn't feel well."

Feeling weighted with doom, Cassie retrieved her purse from the cabinet drawer.

Tanya said, "Make sure you stop at the store and get you a pregnancy test."

This wasn't supposed to be a depressing moment of her life. She was supposed to be happy about her pregnancy. There was nothing happy about it in the moment.

It took Cassie ten minutes to convince herself to go into the drug store to buy a test. She didn't want to have to face what she already knew. After getting an associate to open the case for a pregnancy test, she perused the candy aisle. She was in the mood for some sour candy.

"I thought I seen you."

She looked up and rolled her eyes. Why did he always find her?

"I think you're stalking me," she said.

Sean smiled down at her. "It seems that way."

He looked down at the items in her hand. She flushed with embarrassment and hid the pregnancy test behind her back.

"So why haven't you called me?" Sean asked.

"Excuse me? What am I calling you for exactly?"

"I thought you would have called me to see if I was okay. And maybe some other things."

"Why are you fucking with me? Why are you still showing your face around us? Just to get under everybody's skin? And what other things? Boy, if you don't go on away from me."

"After all that went down I'm still a little salty. If I can aggravate the hell out of ya'll I will."

"At least you admitted it," she said.

"I still can't stand Jah's ass."

"Sean, you need to let that go. Everybody has moved on. Jah and Jazz are happy with two beautiful babies. They ain't thinking about you."

He gestured towards the box behind her back. "Speaking of babies...You think you got one in the oven?"

"None of your business," she said smartly.

"Whose is it Cassie?" he asked.

"Don't worry about it," she said trying to walk away.

"You don't think the father should know?" he called out to her.

Forgetting her candy, she turned around and plucked up a bag of sour Air Heads Extremes, sour Gummi Worms, and Lemonheads. She looked at Sean still standing there. "Leave me alone."

"What about them other things? When will you come back to the club?"

Cassie walked away giving him the finger over her shoulder.

When she got home, Colette was asleep. She tried to be quiet so she wouldn't wake her. The last thing she wanted to deal with that day was Colette teasing her about them being pregnant at the same time.

As soon as Cassie got comfortable, she went to the bathroom. She stood there reading the instructions for ten minutes. She had never taken one of these things before. It couldn't be that hard to do.

Doing as instructed, Cassie used the restroom then placed the test on the edge of the tub. She didn't look at it as she completed her business and washed her hands. In the mirror, she glanced at the reflection of the test sitting peacefully. She turned around and swiped it up, but still hesitated to look at it.

She looked at the results in the tiny window display. She referred back to the instructions again. She placed the test on the vanity. She went to her bed in a daze and sat down. She was torn. It was something she always wanted, but she wasn't sure she was ready.

She picked up the phone and placed a call.

"Hello?" Tanya answered.

"It's two lines."

There was silence.

Tanya finally asked, "So what are you gonna do?"

"I guess go to a doctor so I can start prenatal care."

"Yay!" Tanya cheered. "Can I tell Jazz? She's gonna be too excited."

Cassie smiled nervously. "I guess."

They ended the call. She looked at her phone and waited. As expected it rung. "What Jazz?"

Jazmin shrieked in the phone. "Can I be God-mommy? Tanya is God-mommy to everybody's child. Pick me!"

Cassie smiled, happy that she had two friends that loved her so much.

———

Her first appointment had her on edge. She didn't know what to expect. She didn't know what to ask. Her leg bounced uncontrollably until she was called to the back. She provided her urine, they took her weight, and got the rest of her vital signs. She was then placed in an exam room and instructed to remove her clothes.

It seemed like forever before the doctor came in. She looked up into his sparkling blue eyes that smiled when he smiled.

"My name is Dr. Bradshaw and you Ms. Daniels are definitely pregnant."

There was a sense of joy that made her have to blink back tears. It was official since the doctor's office confirmed it.

After talking and explaining some things, he gave her a physical exam which was so uncomfortable for her. He was puzzled because of the information she provided about her cycle; it didn't necessarily match the results of the physical exam. He referred her to get an ultrasound so he could have an exact gestational age and due date.

That didn't make her feel all that great. But she made her way to the check-out window and waited on the lady to schedule her next appointment and to set up her ultrasound appointment. As she waited, a couple walked into the office laughing and holding hands. They seemed happy and she longed for that. She wished she had the father to accompany her to her appointments.

As the girl stood at the check in window, the guy stood close behind her with his hand at the small of her back. He seemed very protective of her. She didn't look very pregnant but Cassie noticed she signed in on the clipboard for prenatal visits.

When they walked away, the lady at the check-in called out, "Oh...Mrs. Masters...you forgot your insurance cards."

When Cassie heard what the lady called her, she made sure to get a better look at the girl. How did she miss that? She was looking at Kris and her lover, Brother Yosef.

Shame on it all, Cassie thought. She was sure Kris was using insurance that Eli provided for her to get care for a baby that wasn't his...again.

Chapter 17

Two weeks—fifteen days to be exact—had been enough time to clear his head. Although he told everyone he might not come back, he couldn't wait to get home. Italy had been great and the kids enjoyed it. He even spent time with Cosimos getting to know him. And perhaps later, when the kids were older, he would consider moving there permanently, but not now.

Eli found it very weird and almost funny that when he and the kids got to the house, Kris was there waiting for them.

Avani was happy to see her. She ran over to her, "Mommy!"

Eli looked at Bria and Bryce, " Take your things to your rooms." He neared Kris with suspicion and caution.

"Why are you here?" he asked.

Kris gave Avani one last hug and then put her down. "Give mommy and daddy a second okay?"

"Okay," Avani said. She ran to the stairs and stomped up them.

Kris turned to Eli with an unsure smile. "Hey."

"Don't hey me. Why are you here?"

"I wanted to talk. I had no idea you had left. I called Sarah and she told me where ya'll were at. Was it a nice trip?"

Now he wished he stayed in Italy. "It was nice. What do you want?"

Apprehension etched across her face. Carefully she said, "I think I made a mistake."

"Made a mistake about what?"

"This...us."

"Oh really?" he said with sarcasm.

"C'mon Eli," she said. "I knew you weren't going to make this easy for me. And I probably deserve it."

"Probably?" Eli thought she must be crazy.

"I messed up," she said apologetically. "I messed up and I want to stop the divorce."

He shook his head dismissing the notion. He began walking past her toward the kitchen.

Kris followed behind him. "Will you hear me out?"

"No." He was firm in his reply. He glanced at her hand and noticed she had placed her wedding ring back on. He asked, "Who told you to go in *my* bedroom and get that?"

"It's mine, isn't it?"

"No, not after you took it off and placed it on that table as a dramatic goodbye exit. But I don't care. You can keep it. It ain't like I would give it to the next woman anyway."

She smiled softly. "Well, there shouldn't be a next woman."

Eli was annoyed. "This isn't how I expected my first day back home to go. Why now Kris? When I tried to talk to you about us, wanting to fix us...you refused to."

"I know. And Eli, I'm sorry. I messed up. I just wanna come back home. Me and Elijah."

That made him cringe. "Ain't he with his daddy?"

"No."

"Well, where is he?"

"I'm saying you're his daddy."

Eli released a frustrated breath. "Don't do this Kris. Don't do this to me. I went to Italy to clear my mind and now here you come fucking with it again. I was really hurt behind what you did. And it wasn't because Elijah wasn't my son. I could have dealt with that. That lil nigga got my last name. It was how you went about it. And you were willing to abandon Avani for some slick talking, ol' skinny incense-burning, Sahara-desert-sand-kicking sandals wearing nigga."

Kris lowered her eyes with dejection. "How many times can I say I'm sorry. I wasn't thinking."

"I know you weren't. But I couldn't wait around for your brain to start working. I got to move on."

"With someone else?" she asked.

"No. I'm talking about dealing with the feelings you left me with. I couldn't just wallow in them and be depressed. And now that I'm at a point of acceptance, here you come with this shit."

"Eli, all I know is...that when I left, I realized I missed ya'll. I missed you, even the fights. I missed Bria's smart mouth. I missed Avani's affection. I missed Bryce's silliness. I missed our home. I missed my family." Tears came to her eyes as she walked upon him. "Please forgive me and give us another chance."

He didn't know what he should do. He didn't prepare for her wanting to come back. Did he want Kris back? Did he want his complete family? What would happen if she got brainwashed again?

"I love you Eli," Kris spoke softly. Her arms circled around him and she placed her head against his chest. "I miss you so much."

He hated to even acknowledge his feelings, but it wasn't that he missed her. In fact, he didn't miss her at all, but he did care about her wellbeing. He finally admitted to himself that his feelings for Kris were not in a way that a man should love his wife. Nonetheless, he felt a need to console her.

She lifted her head from his chest and smiled. "Can we make love?"

It had been a few weeks for him, so he wasn't exactly pressed. Besides the idea of her being with Yosef turned him off.

"Can we just see how things play out?" he asked.

Disappointment covered her face. "I was looking forward to being with my husband."

Eli countered, "Just like all of those nights I was looking forward to being with my wife."

"If we are going to work on fixing things you can't say little things like that," Kris said.

"Okay Kris," he said flippantly.

She moved out of his hold and took him by the hand. "Will you at least let me try to change your mind?"

"You can try," he said. He couldn't put his finger on it, but something seemed off about her behavior. He didn't trust it, but he would go along with it for now.

———

Cassie went into work late because of her ultrasound appointment. It was much too soon to detect the sex of the baby, but she seen it. It was a bean/cashew-shaped mass in the corner of her uterus all by its lonesome. It made it even more real to see what was actually growing in her womb. She was already in love with her baby. She was determined to be a better mother than Colette had ever been.

Seeing her baby, started her morning off just right. She didn't care about anything else except making sure she was mentally prepared for a baby. Damn a man! He would probably be more of a headache anyway.

As she made her way to her desk, she noticed that Eli's office was lit and there were a few of the owners in there talking and laughing. Cassie assumed it wasn't anything serious or the door would have been closed.

She sat down and prepared herself for a day of work. Tanya came walking over to her desk with a McDonald's bag in hand.

"When you get here?" Tanya asked sitting in her seat.

"Just now," she said. She couldn't contain her excitement. She pulled out the 3-D sonogram and showed it to Tanya.

"That looks scary," Tanya grimaced. "I hate 3-D ultrasounds."

Cassie laughed.

"So how far along are you?"

"According to this, I'm seven weeks and one day."

"Damn, your ass is damn near two months pregnant," Tanya said excitedly. "So we got seven months to prepare for this baby. How do you feel about it now?"

"I'm happy and looking forward to being a mommy," Cassie said. She eyed Lu, Antino, and Stefano as they walked by.

"Have you told Colette?"

Cassie shook her head. "I don't want to. It might make her wanna keep hers."

"She ain't got an abortion like she said she was?"

"No, and I don't think—" Cassie stopped mid-sentence with her mouth gaped open. She watched Kris come out of Eli's office laughing. She was holding onto his hand, pulling him along. They looked happy. Eli had a relaxed and care free aura. Cassie didn't see the Eli that she had grown close to for the past couple of months. She saw the one who wouldn't have paid her much attention because she was a nobody. She saw the one that was capable of not giving a damn enough to call and check on her.

Even when he looked at her, his mood didn't waver. Still holding onto Kris, Eli said, "Hey Cassie. Nice to see you. I'll be right back; grabbing something to eat. You want anything?"

Cassie's first instinct was to hide the sonogram. She swiftly swiped it off the desk and tucked it in the pocket of her pants.

"Hey Cass," Kris smiled.

Cassie noticed right away, that they both were wearing their wedding rings again. Dismal and devastated, Cassie murmured, "Hey. No, I'm good."

They moved on, acting like two teenagers in love.

Tears welled up in her eyes and the hurt was overwhelming. She should have just stayed out the rest of the day. She wasn't prepared to see him. Not with Kris and looking so happy. All of the joy she felt that morning, was gone.

She tried to focus on work but it was hard. She avoided Tanya because she didn't want her to see the hurt in her puffy eyes.

An hour later, Eli returned by himself. He was still in an upbeat mood. She wondered if he and his wife bid one another farewell with some physical fun. That tortured her soul even more.

As he passed by her desk, he tapped her back. "Come in my office."

She didn't want to. She didn't want him to see she had been crying. But she fixed her face as much as she could. She grabbed her tablet, pen and paper before walking in there. She took the seat before his desk as usual.

"How have you been?" he asked.

She shrugged her shoulders in a dispirited manner. She avoided eye contact, but she could feel him staring at her intensely.

"Cassie, I'm sorry for not talking to you while I was gone. I didn't want anything to distract me or cloud my mind. I had a lot of thinking to sort through," he explained.

"So I would have been a distraction?" she asked.

"Don't take it personal. I didn't talk to anyone."

Bullshit, she thought. She asked, "I thought you were staying. What happened?"

"Just missed being home and it didn't feel like the right time."

Her eyes fell to the ring he had on display. She offered him a weak smile, "You and Kris working through your problems?"

"Maybe. We finally talked and she's talking about coming back home."

"What about the divorce?"

"As of now, the process has begun. But depending on how things go, we'll get the process stopped."

"I guess that's a good thing, huh?"

The brightness in his face disappeared and he searched her face. "Are you alright?"

She nodded.

"Cassie, can we talk about what happened—"

She shook her head emphatically. "It's in the past so it's not necessary anymore."

Obliging, he said, "Okay."

She hesitated when speaking her next words. "I uhm...while you were gone...I was dealing with a lot. My daddy showed up out of the blue wanting a relationship. I'm so mad with Letty right now about that whole situation. It's just a lot of stuff."

"Wow. So your daddy just showed up like that?"

"Yeah. And Letty discovered she's pregnant."

"Wait. Time out. Colette's hoe ass is pregnant?"

"Yeah. She's talking about an abortion though, but I don't see her trying to make it happen. And I'm torn because I wanna put her out but she don't have anywhere else to go."

"Damn, that's messed up," he uttered.

She nodded to agree with him. "It is messed up."

She let her eyes wander his face, searching for anything that might hint at him wanting her. She finally said, "You look good. You look refreshed. I need to take a vacation like that."

"You probably do," he said. He asked, "Is there anything else I missed."

"Personal or work related?"

"Anything."

She thought about it. In a way, she didn't want to burden him with the news of her pregnancy, but at the same time she felt like he should be aware of it. She took her time speaking.

"Well, remember that guy I was telling you about? The one I was falling for. I haven't been with him or seen him in a while. He stopped speaking to me because I flipped out one day."

"Why did you flip out?" he asked.

"Because...his wedding ring was on his finger. It hadn't been there until this one particular time. To me it was a reminder that nothing would ever come out of what we had going on. It reminded me that he wasn't mine. And..." her voice trailed while she tried to compose herself. She didn't want to cry because she probably wouldn't be able to stop. "I should have just told him that. And I should have let him explain why he had it on, but I shut him out. And in return he shut me out. And now I wish I could talk to him just one more time, but it's too late."

"Why would you need to talk to him one more time?"

She looked at Eli's face. She could tell he was becoming unsettled. The smile he had been wearing had disappeared and his brow was pinched in pensively. She hated that she had to do this. She reached in her pocket and pulled out the sonogram. She placed it on the table.

She watched as he looked at it and his face frowned with puzzlement. Then he picked it up to examine it closer. He placed it back down in front of her. He asked, "You're pregnant with his baby?"

Cassie nodded. She could tell Eli was effected by the news, but he tried to maintain his indifference. It was evident he was bothered, and the enthusiasm that was present before was gone.

"I wish I could tell him, but he hasn't talked to me," she said. "I don't even know how he would take it, but I feel it's only right that he should be aware of it." She plucked the sonogram up from the table.

She stood up wearing a melancholic smile. "So those are all of the things I've been dealing with while you were gone. It's a lot all at once, huh?"

"It is," he said absently, as he sat there in thought. It seemed like all of the joy had been sucked right out of him. He couldn't even look at her.

She headed out and went back to her desk. She sighed with relief as if some weight had been taken off of her shoulders.

Chapter 18

When Eli came home, which was later than usual, he was stressed out. He didn't do a lot of talking. If he did, he was very despondent even when he spoke to the kids. He even went to bed earlier than usual. And now Kris was looking at him, waiting for an explanation to his behavior.

He couldn't really explain it. As a matter of fact, he was trying to push that situation out of his head and pretend it didn't happen. He wasn't prepared to hear Cassie tell him she was pregnant. That really fucked him up. He couldn't deny he had feelings for Cassie. But would her having a baby change up everything?

"What's wrong Eli?" Kris finally asked.

"Nothing," he mumbled. He flipped over on his side, giving her his back.

"I thought we said we would work on our communication," she said.

"I don't feel like talking right now."

"But you're bothered about something. What happened at work? Did you get into it again with Stefano?"

"No."

"Are you having second thoughts about us?"

His initial response was to answer her with something neutral. But why should he care about her feelings when she hasn't cared about his for the past few months. He said, "I don't think I had a first thought about us. As a matter of fact, I know I'm not giving us any further thought."

"Really? That isn't what you were saying last night. Something or someone must have changed your mind," Kris said with disappointment. She asked, "While I was away, did you meet someone else?"

"Yup," he answered.

"And you didn't even hesitate to answer that. It must be serious." She huffed with contempt.

"Was your involvement with Yosef serious?"

"Eli, you said you weren't going to keep throwing his name up," she said.

"Okay, I won't bring it up anymore." He rolled his eyes.

"Can you turn around and look at me?"

It was funny because when their marriage began unraveling, Eli blamed himself. He felt like he wasn't everything Kris needed him to be. He compared himself to his brothers and wanted what they had. However, it didn't take much into the marriage to realize it wasn't what he truly wanted. But rather than admit that, he tried to make it work. Even though he done what was expected of most husbands, it was something missing. He should have let it go instead of failing Kris as a husband; therefore making it easy for her to fall into the arms of someone like Yosef. He assumed she would accuse his actions as payback, but it really wasn't.

He blurted out, "The person I met is about to have a baby. I just found out today."

"Really?" she asked in disbelief.

He was about to turn around so that she could see he was serious, until she said, "So I guess he made the decision to stay with his girlfriend or wife."

That aggravated the hell out of Eli that she would say something so stupid. He hopped out of bed, completely annoyed. "I ain't talking about a goddamn man Kris. Why the fuck would that be the first thing you think? I can't believe after all this time you think that about me. You never did at first until Yosef got in your head."

"Well..." she said as she watched him walk out of the bedroom. She went after him. "Where are you going?"

"Upstairs."

"Wait, I'm sorry," she said. She grabbed his arm before he hit the corner. "Who is she?"

"It doesn't matter," he said.

"Is the baby yours?"

"Did I say she was having my baby?"

Kris searched his face to see if there was any truth. She said, "So she's having a baby by someone else and what...that's bothering you? You wished it was your baby or something? Is this because you wanna replace Elijah with a baby that's biologically yours?"

"No. I don't even want anymore kids. And because of you, I don't think I want to ever get married again. Hell, I'm not sure if I wanna give another relationship a chance. But I have feelings for her."

"So now what? You don't wanna work things out with me?"

"I don't," he said without hesitance. "I left and thought I had everything figured out. I'm ready to let you go. I was a single father before you, so it ain't nothing new. I do however want to see where things could go with the new person."

"Well, I'm not giving up. I'm your wife and although I hadn't behaved like it recently, you should give us a try first. Let's go ahead and stop the divorce and go to counseling. We gotta give this a real try before we just give up."

Eli released a frustrated breath. "Did you not just hear anything I said?"

"I heard all of that Eli," Kris said firmly. "But what I'm saying to you is that we are married and before getting a divorce we should seek counseling."

That was supposed to make sense. It was the right way to approach it, but the idea of doing that didn't move him. The only thing that was on his mind was Cassie being pregnant.

Eli shook his head. "Why weren't you interested in seeking counseling before Yosef?" He didn't give her a chance to respond. He went upstairs to the guest bedroom and let his mind wander, until he succumbed to sleep.

———

The following morning, Eli got up early. He wasn't able to sleep much. He tossed and turned thinking about what he needed to do.

Two hours before his alarm was due to go off, he went ahead and got up. As he entered his bedroom, the sight of Kris sleeping peacefully disgusted him. So many times he wanted to mush her in her face or thump her in the throat just because.

On his way to the bathroom, he bumped into a chair causing Kris' purse to tumble over. Half of the contents spilled and he looked back at Kris to see if she had awakened. When she didn't move, he bent down and quickly looked through only the things that spilled. This way she couldn't accuse him of invading her privacy. At least that's how he looked at it.

She sure did have a lot of receipts from different restaurants. She was feeding musty niggas with his money. That made him mad. He scooped those back in her purse along with her keys. Then a folded piece of paper with handwriting on it caught his attention. He carefully unfolded it so it wouldn't cause too much noise. It read:

Sister Kristen M.

I'm so hurt by your actions. Your behavior, which was embarrassing, at the second Sunday supper along with other outbursts of yours is not congruent with The Family's practice. I can no longer allow you to destroy the harmony of what we've built here. Furthermore, you are risking the lives of the children by fighting. Isa, Gwynn, and Annette are all carrying my children, who are The Family's future. You were fully aware that you were not the only one. You've been the leading lady for a year and somehow you have forgotten the rules. You are no longer fit to continue that role. Gwynn has earned her position. I do expect a formal apology to all of my spiritual wives and to those who witnessed your hostile behavior. Also, I will need you to reimburse The Family for damages you caused to the main house. You are to leave Elijah with me and when the new baby get here, I expect you to hand it over. You have officially been expelled from The Family. Your presence is no longer wanted or needed.

Brother Yosef

Eli looked over at her sleeping. He wanted to wake her up and ask her about the letter, but instead he stood there and killed her a thousand times in his head. Was this her plan? Now that she had been expelled, and no longer fit the role of Yosef's leading lady, she thought she could come back home and act as though everything was okay. Eli was done with this situation.

He grabbed the pill bottle that also spilled from her purse. It was an over the counter bottle of prenatal vitamins.

Eli threw both the letter and bottle back in her purse. That just ruined his mood completely. Since he was up, he went ahead and got the kids up and ready. They were cranky and uncooperative because he interrupted their sleep too soon.

"You can leave Avani here," Kris said with a yawn. She sat on the bed watching Eli move about.

"She's already ready to go. Besides, I've always taken her to Lovely's," he explained.

"Well...okay," she said. "Me and Elijah might stop by for lunch. Will that be okay?"

"No, it won't be okay," he said. "I'll probably be working through my lunch. I got a lot of shit to do."

"Well, maybe I can just drop something off for you so you won't have to leave out."

"No Kris," he said firmly. "I got an assistant for that anyway."

"Cassie?"

He didn't like the way she said Cassie's name. He looked at her. "Yeah, Cassie. What's the problem?"

"If I didn't know any better, I would think ya'll had something going on. She wouldn't be the person you've fallen in like with is she? And that Rock guy...he's the one that got her pregnant."

Perturbed, Eli said, "You know what you need to be doing instead of worrying about what I shared with you? How about you get all of your shit and your baby's shit out of this house."

"Are you serious?" Kris asked flabbergasted.

He cut his eyes at her before he walked away. He could hear her yelling something out, but he tuned her out. He found her annoying now. Or maybe he was easily irritated because of the Cassie situation. This girl had him bothered way more than he thought she would ever be able to do.

Eli got to work before the others. He didn't do anything because he couldn't focus. The image of Cassie's sonogram kept flashing in his mind. He kept replaying the past two and a half months in his head. Something wasn't adding up.

He didn't know how long he had been sitting in his office lost in thought when he became aware that the workplace had come to life. He looked out the glass wall and could see Cassie, Tanya, and Jazmin having their usual catch-up morning talks. He focused on Cassie.

For over two months, he watched her. She caught on to her job fast. She was dependable. Sometimes she motivated him to actually work when he didn't want to. She kept him in check. She paid attention to all his quirks. She was a great listener. She was a good friend.

If a person had been watching them, they would know that Eli's attraction for Cassie began before she started working for him. He watched her on the boat during last year's Fourth of July celebration. He found it amusing when Tanya and Cassie fought that girl. But he could tell she went hard for her friends. After getting to know her, he understood why her friendship with Tanya and Jazmin meant so much.

Cassie was wearing a coral sleeveless sheath dress with ankle strap nude heels. He liked that color on her. It softened her demeanor. And it complemented her mocha skin. He told her to stop dressing so drab as if she believed she couldn't be beautified. Right before his eyes, she blossomed. She walked around with more confidence and smiled more. The only problem he had with Cassie was not allowing herself to be loved.

Cassie finally decided to come into his office. It was like she flipped a switch, and her smile disappeared. Now she wore a look of apprehension as she approached his desk.

"Hey, I wanted to discuss something with you," she said. She didn't bother to sit down.

"What?" he asked.

"Uhm...I think it would be a good idea if I didn't work so close with you anymore," she said and averted her eyes.

He wasn't expecting that. "Why is that?"

"Just so we both can have a peaceful working environment. No distractions. No tension."

"You're still running," he pointed out.

"There's no reason for me to stop," she countered. She shifted her eyes to his.

"You gotta slow down first. You're running so fast, you don't pay attention to the reasons telling you to stop."

She released a frustrated breath in defeat. "I don't wanna talk in riddles with you. As a matter of fact, I'm done pretending. I got a baby on the way. And I need to get myself together."

"I wanted to stop pretending a long time ago."

She wanted to get back to the original subject. "I'm asking you for permission to work elsewhere in the company."

To satisfy her he said, "I'll look into it and let you know something."

"Thank you," she said. She turned around to walk out.

"Cassie," he called out.

She turned back around and waited for him to speak.

"We need to talk—"

She cut him off. "No, we don't."

He blurted out, "Who's the daddy?"

A wave of bafflement crossed her face. Slowly, as she realized his words, she said, "None of your business."

———

Cassie refused to let Eli's words get to her. In the back of her mind, she had a feeling that was how he felt. But this wasn't just about him. And then he wondered why she wanted to work somewhere else. She couldn't deal with looking at him and working so physically close. In order to move on, she needed to push him out of her head and her every day life.

For the rest of that week, she asked him about transferring somewhere else. He gave her the same dry ass answer: looking into it. Was he trying to force her to quit? Knowing him, he was getting a kick out of aggravating her. But she refused to let him get to her. She kept a positive attitude and continued to smile in his face.

"What's up Cassie?" Rock asked. He took a seat beside her on the steps of Jazmin's deck. It was Father's Day, and Jah and Jazmin decided at the last minute to have a small gathering and put some food on the grill.

The smell of the beer seeping from his pores, was nauseous. Frowning, she said, "You stink. Get away from me."

"You don't never want to talk to me anymore," he said feigning hurt.

"I just be preoccupied," she said.

"You can't be that damn preoccupied. What's up though? I miss your ass," he smiled.

His crooked smile and chipped tooth, made her smile. It was one of the things she found attractive about him. "You don't miss me."

"Yeah, I do," he said. "With your hateful tail."

"Well, I don't miss you," she said playfully.

"I know that. That's why you ain't bothered to call a nigga," he said.

"I meant to call you and ask you how things went in court."

He was confused. "In court?"

"Yeah, you know, the money?"

"Oh...Yeah. It went good. Thank you again," he said.

"That's good. So how are things with you and Melody?"

"I don't wanna talk about her ass. Let's talk about me and you."

Cassie giggled. "There ain't nothing for us to talk about."

He looked her over. "But you looking good. You smell good. And is them titties tryna grow?"

She started laughing. She nudged him. He wrapped his arms around her and tried to grope her breasts. "Stop," she laughed. "They hurt."

"Well, let me rub them and make them feel better. I can kiss them later if you need me to," he joked.

"I'm sure you would love to do that," she said.

"For real though," he said as his arm snaked around her. He squeezed the side of her ass. "I miss this."

She looked him in his eyes. Rock wasn't the one for her. His eyes spoke it. All he wanted was what he could get. She wanted a deeper, meaningful relationship. And she didn't want to sleep around having casual sex. That was Colette, not her.

"The only way I'd sleep with you again is if we were in a committed relationship heading towards marriage," she said.

"Look...I fucked up before. But we can try again. Start things off slow and let shit grow."

"I don't know Rock," she said with uncertainty. She stood up and wiped the seat of her maxi dress. He stood up with her. When she turned to walk back in the house, her eyes landed on Eli. He looked her way briefly then turned his attention back to Romyn and Jazmin.

She was almost tempted to go home when she first discovered that he was there. He wasn't alone either. Kris and the kids accompanied him. So far, he hadn't said anything to her.

"Where you going?" Rock asked.

"Back inside," she said. "It's hot." As she headed towards the back door, Eli looked her way again. She was thankful that Rock decided not to follow her or he would have had something to say about the look she and Eli shared.

She turned away from his gaze and proceeded inside. Since the den was occupied by the older adults, Cassie went upstairs to the bonus room. It was cool and the ceiling fan was going. She picked up the remote and turned the tv on. She sat back propping her feet up on the ottoman while she channel surfed.

She settled on *The Martian*. She was fifteen minutes invested in the movie when someone came to ruin her solitude. She glanced towards the doorway. Instead of turning away with detest, her eyes lingered and appreciated how sexy Eli was. He stared at her. She stared back. It was as if he was contemplating even coming in the room.

She finally turned her attention back to the tv. She missed something and had to rewind it. She tried to focus on getting back to what she missed as he came in and sat beside her. The hairs on her arm stood up and she fought against the shiver coursing through her body.

"You okay?" Eli asked.

"I'm fine," she said keeping her eyes on the tv.

"I'm not."

"I don't think I asked if you were," she retorted. "Shouldn't you be downstairs with your wife and kids?"

"I will be, but I needed to talk to you first."

"I don't wanna talk. I just wanna move on. Hell, I wanna forget things even happened."

"Cassie, that was my problem with you. You want to forget that it happened, but hell you didn't even want to acknowledge it while it was happening. It was a game of pretend for you."

"Whatever Eli," she said dismissively. She cut the volume up hoping to either drown him out or send him the message that she didn't want to hear him.

"And now you want to shut the conversation down."

"I wasn't trying to have one," she said angrily. She turned to him and snapped, "And how you gon' say it was a game of pretend for me. It was one for you too. I wasn't pretending by myself."

"No, it never was about pretending with me. I was going along with it until you felt comfortable with what we were doing. My feelings for you were very real; but I realized you didn't want me. All you wanted was dick to temporarily make you forget about your problems. Between you and Kris, I've been on this rollercoaster ride of emotions. And I don't wanna ride it anymore."

"Fine," she said. "I was trying to help you out by moving on, but here you are up here talking to me. Seems like you ain't hopped off yet."

He placed his hand on her stomach. "This is why I'm up here."

Why did he touch her? Her body came on like a motion sensor. She would be lying if she said she didn't miss him. She missed him, she craved him, she wanted him, and she loved him. She didn't think it was possible, but Cassie had tripped and found herself falling in love with someone she wouldn't have imagined. The attraction was always there, but the thought of him actually wanting her was unconceivable. Until it happened; and things accelerated like a wild fire.

"Is it Rock's baby?"

"I told you whose it was," she said throwing his hand off her.

"Are you sure? That sonogram said you were seven weeks. I didn't start cumming in you until about five weeks ago."

Cassie groaned and rolled her eyes. "The way it's calculated you're already two weeks along in gestational age when you conceive. The doctor broke it down for me cause I was confused too. According to what he told me, I likely conceived around the time we went to the hotel, or at Saint Anejos."

He didn't say anything.

"And I stopped fucking with Rock right before I started working at BevyCo," she added. Her voice lost the attitude and was now dismal. "I ain't getting rid of it. I'm thirty years old and I've been wanting a baby. I wanted a husband too but shit don't always work out like you want it to. Why it was you, I don't know. But you can pretend like it's not yours. Just don't—"

"There you go with that word again. I didn't want anymore kids, but at the same time, I didn't try to prevent it. And I understand your reason for wanting to keep it. But are you really ready to be a mother?"

What angered her most was not his questioning of her motherly capabilities, it was the fact that he was hinting at abortion. She didn't answer him. She placed the remote down and hopped up.

Eli grabbed her arm as she tried to step around him. He pulled her down unto his lap. "Don't fucking run. Talk to me."

"You want me to get rid of it. You don't want it," she said trying not to cry.

"Cassie, you just told me I could pretend that it wasn't mine. Make up your mind. Do you want this baby?"

She nodded.

"Do you want me to be a part of this baby's life?"

She hesitated.

"What do you desire? If you could have it your way. What do you want?" He searched her eyes looking for an answer.

She thought about it. "You."

"Okay...and you can have me as long as you're willing to give me you too," he replied.

"I thought you were done. I thought you and Kris were—"

He shook his head emphatically. "That's dead. I don't want her. I only told you that shit because I wanted to see if you would stop the pretending. And I've been trying to put her out for the past few days. She's been acting real stupid. But you fucked my head up when you showed me that ultrasound."

"I felt like you should know. I didn't show it to make you choose me or anything."

"I know, but I chose you a long time ago. And while I was in Italy I realized that. But that was also why I didn't want to talk to you while I was there. Cassie, I was missing the hell out of your bipolar ass. And it wasn't about sex only. I felt malnourished, like I was starving for your company. I was supposed to be enjoying Italy, but all I could think of was how much you would enjoy it. The color purple made me think of you. I missed your bouncing knee when you get bothered. I missed seeing that look in your eyes that made me wanna hold you forever. When it comes to you, I don't think of the past, I'm not afraid of the future...I just want the right now. And I..."

His voice trailed as he searched for words to best describe how he felt. "You know how kids are excited about going to Disney World? They can hardly sleep the night before because they're so anxious. When they finally make it there, they're overwhelmed with this rush. And they just wanna scream how goddamn great it is to be surrounded by all of their fucking favorite Disney characters...Whether I'm mad at you or if we're making love, or when we're working side by side...You're my Disney World."

Cassie started tearing up as her heart ballooned. She was speechless and couldn't contain her enraptured smile.

He placed a soft kiss on her lips. When he pulled back, they stared into each other's eyes speaking to one another as they always have done. He said softly, "I never knew what being in love felt like, until you. Hell, I didn't even think I was capable of falling in love."

She lightly chuckled through her falling tears, "Me either. And I feel sick when you're not around."

Eli wiped the fallen tear from her cheek. He spoke soothingly. "For the record, your *maestro* had that ring on that day because his three-year-old doesn't understand what's going on between her mommy and daddy. She saw it on the nightstand in my room. She handed it to me and told me to put it back on that morning so her mommy would come back. But she didn't know Mommy had already taken hers off."

Cassie grew angry and tried to hop off his lap, "I'm about to kick Kris' ass."

Eli laughed while holding her down. "No, you're pregnant remember? And so is she."

Cassie let her shoulders drop and looked at him with sympathy. "She told you?"

"No, I accidentally found out. I haven't even told her that I know."

"I was gonna tell you I saw her with that Jim Jones fucka at the doctor's office, but again, I didn't want you picking me as your next option."

As he absorbed the news, Eli contemplated telling her what he knew about Rock. He decided against it; it wasn't the right time. And with Cassie's little ass possibly turning into a Tasmanian devil, he didn't want her putting the baby at risk. Besides, he knew it would devastate her.

"I'm not worried about her or her problems anymore. I just wanna make sure you're okay. So I'm asking you again, what do you want?"

A big smile spread on her face and without thought or hesitation, she replied again, "You."

Chapter 19

Jah observed the way Cassie and Eli had been dancing at the 90s party. He also witnessed the exchange between Cassie and Eli at the party before she left. He saw the way Eli touched her and how Cassie walked away. If the person standing in front of him had been someone other than Rock, he would have told them to look, but he kept it to himself. That was until he made his way back to Jazmin that night at the party.

He told her, "I think Cassie and yo' cousin got something going on."

"Who? Eli?" Jazmin asked with her face scrunched up. "Why would you say that?"

"Just watch they ass. Them niggas think they slick. How they be acting at work?"

Jazmin gave it some thought. She one-shoulder shrugged, "They're cool. I mean we all act silly. They just work. Nothing special."

Jah grimaced, agitated by Jazmin's inobservance. "Juicy, you don't pay attention to shit noway. A mothafucka can be robbin' yo ass right in yo face...and you'll watch his ass take yo purse and walk off and then yo monkey ass'll be lookin' for yo shit askin' me where it at. And I'ma tell yo ass, ask the nigga that just rob you."

Jazmin laughed, "Shut up Jah. I am not that bad."

"Shit," he mumbled under his breath.

That was when Cassie walked over to tell Jazmin she was leaving. Unable to be convinced to stay, Cassie left.

Jah turned to her and said, "Didn't you see her ass was upset? Look over there...See who watchin' her ass?"

Jazmin looked in the direction Jah was gesturing towards. Yes, she saw Eli following Cassie with his eyes, but that didn't really mean anything. She said, "So. Cassie been getting a lot of looks tonight. And Eli always looking at people trying to find something to make fun of them about."

Jah gave Jazmin one of his "you stupid" looks, but he didn't want to call her that. He decided a while ago that he wouldn't refer to his wife as stupid anymore, but she was still retarded as hell.

"Wait," Jazmin said. "On second thought...Him and Cassie do be acting all secretive. They both stay gone really long times for lunch. And when Cassie come back she be starving. " Jazmin laughed.

"That's cause Eli breaking that back in. How you go to lunch and yo ass still hungry?"

"Well, I thought she was just running errands and didn't have time to eat," she said. "Oh wait! Sometimes Eli calls her in his office and she shut the door. The blinds be closed...Oh my God! Have they been fucking at work?"

Now, at his house and out of curiosity, Jah wanted to know if he and Jazmin were right. While Rock had been talking to Cassie out on the deck, Eli's attention kept going to them. At one point, Jah could see a glint of anger cross his face. When Cassie got up they gave each other a look. Jah didn't see this because Rock's big-headed ass came over talking to him. This was what Jazmin whispered to him minutes later. Rock walked away to take a phone call and talk privately. Eli then went in the house.

"Go see," Jazmin whispered excitedly.

"Naw, Rock might come lookin' for my ass."

"I'll tell him you went to get something out of our bedroom."

Jah went in the house and didn't see Cassie or Eli right away. He even looked in his man-cave where the others had migrated to. They weren't in there. He didn't see them in the kids playroom either. Trying to be discreet he looked in the guest bedroom on the main floor; still not there. Quietly he went upstairs. It wasn't even necessary to go all the way up. He halted as soon as they came into view. The bonus room's door was wide open and they didn't give a fuck about being caught. Or maybe they were just caught in the moment.

They were only kissing, but not in a way as if it was their first. It was obvious they were already familiar with each other and it was something deeper there. As quietly as he ascended the stairs, he descended them just as quiet backwards.

By the time he got downstairs, Rock was coming in the house. Jazmin was right behind him. "Hey Jah, did you find it?"

"Uhm...naw. You go find it," he told her.

"Where's Cassie?" Rock asked.

"She probably down there with everybody else," Jah lied. He looked at Jazmin and gestured with his eyes upstairs.

"Oh. Yeah, I'm gonna go look for it," Jazmin said. She ran upstairs still yelling, "I'm gonna find it Jah!"

Jah shook his head in disbelief. Jazmin was hopeless.

"What the hell wrong with Jazz?" Rock asked.

"Retarded," Jah answered. He nudged Rock in the direction of his man-cave. "C'mon nigga so we can watch Golden State get they mothafuckin ass whooped."

———

Cassie should have gone home before she got sleepy, but she ended up entertaining a drunk Rock on Jazmin's sofa. He kept trying to persuade her to go in the guest bedroom so they could have sex. She wasn't trying to sleep with his ass. But he was funny. Tanya had gotten tipsy herself and was feeling Ricky up. And unlike his brother, Ricky was a respectful man. He knew Tanya wasn't trying to go there with him, and he didn't take advantage.

Cassie asked Rock, "Why didn't you have your kids with you today? It's Father's Day."

"Cause Melody ass trippin. She talkin' bout they had plans to go to Michigan to see her daddy. And Jerrica...you know that bitch crazy. I went by to visit him but she wouldn't let me take him."

"Rock, you've fallen off. You were doing so well at first with the kids," Cassie said.

"I'm still doing good."

"Yeah, when it comes to just Rodney. But you done got off track somewhere along the line."

"I felt like I was doing better when we were together," he said. "Then your crazy ass started being even more crazy."

"We started off good, but—"

"Your ass was a bitch."

"Really Rock?"

He gave her a drunken grin then rested his head against her shoulder. "I miss you Cassie."

Jah entered the den shaking his head. "Ya'll mothafuckas still in my house?"

"He ain't gon' be able to drive Jah," Cassie said.

"Leave his ass there or take him in the guest room," Jah said. "And what the hell wrong with her big ass?" He pointed to Tanya who was snoring on the loveseat.

Cassie laughed.

"Where Ricky ass at? He need to get his brother and his play-tonic friend."

"Platonic Jah," Cassie corrected.

"It's what the hell I say it is," he mumbled. "I'm takin' my ass to bed. Me and Jazz tryna make anotha baby."

Cassie covered her ears and shook her head. "I don't wanna hear that."

Jah chuckled before heading back around the corner.

Cassie heard snoring in her ear. She looked at Rock and saw he had fallen asleep. She allowed him to rest against her, while she closed her eyes. She started dreaming immediately about being with Rock and arguing with Melody. Cassie and Rock were supposed to be getting married but Charles, her daddy didn't want her to. So he was trying to call her. She wanted to ignore the phone but it kept buzzing. It wouldn't stop buzzing.

Cassie jolted out of her sleep. Her phone was buzzing in her lap. She picked it up and answered quietly, "Hello?"

"When are you going home?" Eli asked.

"I don't know," she said.

"Can you come to the door?"

"Jazz's house?"

"Yeah."

"Hold on," she said. She ended the call. She eased away from Rock letting him slide down to the sofa. He stirred a little but didn't wake.

Careful not to cause any disturbances, she went to the front door to let Eli in. She asked, "Did you forget something?"

"Yeah, you."

"Uhm," she said looking over her shoulder. "You know, some people are still here."

"I know. I seen Rock's car still out there. Where he at?"

"He's in the den," she said.

Eli took her hand and led her to the guest bedroom, shut the door, and locked it. Cassie didn't object to anything. She let him back her up to the bed. She reciprocated the same aggressive hunger for him as he had for her. And even though she knew there was a possible chance they could get caught, she really didn't care. Just like she got a thrill out of sneaking around in his office, she was getting a thrill out of this. She missed him so much and earlier, as they kissed, reignited a fire that got out of control fast.

With her dressed hiked up and her panties at her knees, he had her bent over the bed. He only had his pants and boxers down enough to be free. She was already wet and ready. His entrance had her body trembling and she released a long moan. He started slamming into her. She cried out.

He stopped. "You gotta be quiet."

"Okay, okay," she whimpered. He started doing it again. She couldn't help it. He stopped again.

He grabbed a pillow. "Bury your face loud ass girl."

She chuckled grabbing the pillow just in time as he drilled into her. She bit down on the pillow trying to bear through it.

"You want me to make it hurt, Princess?"

"Mmmhmm," she groaned.

"But you gotta be quiet."

"Mmmhmm."

No matter how much she cried into that pillow, or how much she tried to inch away, he wouldn't let up until she was soiling the comforter. She forgot about the pillow and screamed out. Eli had to cover her mouth with his hand.

"Didn't I tell you, you'd have to be quiet?"

She was spent, but she knew he wasn't done. All she wanted to do was go to sleep. He ordered her to lay on her back. Not bothering with removing her panties completely off, he held her legs together by the ankles and rested them over one shoulder while he went to work.

Cassie loved to look up into his face while he stroked her good. She could always tell when it was feeling good to him. His lids would lower lazily while he looked down at her. It made him sexier and it caused her loins to quake.

Her maestro, she thought. Her master. Mr. Elijah Masters. She smiled and warmth swelled within, followed by her body trembling from a small orgasm. What would become of them? They didn't know just yet, however, they knew they weren't ready to walk away. With a baby on the way, it would change the dynamics of their relationship. But if he was willing to try, she would be willing as well.

She felt him shudder as his pace slowed. He pulled out and she could feel their fluids running down her cheeks.

"You know Jah and Jazz gonna get you for fucking up their bed," Eli said.

"You too," she said. She remained on her back. He leaned on her and kissed her. She pushed him off. "Boy, get away from me."

He rolled over on his back. "Get something for me to wipe off with."

"You get me something. My legs are stuck," she joked.

"You kill me, lazy ass girl," he said. "I always—"

There was an angry pounding on the door and displeased voices could be heard coming from the other side.

Eli and Cassie turned to each other both wide-eyed.

Eli chuckled, "Looks like we're caught."

———

This was the shit Jah was talking about. Ja-ja woke up and Jazmin nudged Jah out of his sleep. "Can you go get him a bottle? I forgot to put one up here."

"Do it yo'self," Jah barked at her. And he turned over giving her his back. Ja-ja's cries started sounding as if he was accusing Jah of not caring about him. Hell, he didn't, not while he was trying to sleep.

"C'mon Jah," Jazmin whined.

He got out of bed. This was what he signed up for, and though he acted as if it all got on his nerves, he wouldn't have it any other way.

"Why won't he sleep? Genni didn't do all this. He get this shit from yo' side of the family," Jah griped as he headed out of the room.

He went downstairs and straight to the dimly lit kitchen to fetch the baby's bottle. Just as he was about to go back to the staircase, he heard what he thought was moaning coming from his guest bedroom. He stopped and looked towards the door. The moaning grew louder and became a stifled scream. Who the hell was fucking in his house that wasn't him and Jazmin?

Then he remembered Rock and Cassie still being there before he went to bed. It was their business, but he knew shit was about to get out of hand sooner or later. First, Rock was fucking Cassie's mama. Second, Cassie and Eli have been fucking. Third, now Cassie was fucking Rock.

As he went to ascend the stairs, a heavy knock came from the front door. Who the fuck was this? They knocked again.

Jah went to the door and snatched it open. "Why the fuck you knocking on the do' like that?"

Kris stepped in brushing past him. Her face was tight. "Where is he?"

"Who?" Jah asked, completely annoyed. "Hol' up though. Did I invite yo' ass in here?"

She ignored him. "Eli. I know he's here."

"Eli ass ain't here. Lady, you betta take yo' ass on back to yo house," Jah told her.

Now Jazmin had come to the top of the stairs holding Ja-ja. "Who is that?"

"Kris ass looking for Eli," he said.

"Eli ain't here," Jazmin said.

"I know that. Go back to the room," Jah said. Then he heard feet shuffling towards them. It was Rock looking like he just woke up.

"What the fuck going on?" Rock asked.

Kris asked him, "Have you seen Eli?"

"Naw, why the fuck would I know where that nigga at?" Rock grumbled. He looked at Jah. "Where Cassie go? Did she leave?"

"Nigga, wasn't you just in the room with her?" Jah asked. Everybody was getting on his nerves now.

"Naw, I've been on the couch in there knocked out," Rock answered.

The look on Jah's face was enough for Kris to put her own conclusion together. She stormed in the direction of the guest bedroom before Jah could stop her. She started pounding on the door.

"What is it?" Rock asked, trying to figure out the reason for Jah's expression and Kris' behavior.

Jazmin came to the bottom of the stairs with the baby. "What's wrong with Kris?"

Jah went after Kris with Rock following.

"Hey...hey!" Jah hollered angrily. "Don't be doing all this shit in my house, man."

Kris ignored him and pounded on the door again.

319

"Who the fuck is in there?" Rock asked. Jah could see he was starting to get edgy.

The door opened.

"What are you doing Eli?" Kris asked angrily. "So this is what you snuck out the house to do?"

"I didn't sneak out, I walked out the front door. You saw me," Eli said with an insouciant shrug.

Rock said, "Hold up! What the hell you doing down here?"

"Go back to sleep," Jah told Rock. "It's all a fuckin' dream."

Now Kris was trying to get around Eli and screaming, "Is this why you wanna go ahead with the divorce! I knew you were fucking her!"

Rock saw Cassie behind Eli and it took a minute for it to register. Before he could snap and attack, Jah already had him blocked. Eli remained in place unbothered.

"Ya'll ain't finna do this shit in my house," Jah said. He pushed Rock back. "Take yo' ass on Rock!"

Cassie stepped out of the room and moved away to ensure her safety.

"You fucking that nigga, Cassie?" Rock asked. He was incensed and trying to figure out how he could get around Jah.

Cassie didn't say anything.

"Just answer the question," Rock said with spittle flying.

"What difference would it matter Rock?" Cassie asked. "We're not together. I can do whatever I want."

"But him though? I knew there was a reason I didn't like yo' ass," Rock hissed towards Eli.

"How you gon' say 'but him though'?" Eli asked. He was amazed at Rock's hypocrisy. "Who you been fucking? *But her though.* What about that? Don't fuck with me."

"Fuck you!" Rock spat.

"Ya'll need to fuckin' calm down," Jah said.

As if she was hurt and on the verge of tears, Kris asked, "How long Eli?"

"Not as long as you've been throwing your twat at Brother Yosef," he countered.

"Yeah, how long?" Rock asked Cassie. "Is this mothafucka the reason you keep brushing me the fuck off?"

"I keep brushing you off because there's nothing there," Cassie stated definitely.

"But it is with him though?" Rocked tried to step closer to Cassie, but Jah wouldn't let him.

"Don't get in her face," Eli told him in a threatening tone.

"Or what? Nigga, do something!" Rock challenged turning his attention back to Eli.

"I've already done something. A whole lot of something to Cassie," Eli taunted. "Now you do something."

Jah shook his head not believing this shit. He looked at Rock, "Nigga, I ain't letting you go until yo ass calm the fuck down. Ya'll not finna tear my shit up. And if ya'll wake Genni up, I'ma kick everybody's ass."

Rock looked around Jah with fire in his eyes. "The only reason yo ass is still standing is cause of Jah. You know he ain't gon let me fuck you up."

Kris interjected, "Whatever it is ya'll had going, ends today. Eli, let's go home and talk about this."

"Naw Kris," Eli shook his head. "You're not even supposed to be here. Didn't I put you out like five times today already? You're talking as if you matter. And I know what your ass is up to."

"What I'm up to?" Kris asked innocently.

"Get out of my face Kris," Eli said nastily.

"No, what am I up to?" she demanded to know.

"You're trying to pull some fucked up bullshit again. Why would I want to take you back? You were willing to leave your daughter to be with a dusty ass nothing having ass nigga. And now he don't even want you. You're pitiful and you get no more chances with me. Aren't you pregnant with his child anyway?" he asked.

"No," she lied. "But isn't she pregnant with yours?"

"Isn't she who?" Rock asked.

They all looked at Cassie.

"You pregnant?" Rock asked in disbelief.

Cassie ignored him and spoke to Kris. "I saw you at the ob/gyn doctor I go to. You were there with Yosef and this was a couple of weeks ago."

"You didn't see me," Kris said maintaining her lie.

"Yeah I did. They even called your name, Mrs. Masters," Cassie said.

Rock was still in disbelief. He was hurt. "You pregnant by him?"

Cassie answered him with her eyes.

Rock tore away from Jah and got in Cassie's face. "You got pregnant by this nigga! You let this nigga go up in you mothafuckin' raw!"

At this point, Eli was trying to make sure Rock didn't try to put his hands on Cassie, but Kris had a hold of him, whispering and begging for him to please come home. Jah pulled Rock out of Cassie's face.

"Leave Rock," Jah told him. "I ain't finna let you get in Cassie's face like that. Nigga, you need to leave and chill the fuck out."

Eli pried Kris' fingers from his shirt. "Will you let me fucking go? Get away from me...Bye Kris. And who's at the house with the kids anyway?"

"You can have this dry pussy bitch," Rock snarled. He glowered at Cassie one last time before he turned away.

"Dry?" Eli asked as if he was insulted. There was a hint of humor in his voice when he said, "Aw nigga, you must have not been able to get that fountain going. You gotta hit that spot right. Pussy stayed wet for me. Don't be hating on Cassie nigga. As a matter of fact, Jah, ya'll need to replace them covers in there. We made a mess."

Jah wanted to kick Eli's ass himself. Why couldn't he just be quiet? This time Rock used enough strength to get past him and attacked Eli. Both Kris and Cassie had to hurry out of the way as the two men fought. Jah tried his best to separate the two. Eli lost his footing on the runner, and it seemed as if Rock was going to fuck him up. But Eli grabbed a ceramic vase from the bottom shelf of the hallway table and crashed it upside Rock's head.

Jazmin, who had been watching everything at the end of the hall, cried out. "No! Not my vase!"

It didn't knock Rock out but it dazed him enough for Eli to get away from him. Eli was angry, "That mothafucka bit me. Now I need a goddamn shot."

Jah helped Rock up and pushed him towards the kitchen. He had a gash where the vase connected with his head.

Kris was crying. "My husband is fighting with a man for another woman. You didn't fight Yosef for me!"

Eli waved her off as he went back in the guest bedroom. "You sound stupid Kris. Go back to the house, get your shit, and get out."

Kris followed him in the room where they started going back and forth with heated words.

Cassie looked at Jazmin, who was cradling Ja-ja. Jazmin carefully walked over so her bare feet wouldn't step on any glass.

Jazmin whispered, "Are you okay?"

Cassie nodded.

Sympathizing, Jazmin said softly. "Why didn't you tell me that Eli was the father?"

Cassie shrugged.

"So wait," Jazmin said. "At the party...When you explained to me and Tanya why Sean kept bothering you, you said it was because he witnessed you at the club having sex with someone that was married. You said he kept messing with you and threatening to tell people how nasty you were. Was the person Eli and you just didn't want to tell me and Tanya?"

"Yeah," Cassie said with contrite.

"So all this time?"

"Pretty much," Cassie answered with a hint of shame.

A grin spread across Jazmin's face. "Never would have thought...well...until Jah said something to me at the party. He said he had a feeling ya'll were messing around."

"Jah thought we were messing around for real?" Cassie asked.

"Yeah," Jazmin said. "But you're about to have a baby with my cousin. This is gonna be so weird but great."

Cassie smiled. "You're so silly."

They heard heavy shuffling coming towards them. They both turned their heads in the direction it was coming from. Tanya was yawning. "How come ain't nobody woke me up and told me to take my fat ass home?"

Jazmin's face scrunched up in surprise. "You've been here all this time?"

"Yeah, what ya'll doing? What time is it?" she asked.

Jazmin looked at Cassie and laughed. "She slept through all of that?"

"Through what?" Tanya asked looking between Jazmin and Cassie.

"Nothing," Cassie laughed.

Tanya looked on the floor at the shattered vase. Then she paused and could hear Kris and Eli still going back and forth. She heard Jah and Rock talking from the kitchen. She furrowed her brow with question. "What the hell I miss?"

Chapter 20

For it to have been such a nice sunny beautiful day on Father's Day, the following Monday was complete opposite. Where did the dark clouds come from?

Cassie could hear the thunder as she stirred out of her sleep. It sounded as if it was really going to storm. She thought, it couldn't be any worse than the night before though. The events replayed in her head.

Eventually, Eli left with a quick bye. Kris trailed behind him pointing out all of the reasons their marriage should come before Cassie and her baby. Tanya kept asking, "Who she talking about? What baby?"

Then Rock, still glaring at Cassie and upset that his head had been busted, left. Tanya asked, "Who busted him upside the head?"

Jah fussed at Cassie and made her redress the bed in the guest room. She didn't mind. He told her to take the other bedding with her since she christened it. Tanya asked, "Why he got you doing that?"

Cassie just laughed through it all while Jazmin tried to give Tanya a play by play. Jah got irritated all over again and took his son from Jazmin to feed him.

She was somewhat looking forward to getting to the office. She wanted to see Eli to make sure he was okay. She kept thinking that he would reach out to her by text or something, but he didn't. She said she wouldn't bother him because he and Kris were probably still going at it.

Cassie got up and got dressed for work. She purposely selected something bright because it was what Eli liked on her. She had to admit, his advice on the clothes she should wear did do something to boost her confidence. Normally she would wear something dark never realizing she was subconsciously detracting from herself. Now she wore colors and patterns that demanded attention.

As she slipped on her heels, she could hear thumping and moaning coming from Colette's room. She rolled her eyes. She wished that woman would leave. And she still hadn't bother to get an abortion.

Cassie grabbed her purse and headed out of her bedroom. She threw her purse over the dinette's chair upon passing and walked into the kitchen to grab her individual bottle of orange juice like she did most mornings.

She heard Colette's door open. Colette's voice yelled, "You ain't shit, you know that!"

328

As Cassie stepped out of her kitchen space, the sight of Rock's smug expression greeted her. She froze trying to make sure she was seeing what she thought she was seeing: a bandaged-head Rock in his boxers making his way to her kitchen.

Before she could question anything, Rock said, "Yeah, I'm on some shit too. You can call me yo stepdaddy. I might be your little brother or sister daddy."

Cassie blacked out in a rage. She threw her juice at him first then pounced on him. "You dirty mothafucka!" She hit on him everywhere she could. She even went for the bandage to bust his wound open. She kicked, scratched, slapped, punched, and spit on him.

Colette ran into the open living room area to pull Cassie off of Rock. Cassie turned around and gave Colette the same treatment.

"Get out bitch! You dirty sleazy slutty no good ass bitch!" Cassie spat as she slung Colette towards the door. "I hate you and don't you ever come near me again. And Rock! You're fucking dead to me. You're the fucking scum of the mothafuckin' earth! Get out!"

When Rock didn't move fast enough, Cassie went to attack him again. He pushed her causing her to stumble backwards. It didn't phase her. Her five foot two inch frame bounced right back up and grabbed the floral arrangement on her dinette table and hurled it at him. It brazed him, but he managed to get out of the way before it shattered.

She yelled at the top of her lungs. "Get out! Get out, now! And take your slutty ass cum bucket with you."

She stormed to Colette's room. She first went to the window to open it. She then started grabbing any and everything in sight that she could get her hands on to toss out.

"Hold up. Let me get my clothes," Rock said hurrying into the room. He looked around for his jeans. "I know you ain't throw my shit out there."

Cassie continued tossing things out the window while Colette and Rock were trying to scramble for their clothes to get dressed.

Colette tried to stop her. "Cassie, we can talk this out."

Cassie ignored her. She looked at Rock. "You have five seconds to get out."

"We even now Cassie," Rock said in a righteous tone.

Cassie stormed to her kitchen and pulled out a large carving knife and lunged at him.

Rock managed to get out of the way. He mocked her, "I knew your ass was crazy."

Colette got in between holding her hand out towards Cassie. "You don't want to stab him Cassie. He ain't worth it. He ain't never been worth it and I was so glad you moved on from him. He ain't shit Cassie. I mean, I know I ain't shit. That's already been established. But if he was willing to fuck your mama, then he would have

330

fucked you over in so many other ways. You can do way better than him. But don't get no damn charges over this nigga."

Cassie lowered the knife. She was still raging inside. "Get out!"

Five minutes later, Cassie was alone. She placed the knife back in the kitchen. She suddenly got nauseated, and started dry heaving in the sink. The force of her gagging caused tears to form. Once they started, she fell to the floor and started sobbing. She beat the floor and whipped her body back and forth as she had an emotional tantrum.

After about ten minutes of just sitting on the floor, she managed to get up and go to her bedroom. She didn't bother undressing. She got in her bed and pulled the covers over her. She shut the world out.

———

It was the middle of the day, when Cassie decided to get out of bed. It was pouring rain outside and the thunder boomed across the sky.

She went to the living room to find her phone. She retrieved it from her purse. She had so many missed calls, too many texts, and several voicemail messages. She didn't care who they all were from. She wondered who had been at her door the few times she stirred in her sleep. She heard the knocks but she ignored them.

If Rock wanted to hurt her and get even, he definitely achieved that. She wondered if he mentioned that he could be Colette's unborn baby's daddy just to add more salt to her wound. And if it was the truth, then that meant he had been sleeping with Colette for a while to be a possible father. Then it dawned on her...Colette was wolf bat Arby's pussy. Mortified, she cringed with repulsion.

Her phone started going off again. She looked at it and saw that it was Tanya. She ignored it. She cleaned up her kitchen and straightened up her table and chairs that were knocked over during their scuffle.

She needed to get out of the apartment. She decided to change into something more comfortable: a plain v-neck tee with black leggings. She slipped on her black Vans. She pulled her hair back into a low ponytail, grabbed her phone, purse, keys, an umbrella, and headed out to her car.

She really didn't have a destination in mind, but she felt like she needed to get out and go somewhere. Her phone continued to buzz and beep.

She ended up outside of the Stephenson & Reagan Law Firm building. She had second thoughts about going in, but since she had drove the distance there, she might as well go inside.

When she went in she immediately sensed that this place was loaded with money. The inside of the building looked like a luxurious hotel. It was just as posh as BevyCo and she knew their asses had plenty of money.

Straight ahead was the double glass doors with the Stephenson & Reagan logo on it. She passed the elevators and went straight into the suite. The receptionist smiled, but Cassie could sense she was leery of her presence.

"Can I help you?"

"I'm here to see Charles Stephenson," Cassie said.

"Is he expecting you?"

Cassie shook her head.

"Well, he doesn't take walk-ins. You have to make an appointment. I'll be glad to set that up with—"

"I ain't here for that. I'm his daughter," Cassie said evenly.

The receptionist was taken aback. She produced another leery smile. "Oh. Okay. I'll call him right now."

Cassie turned around while the lady spoke on the phone. She could hear the uncertainty in the lady's voice when she said, "Ugh...there's a lady here to see you...She says she's your daughter...I...uh...What's your name sweetie?"

Cassie turned to her. "It's Cassie."

Before the lady could repeat it, he must have said something on the other line. She replied in a chipper tone. "Okay...Okay. Sure."

She hung up and said, "He said wait right here and he'll be here shortly."

A few minutes later, Charles was coming around the corner. He greeted Cassie with a warm smile and a hug which was surprising. She didn't think he would show her any affection at his workplace.

"It's nice to see you," he said. "What brings you here?"

Cassie shrugged. "I don't know."

It was then that Charles saw that she was distraught and had been crying. "Well, let's go to my office."

She followed him, bypassing other offices and cubicles. He spoke to a few people as they journeyed to his office. Much like Eli's office, Charles' was enclosed by glass walls too. He had a big executive desk and nice decor. Photos of his white wife and their mulatto kids were perched here and there.

"Can I get you anything?" he asked.

Cassie shook her head as she sat in one of his chairs. She asked, "What kind of law do you practice here?"

"Mainly corporate," he answered.

"So if I needed to kill somebody, you wouldn't be able to defend me?" she asked seriously.

Charles chuckled. "I know some good criminal defense lawyers. Who exactly are you trying to kill?"

Since he had a sense of humor, it allowed Cassie to be at ease. She relaxed a little. She said, "I wanna kill Colette. She is the absolute worse. I just found out today that she's been sleeping with my ex. She tried to sleep with my sister's husband too. But what makes it so bad is that they were in my apartment."

Charles winced. "Ooh...That's awful. I see Colette hasn't changed much."

"How did you end up with her?" Cassie asked.

He gave it some thought before answering. "Well...let's just say, I indulged in activities outside of my marriage that I shouldn't have been doing in the first place. I was foolish and let lust get the best of me. And that's how you got here."

"But she slept around so much, how did you know I was actually yours?"

"I could see it then like I can see it now. But we got tested and I agreed to take care of you but from a distance. When she tried to get me to take you and I couldn't that's when she turned into a witch. So she tried to cut me off completely unless it was to benefit her. And by then she had so much over me that if I didn't comply she would run her mouth."

"She's just low down."

"So are you trying to kill just her or kill them both?" he laughed.

As they talked more and more, Cassie realized Charles wasn't such a bad guy. He had a soft amiable personality. She just couldn't understand how someone like him could get caught up with Colette.

He canceled all of his appointments and took the day off. He and Cassie went out for lunch where they continued to talk. Brenda, his wife, had recently died of pancreatic cancer. He told her siblings about her and they were looking forward to meeting her. His mother also wanted to meet her. He was delighted about her news of pregnancy, although he was already the grandfather to four.

Visiting with him lifted her spirits, and despite the weather, it brightened her day.

She went to the mall later that day, perusing through all of the babies' and children's stores. All the while, she still continued to ignore her phone. At one point she had powered it off. She just needed to clear her head although she really wanted to talk to Eli. When she scanned the missed calls, voicemails, and texts, none of them were from him. If she couldn't hear from him, she really didn't want to be bothered with anyone else.

When she got back to her apartment, she decided to call Eli. All of this stubbornness had to stop. She dialed him but it went straight to voicemail, which put her in a deeper depressed mood.

She was in her living room watching tv when her front door opened. The only person who had a spare key to her apartment was Romyn.

Once a frantic Romyn came into view, he said, "Where have you been? Your friends have been trying to get in touch with you. Tanya finally got in touch with me and I've been calling and calling."

"What is it?" she asked.

"It's your baby daddy," Romyn said. "That wife of his stabbed him last night."

"What!"

———

Cassie was so mad at herself for being all in her feelings and not answering her phone. After Romyn told her the news, she jumped up, grabbed her purse, keys, phone, and ran out the apartment with him. She started going through her phone and realized everybody was trying to get in contact with her. Tanya, Jazmin, and Romyn had left several frantic voicemails and text messages. Even Jah's non-spelling behind sent her a few text messages cussing her out for not answering the phone.

Romyn drove her to Vanderbilt. He didn't know Eli's condition so he couldn't update her. She called Tanya first but she didn't answer. She tried Jazmin.

"Oh my God! Cassie, where have you been?" Jazmin screamed into the phone. "That crazy bitch stabbed Eli!"

"What happened?" Cassie asked.

"She flipped out because he said he was done with her; and he told her period, point, blank, that he wanted you. According to what Bryce and Bria said, they were arguing to the point it woke them up. The twins don't play when it comes to their daddy. Bria called the police so they could remove Kris from the house. She got that shit from her daddy. They still went to be nosy. Bria said when they got to the kitchen, Eli turned to them to tell them to go back to bed and that's when Kris stabbed him in the back. They said she drew it back and stabbed him again. Eli was able to turn around and prevent her from retracting the knife and stabbing him a third time but by then they said he kinda went down but told them to call 911. Thank God Bria had already called the police. Kris realized what she had done and ran."

"Oh my God," Cassie was stunned. "Is Eli...is he...Where is Eli?"

"He ain't dead Cassie," Jazmin reassured. "They had to do emergency surgery. It was like his side and back. She messed up one of his kidneys, but they were able to repair it. He's in the trauma intensive care unit for now."

"What floor?" Cassie's heart was beating profoundly.

"Come to the tenth floor family waiting room," Jazmin told her.

"Okay," Cassie said and ended the call.

Cassie became nervous and the thought of losing Eli had her emotional. After Romyn parked and they got out, Cassie remained quiet. She didn't know what to think or how to feel. So much had happened in just two days. She didn't think she could take much more.

Arriving on the tenth floor, they went up to the unit's nursing station. They were given visitors passes and instructed to go to the family waiting area.

"Cassie," Jazmin called out. "You got here fast."

"We were already on our way," Romyn said.

"Heifa, I tried to call you," Tanya grumbled.

"I know," Cassie said. "I was kinda going through something."

They looked up as a very pretty, very pregnant Lovely came in the room followed by Luciano Pavoni and his wife Cece. Right behind them was the tall slender built and beautiful Grace. Her hair reached the jut of her ass. She explained to Cassie and Tanya once, that she was growing her hair so long to only cut it and donate it to Locks of Love to make wigs for kids with medical conditions, such as cancer.

"Ya'll, we're going home," Lovely announced. "That crazy boy won't stop talking. He's okay and he should be going to the step-down unit tomorrow."

"Hello Cassie," Lu said with a smile.

"Hey," she said.

"Cassie's here?" Lovely asked turning in the direction of her voice. "Cassie, if you don't hurry your tail in that boy's room. He's been asking for you all day. I think he was out of it maybe an hour after surgery, but he's been up since asking about you."

"He has?" Cassie asked as if it was unbelievable.

"Yes," the majority of them answered all at once.

"The only person in his room right now is Lulu," Lovely said. She turned to her daughter. "And please don't drive crazy when you bring her home."

Grace giggled. "I won't. Lulu just sensitive to speed. She'll be a'ight."

Lovely kissed her daughter bye then held onto Lu's arm as he escorted her out the family room.

Grace said, "I'ma drive like a bat out of hell. Lulu gon' shit sweet and sour chicken and finally quit."

Jazmin laughed. "You're terrible."

Cassie inhaled a deep breath. "Well, I'm going in here to see him."

Grace told her the room number. She didn't hurry, as a matter of fact she walked slow. The curtains were drawn on his room, but the doors were opened. She stepped around the curtains. Lulu looked up at her when she entered. Eli turned his head to see who she was looking at.

He said in a drugged stupor, "Get this oriental out of my room."

"I no oriental," Lulu said in a playful angry tone.

"But your ass is flat as an oriental rug," Eli told her.

"You high. You high on drugs. But you no sleep. Why?"

"Lulu, I need some of that shit you be smoking. I know your ass be hitting that bong. I seent you."

Lulu laughed. "Oh hush Fruitcake."

"Lulu...Lulu," he said pointing to Cassie. "That's my new babymama. Her name Cassandra. Cassie, this is the oriental that won't go away."

"Oh. You Cassie," Lulu grinned. "He been asking for you. Where Cassie, where Cassie! Glad you here; now he shut up."

Cassie giggled. She watched as Lulu kissed Eli's forehead and ruffled his hair. She said, "Get better Fruitcake."

"Don't touch my hair," he mumbled. "You be playing with fish heads and shit."

Lulu could do nothing but shake her head.

Cassie waited for Lulu to exit before getting closer to his bed. Her eyes roamed over him as if she was examining him. His once vibrant honey toasted complexion was dull and his eyes looked tired. The laziness of his eyes were a clear sign he was feeling the effects of the drugs pumping through him. He had tubes coming from under his blanket.

She could feel him staring at her. She finally made eye contact with him. And like he usually done, he gave her one of those stoic looks of his.

"Where you been?" he finally asked.

"With my daddy," she answered.

"Daddy?"

She nodded. "I went and saw him today."

"How that go?"

"It was good actually. We talked. I think I like him."

"That's why you didn't go to work?"

"How you know I didn't go to work?"

"Cause they said you didn't show up today."

"Oh. Well, I got ready to go and was about to head out the door until Rock came out of my mama's room," she said.

His eyes opened up. "What?"

She sighed. "Yeah. I fought both of them and put—"

"Fought?" he questioned. His brow furrowed in a frown. "Don't be fighting nobody with my baby in there."

She gave him a guilty smile. "Okay, that'll be the only time. But I put them out, and needless to say, I didn't really feel like working or being bothered with anybody. Then I got mad at you for not calling me, but I feel so bad now because you were laid up in the hospital."

"That's okay. You get a pass after that shit," he said. "He wasn't shit nor was your mama. Speaking of not shit; did you see Sarah out there?"

Cassie nodded. "I think she was about to leave though. Lu, his wife, and Lovely just left."

"I think Lovely getting blinder," he said. "She bumping into all kinds of shit. I told them take her ass home 'fore she fuck up that baby."

Cassie tried not to laugh. She asked, "Eli, why aren't you sleeping?"

He shrugged. He said, "Hey, you know this the second time a bitch stabbed me."

Cassie laughed. "Yeah, you told me about the first time."

"When I tell you that?"

"A few weeks ago," she said.

"Oh," he murmured.

"What's gonna happen to Kris?"

"I don't know but she better come get her lil boy. I ain't taking care of his ass after this shit."

Cassie started laughing. "I can't stand you."

"Brother Yosef—somebody better come get that raggedy head boy...But she turned herself in. Depending on how I feel...I don't know...Even if I don't press charges, the state will. And I ain't got shit to do with it after that."

"That's really crazy," Cassie said in disbelief. She tried her best not to give in to the laughter she was fighting. She couldn't help it though "Eli! Why you call that boy raggedy head?"

Eli chuckled goofily. "Cause he is...hell...you seen him. They needa throw some dreads up in his head...real quick. Nappy hair look better in dreads...Maybe that's what you should do too."

"Ooh I can't stand you!" she laughed.

He smiled as his eyes got heavier. "I'm just kidding...Ain't nothing wrong with my baby's hair...long as you take care of them edges."

"Eli!"

"Okay, okay...I quit." He stared at her for a second before he asked, "So what we gon' do Princess?"

Curious, Cassie asked, "Why do you call me Princess?"

His eyes started getting heavier. "Cassandra...was the Princess of Troy...She tried to tell them niggas bout them other niggas in the Trojan horse but they ain't believe her...That's cause Apollo spit in her mouth and cursed her or some shit so nobody would believe shit she said...And some more stuff."

"How you know all of that?"

"Cause I'm not stupid...I may act like I'm stupid...but I remember some shit I learned in school..." he said. His eyes fluttered open. "You haven't answered me."

"About what we're gonna do? I don't know. What do you wanna do?"

"I wanna fuck you but I got this damn tube up my dick."

Cassie chuckled. "I really can't stand you."

A slow, lazy smile spread across his lips. "Give me a kiss so I can finally go to sleep...Don't stick your tongue in my mouth though...My breff a lil tart."

Cassie shook her head. She leaned over and placed a soft kiss against his lips. She pulled back to look at him. He was drifting to sleep. She whispered, "I love you."

Without opening his eyes, he mumbled, "I love you too."

Cassie stared at him as he slept. She smiled as an overwhelming presence of something she couldn't quite name filled her. She didn't know if it was happiness and joy, or just knowing that things would be okay. And she also knew that the man lying before her really loved her. They were a pair no one would have imagined putting together on purpose. She didn't know what would become of them, but she was willing if he was willing to give it a try, and see what becomes of them.

*** *The End...but not the end of them......an update to come later...* ***